Suspic̶̶̶̶̶̶̶̶̶ ̶̶̶̶̶̶̶̶̶̶̶̶̶̶̶̶̶ ̶̶French chef who
prepare̶̶ ̶̶̶̶food eaten by the unfortunate
victim. Auguste must defend himself not only
from the accusation of murder, but from the
insult to his fine cuisine.

EDITH HANKEY?

The housekeeper thought she had an "understanding" with the pompous Mr. Greeves—
until she discovered she wasn't the only lady in
his life.

MAY FAWCETT?

The 28-year-old lady's maid had more than an
understanding with the silver-haired steward—
until she discovered him fondling the scullery
maid.

ERNEST HOBBS?

The butler had been bullied and harassed by
Greeves for ten years, and with Greeves out of
the way, he was the natural successor.

ETHEL GUBBINS?

The head housemaid might have had her own
secret motive for murder.

EDWARD JACKSON?

Why had he been quite so sure someone had
done Greeves in?

JOHN CRICKET?

The valet plainly walked in fear of Greeves and
had plenty of reasons to dislike him.

Other Mysteries by
Amy Myers
Coming Soon from Avon Books

MURDER IN THE LIMELIGHT

MURDER IN PUG'S PARLOUR

AMY MYERS

AVON BOOKS ◆ NEW YORK

AVON BOOKS
A division of
The Hearst Corporation
1350 Avenue of the Americas
New York, New York 10019

First Avon Books Printing: April 1992

AVON TRADEMARK REG. U.S. PAT. OFF. AND IN OTHER COUNTRIES, MARCA
REGISTRADA, HECHO EN U.S.A.

Printed in the U.S.A.

RA 10 9 8 7 6 5 4 3 2 1

To Dot with gratitude

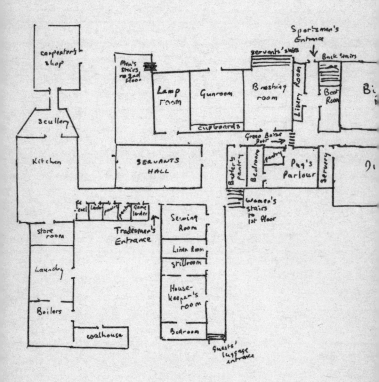

To the dairy
↑

carpenter's shop

Men's stairs to 2nd floor

Lamp Room

Gunroom

Brushing room

Library Room

Sportsmen's Entrance

servants' stairs

Back Stairs

Boot Room

Bi

Scullery

Kitchen

SERVANTS HALL

cupboards

Green Baize Door

Butler's pantry

Bedroom

pantry

Pug's Parlour

Servery

Di

Women's stairs to 1st floor

cell   larder   pantry   game larder

Tradesmen's Entrance

store room

Laundry

Boilers

coalhouse

Sewing Room

Linen Room

grillroom

House-keeper's room

Bedroom

Guests' luggage entrance

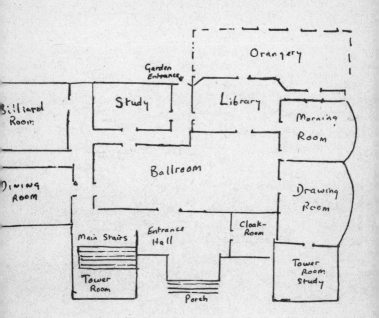

Stockbery Towers
Rough plan of the ground floor
drawn by
Inspector Egbert Rose

Orangery

Billiard Room

Study

Garden Entrance

Library

Morning Room

Dining Room

Ballroom

Drawing Room

Main Stairs

Entrance Hall

Cloak-Room

Tower Room

Porch

Tower Room Study

Chapter One

'Murder?' cried Mrs Hankey, billowing along the corridor towards Pug's Parlour, with the rest of the upper servants following bemusedly in her wake. 'But who'd want to murder Mr Greeves?'

One pastry-cook-cum-baker, one apprentice chef, two kitchen-maids, two scullery maids, one pantryboy, one still-room maid, one junior lady's-maid, one lampboy, five footmen, one vegetable maid, five housemaids, one hallboy, two odd-job men, two sewing-room maids and four laundry maids, could readily have told her. But the lower servants had, naturally, not been present when Edward Jackson, the steward's-room boy, had so unceremoniously burst into the hierarchical fastnesses of the housekeeper's room where the upper servants were partaking of their after-dinner tea in formal ritual, yelling: 'It's old Greeves – he's puking – gorlimy, you gotta come, Mrs Hankey. Someone's tried to do 'im in.'

The housekeeper's majestic figure had risen, delaying the disciplining of Edward Jackson in the interests of Mr Greeves' health, gathered hastily, but with almost unnatural composure, a number of bottles from the oaken cupboards in her still-room, and swept out to bring succour. Only then had the full measure of his words sunk in. 'Someone's tried to do 'im in.'

Once inside the steward's room, any hope she might have

1

nursed that this was some horrible prank dreamed up by Edward Jackson was dispelled. On the carpet a prostrate figure vomited and retched, the face contorted in agony, the body jerking in spasms. Uttering only an involuntary 'Archibald!', Mrs Hankey sank to her knees in a rustle of black bombasine to administer relief. But it was soon clear that mustard and warm water would do little for Greeves, nor the ipecacuanha which followed with shaking hand.

'Madame, I think the doctor – urgently.' Auguste Didier, master chef, bent over her, quietly removed her arms from the unfortunate steward, and drew her to her feet. 'Edward, to the stables with you. Send the governess-cart for Dr Parkes. Ethel, perhaps –' He indicated to the head housemaid that Mrs Hankey should be removed.

But not even this emergency could rob Edith Hankey entirely of her training: 'Put that nasty dirty plate and glass in the pantry, Mr Hobbs. And wash them up, if you please.'

Preoccupied with making the groaning man more comfortable, Auguste Didier paid scant attention to these innocent words.

Which was unfortunate.

'Tea, Ethel,' requested Mrs Hankey faintly, holding a sturdy piece of lace-trimmed cambric to her eyes. It was a sign of the unusualness of the situation that Miss Gubbins immediately busied herself with cups and saucers in the adjoining still-room, entirely disregarding what was due to her position as head housemaid.

With the exception of Auguste Didier, the upper servants, the Upper Ten as they were always known, regardless of their actual numbers, had trailed reluctantly back to the housekeeper's room. Once there a problem of etiquette had to be attended to. This being October and the prime of the 1891 pheasant season, there was a shooting party resident at

Stockbery Towers, and the accompanying servants had perforce to be entertained by their counterparts. Present when Edward Jackson had precipitated himself into the room, they were now difficult to dislodge, and it took all Ethel's powers of tact to persuade them to be about their lawful occupations. It took some time and, by the time Prince Franz's manservant had been dislodged, Auguste was back amongst them, having himself been expelled from Pug's Parlour, as the steward's room was known, on the arrival of Dr Parkes.

'The good doctor will visit us,' he announced, still somewhat piqued that his presence was not considered necessary. He winced as he watched the inevitable milk being poured into the lemon tea; he had long given up protesting. These English – they took the best food in the world and they ruined it by inattention to detail. For times of shock, no, not tea, to awaken the spirits, but a tisane of *verveine*, some chamomile perhaps to soothe the stomach, but not the tea leaf. Or a *chocolat chaud*. Brillat Savarin was right, as always. It calmed the nerves. Yet did any of those present *need* soothing? he wondered. Greeves was no more popular with most of the upper servants than with the lower. The pompous, silver-haired, fifty-year-old steward to the Duke of Stockbery was responsible not only for the smooth running of Stockbery Towers and its estates but for the financial management of Stockbery House in Mayfair. A servant, but not a servant. A Power.

'Such a lovely man,' Edith Hankey whispered. 'No one would want to do a thing like that on purpose.'

There was a pause while the upper servants studiously applied themselves to sipping tea. Auguste, partaking of the same ritual – it was, after all, necessary to conform in such times of stress – looked round at his colleagues; his Gallic shrewdness noted details dispassionately, despite the

3

fact that he was as shaken as they at the day's events. Mrs Hankey's attachment to the steward might have been a subject of merriment among her minions, but Auguste thought he knew her well enough to detect genuine emotion. Though quite what emotion he was not sure. How old was she? Fifty, fifty-five? It was difficult to say. Old enough in her position to worry about her old age, and to welcome with enthusiasm the attentions of any that seemed prepared to share it with her. He was fond of her in a way; she was not a clever woman, and an autocrat when she chose, yet behind her formidable exterior there was a warm enough heart, if it could be reached. She had been handsome in her day; and indeed with her chestnut-brown hair still unstreaked by grey, and her full figure still could lay claim to the term. Only the lips when pressed together displayed the personal disappointment the years had laid there. Instead of a husband, for the 'Mrs' was the usual courtesy title, she had made Stockbery Towers her home, her family, her passion.

'Might have tried to commit suicide, perhaps,' put in Ethel Gubbins incautiously.

Edith Hankey fixed her with a withering look. 'Mr Greeves – suicide? And why would he want to commit suicide, may I ask – when he had everything in life to look forward to? We had, as you know full well, Miss Gubbins, an understanding.'

'Accident then,' put in Ernest Hobbs, butler, hastily peacemaking. He was a Man of Kent born and bred, with the slow determined way of his ancestors; he always had the air of one faintly surprised to find himself no longer the lampboy he had started his career as at the Towers.

'How can you accidentally swallow enough poison to have that effect?' said May Fawcett belligerently, clearly piqued at being omitted from the circle of attention. A

4

sharp-faced intelligent twenty-eight-year-old, she was lady's-maid to Her Grace and it was an open secret to all, save Mrs Hankey, that she and Greeves had not so much an understanding as an actuality yielding more immediate physical rewards than those anticipated in her private moments by the housekeeper. Auguste's sympathies were with Mrs Hankey, but his money he would have put on May Fawcett in the Greeves matrimonial stakes.

'In something he ate most like,' continued Ernest Hobbs defiantly, looking meaningfully at Auguste. Six pairs of eyes turned to the thirty-two-year-old master chef. The usual twinkle disappeared; his dark brown eyes flashed as centuries of French honour were aroused in him. For all he was half English, he had been reared in France. *Something he ate?* Were these blockheads suggesting that cooking supervised and prepared by him, for which *he* was responsible, could poison a man? Yet behind his anger there was a faint chill. These people facing him had but a few hours before been his colleagues, his friends, his family. Now they seemed accusing strangers.

'Mushroom, it must have been a mushroom,' put in valet John Cricket eagerly.

'Or that nasty French stuff you pick, like spinach. Perhaps it was that. Perhaps you put some rhubarb leaves in by mistake. Easily done. Poor Mr Greeves, suppose he –' But the thought was too awful to be put into words and Edith Hankey's white square of cambric was pressed into service once more.

Auguste swelled in fury. He was used to a state of armed professional enmity with Mrs Hankey ever since he had insisted it was his prerogative as chef to prepare the desserts himself, instead of leaving it in her control as mistress of the still-room. He had had no choice in the matter. Ever since he had observed her thickening a *crème bavarois* with

5

cornflour, he had realised that a stand had to be made. Now she was insinuating he could not tell rhubarb from sorrel.

Ethel leapt in as always to lower the temperature. 'But, Mrs Hankey, we all had the spinach at dinner.'

'We didn't all have the mushrooms, though,' put in Cricket doggedly, eyes flickering vindictively. 'And he could have been unlucky. Just got the Death's Cap. Might have been any of us.'

'Monsieur Cricket, would you lay out for His Grace brown boots for a visit to his club?' asked Auguste dangerously, quietly.

Cricket blinked nervously. He had nothing to say on the question of boots.

'Then have the kindness to realise that I do not simply drop an *Amanita phalloides* into *un garni de champignons*.' Auguste's tones were clipped and incisive. This was an affront that could not be ignored.

There was a nervous silence.

'Perhaps it was something he took last night,' put in Frederick Chambers, he of the unfortunate name. As Groom of the Chambers he was perpetually the target of feeble jokes from guests, all of which he suffered stoically, but worse, since the Duke was in the habit of calling all five footmen Frederick on the grounds that footmen at Stockbery Towers had always been called Frederick (way back in the last century one had been) he was in perpetual danger of being taken by surprise and answering to the name, in a manner unbecoming to his status as an upper servant; they were, of course, addressed by their surnames. Hence, Auguste presumed, Chambers' always guarded manner, always watchful for some real or imagined affront.

'Then why was it after dinner that he was took bad?' Mrs Hankey's voice wavered. 'He was all right when we were

6

there. Didn't complain – not more than usual,' she added honestly.

Servants' dinner, as opposed to Their Graces' luncheon, had proceeded as usual. The upper servants and their counterparts attached to His Grace's guests for the shooting party, being My Lord Arthur Petersfield's valet, the Marquise's maid, the Prince of Herzenberg's manservant, and Mrs Hartham's lady's-maid, had partaken of their entrée in the servants' hall, then progressed in stately and duly ordained order of precedence to Pug's Parlour, the hallowed sanctum of the upper servants. There they had partaken of their dessert and cheese. In most households they would also have taken tea or coffee in Pug's Parlour, but Mr Greeves, with a fine twist of the hierarchical knife, chose to underline his highly superior status by taking a savoury and a glass of brandy alone while the rest of the upper servants retreated part way whence they had come and smartly turned left to the housekeeper's room. There they imbibed their own more modest refreshment, before separating to take up their several duties. Usually, that is. Today, their cups had hardly reached their lips before the white-faced steward's-room boy had burst into the room without so much as a knock.

No one had an answer for Mrs Hankey's question. Conversation dwindled, and private speculation rose. Reluctantly one by one they departed to take up their afternoon occupations, each one scuttling past the closed door of Pug's Parlour, half fearful, half hynotised.

The lower servants too seemed to be milling in unusual numbers for this time of day in the humble milieu of the servants' hall, which was conveniently close to Pug's Parlour. There they were indulging in lurid speculations, based on their fascinated study of the deeds of Jack the Ripper, aroused by the occurrence of a sudden drama of life and

7

death in their midst. No hesitancy here about what the outcome of the afternoon would be. In their minds Greeves was already a goner, done to death by an arch-fiend – though about the latter point opinions varied. But had the Duke himself been found with a knife in his back, it could hardly have caused more excitement. The Duke and Duchess were but mere names to the smaller fry of the vast indoor and outdoor staff who might never see them in the whole course of their lives in service, save for Their Graces' fleeting and statutory appearance at the annual Servants' Ball. Archibald Stewart Greeves, on the other hand, had been the ever present tribulation that might at any moment scourge them, a greater fear to these raw Kentish girls than 'being catched' by the Hooden Horse, a threat their mothers held over them still.

The appearance of both Sergeant Bladon and, in due course, Police Constable Perkins changed private assumption to public certainty. Greeves must be dead. The self-important demeanour of Dr Parkes, watch-chain lying with assurance over his paunch, as he emerged from Pug's Parlour confirmed their best suspicions. This was Murder Most Foul.

It was about five o'clock when the upper servants again foregathered, with Ethel bringing them the momentous news that Sergeant Bladon's bicycle had been seen in the courtyard, thus being as usual one stage behind the lower servants.

Scarcely had the ramifications of this news been absorbed than a knock at Mrs Hankey's door revealed an agog lower minion ushering in Dr Parkes. All eyes turned to the portly frock-coated doctor.

He cleared his throat, self-consciously: 'I am sorry to inform you, ladies and gentlemen, that Mr Greeves has – um – passed away.'

A shriek from May Fawcett; a faint cry from Mrs Hankey.

'And I'm not satisfied. Not satisfied *at all*, as I shall be telling His Grace,' he emphasised, glaring at them. He couldn't wait to tell His Grace, it was his big moment. 'I have had to ask for police presence. Mr Greeves' rooms are under guard.'

Such was the eloquence of his declaration that the upper servants imagined the whole of the Household Cavalry galloping up the drive, but reality returned with the news that the police guard was only Ned Perkins, the butcher's youngest.

'Good afternoon, maître.'

The Duchess of Stockbery was always punctilious in her greeting. Sitting in her blue chiffon teagown, she created an air of fragility, surrounded by portraits of the Duke's ancestors in the library. It was an air belied by her purposeful chin. The Duke contented himself with a mere nod and a ' 'Nin, Did'yer'. However enamoured he was of their cuisine, the Duke regarded all Frenchmen as vaguely effeminate and their language as an eccentricity in which they illogically persisted.

'Been killing off my staff, eh, Did'yer?' remarked the Duke, all fifteen stone ensconced in his brown leather-covered chair, surprisingly intelligent eyes glaring out from under the bushy grey eyebrows. 'Had another shot at the old Quoorma, eh, Did'yer, eh?'

Auguste stiffened. His Grace was His Grace, but even he need not have reminded him quite so outspokenly of that early disaster. True, he had not quite mastered the use of spices recommended in Colonel Kenny-Robert's *Culinary Jottings*, but that had been in his early days in England. Now his mulligatawny, his curries were eagerly devoured by

9

His Grace's guests. Why, even Colonel Milligan, on leave from the Indian Army, after the winning of the VC and much in demand by ambitious hostesses as a result, had demanded Didier's curry as a condition of his attendance.

'George,' protested the Duchess, laying her hand lightly on the ducal arm and smiling with practised charm at Auguste. Fifteen years younger than her husband, it was hard to believe she was the mother of a twenty-year-old daughter and twenty-two-year-old son, and Her Grace would have been the first to agree with you. Only she and May Fawcett knew the labour that went into achieving this effect.

The Duke grunted. 'Bad business though. Place gone haywire. The sergeant fellow tells me Greeves was poisoned but they don't know. Even had the impudence to tell me he's leaving a guard. Must have been an accident. Things get left around. It happens.'

Auguste stiffened but His Grace, not attuned to his inferiors' feelings, swept on. 'Easy enough. Organisation gone to pot. Saw a gal skipping around at five o'clock yesterday afternoon.' The Duke shook his head in despair. His dislike of seeing the female members of his staff after noon was legendary. 'What with her not in her black when she should be, and Freds in dress livery before luncheon, I don't know what the staff's coming to. Discipline gone to pot. See to it, Did'yer, there's a good fellow.'

'Certainly, Your Grace,' murmured Auguste.

It was easier to agree than to point out it was now Mr Hobbs and not the chef whose duty it would be to discipline the lower servants. The Duke had this simple idea that an order given to one servant could be passed on to all, that behind that green baize door was one cohesive unit striving only to do its best for the Dukes of Stockbery. So, Auguste supposed, in the last resort it would. But before that last

10

resort, what petty bickerings, what jealousies, what rivalries, what jealously guarded prerogatives and dividing lines. So foolish – except for his own grievance of course. How glad he was that as chef with his two assistants, two kitchen-maids, one vegetable maid, two scullery maids and the pantryboy, he formed a small separate sovereignty within the vast empire below stairs. Or was it just Greeves, with his sly insinuations, his sinister, brooding eye on them that had resulted in that perpetual sense of unease in which they had lived for so long?

'Monsieur Didier' – the Duchess's accent was impeccable – she had had a French lover for the whole of one London season – 'we realise what a blow this has been and how distressed you must be at this unfortunate accident, but, Monsieur Didier, can you still *manage*? It is quite impossible to stop our guests arriving on Friday.'

'Damned cheek,' grunted the Duke. 'Whippersnapper of a policeman suggested we call the whole thing off till he'd finished what he called his investigations. I said I knew old Hobbs could cope perfectly well, and he had the impudence to tell me that wasn't what he'd had in mind. Sent him off with a flea in his ear.'

'*Oui*, madame,' said Auguste, disregarding this intervention and concentrating on the important matters, his eyes brightening as usual at discussions of *les menus*, *le banquet*, which had occasioned this unusual afternoon summons. The morning was his regular time for admission to the Presence. Another fifteen house guests would be arriving on Friday to Monday, not to mention the guests invited for the day only for the shoot and the dance. It was only a small dance, of course, nothing like the ball that would be thrown at the end of the three-week shooting party. The guests on Friday would be arriving by London, Chatham and South-East railway. Only one train was involved for it had a special connection to Hollingham Halt, its voyagers known to the more frivolous of the railway staff as the Tower Trippers.

For the Friday evening to precede an informal dance, a dinner *à la Russe* had been planned. For the Saturday a buffet to excel all buffets. The marble-shelved larders were groaning under the weight of stores awaiting conversion into works of art; the iceboxes would soon be full of the sorbets to quench hot passions aroused by the dancing; the game larders were being stripped of their contents in preparation for the forthcoming culinary delights.

As Their Graces pored with delighted exclamations and the occasional frown over the menus, Auguste wondered how they had taken Greeves' death. Had the dread word of murder been mentioned to them? And, if so, did they feel it pertained to them? Or, as it had taken place the other side of the green baize door, was it to them simply a parlour game of Guess the Murderer, in which they were concerned simply as bystanders? Not that murder was a stranger to this house of aristocracy. There had been murders a-plenty in the past – Ethel had relished telling him of them on the dark nights when they could wander unobserved in the huge park of Stockbery Towers. There had been the unfortunate case of the ninth Duke's sister, a little strange from birth, who had stolen by night to the coachman's dwelling with a long kitchen knife; the third Duke's younger brother whom no one had set eyes on after the horrible murder of My Lord of Lyme, his rival at court in the affections of Good Queen Bess. And the –

'What the devil's this, Did'yer?' An imperious finger was pointed at the carefully written list.

'Crayfish, Your Grace, from the River Len.'

The Duke snorted. 'Why the devil can't we have some of that *écrevisses à la provençale*? Something with a bit of taste.'

'*Ne compliquez pas les choses*, Your Grace. Do not complicate matters,' said Auguste deferentially. 'That's what the maître, Monsieur Escoffier always said. In Kent, crayfish. In Provence, *écrevisses*.'

'Why the devil I ever brought you over, I don't know,' grunted the Duke. 'Haven't had a decent sauce in weeks.'

The battle of the menu won, Auguste made his way to the housekeeper's room where a further pot of lemon tea was being consumed and tongues were loosed in earnest.

'He said he wasn't satisfied,' said Hobbs, alarmed. 'That means –'

'Foul play,' breathed Cricket.

'Nonsense,' wept Mrs Hankey. 'How could it have been? It were an accident. Must have bin the Scotch woodcock. His little savoury he was so fond of. That boy, it's all his fault. He prepared it.'

Auguste shrugged. 'How could one poison someone with anchovy fillets and cream, Mrs Hankey? Accidentally?'

Much as he might privately consider all savouries as a poison, an assault on the tastebuds at the end of a meal, it was difficult to imagine them as a vehicle for a virulent poison, especially at the hands of a fifteen-year-old boy. As steward's-room boy it was Jackson's job to prepare the savoury and coffee in the pantry adjoining the Parlour, but it was difficult to see how poison could have been accidentally added to them.

'You mark my words,' said Cricket, though hardly anyone ever did. 'They'll find he was an arsenic eater – like that Mr Maybrick. Don't you worry, Mrs Hankey. I agree. Must have been an accident. The doctor's wrong. He took a bit too much.'

These words failed to cheer her. 'Arsenic eater,' Mrs Hankey said scornfully. 'What would he want to eat that

13

for? Unless someone fed it to him of course.' Her eyes travelled towards May Fawcett. 'Some people were bent on making his life a misery – knowing he was pledged to me, that is.'

May Fawcett was flushed but uncowed. She venomously spat out: 'If that's meant for me, Mrs Hankey, I would point out, if you please, that far from making Mr Greeves' life a misery, I was the one spot of fun that Archibald had.'

Auguste felt a shiver of apprehension. Every normal day, he and his fellows got on reasonably well, a few sour remarks, nothing special, a united band of upper servants. Then comes a death, a violent one, and suddenly all is changed. It was like a sauce; you add one final ingredient and the chemistry of all the rest is changed. Perhaps ruined . . .

Edith Hankey was staring at May Fawcett as though unable to believe the impertinence of what she had just heard. Finally she burst out: 'Archibald? You dare to call him Archibald. May Fawcett, how dare you! You never would while he was –' Her voice wobbled.

Miss Fawcett turned on her with a triumphant, cruel smile. 'Oh yes, I would. Why not? He was in love with me, see.'

Aha, thought Auguste. Now we shall hear the pheasants fly. The big bang and the birds fly out.

'May,' said Chambers sharply.

Auguste's eyes turned swiftly to him. What was this? *May*, not Miss Fawcett?

Chambers' intervention was ignored.

Edith Hankey had risen to her feet, to tower in personality if not inches above the girl. 'You forget your place, my girl. You taken leave of your senses? In love – with you? It was me with what he had an understanding.'

14

The girl looked at her contemptuously, the crisis having temporarily swept away all thought for the morrow. 'We was in love. We was going to get married, just as soon as we could get a house on the estate.'

Mrs Hankey's face was purple. 'You? You wicked little liar. He was going to marry me, miss. *Me*.'

'You!' retorted Miss Fawcett with withering scorn. 'What would he want you for? A man likes something pretty in his bed, not a ripe old bird like you.' And with that she burst out crying, while Mrs Hankey was reduced to a quivering jelly of shock and rage.

'Who cares how he died anyway?' wept May. 'He's dead.'

This realisation subdued Mrs Hankey's impotent anger and she sat down suddenly, first her chin, then her lips beginning to quiver. Ethel Gubbins rose to her feet and rushed straight to her, casting a scathing look at May.

'You shouldn't say such things, Miss Fawcett. You really shouldn't. We're all upset . . .' She put her arm round Mrs Hankey, an action unthinkable in other circumstances. 'Now you come to my room and lie down, Mrs Hankey. I'll look after you. A good cry will do you good.'

Another scathing glance, this time delivered at the men, presumably for the uselessness of their sex, and Mrs Hankey was escorted out of her room along the corridor and up to Ethel's on the first floor. Her footsteps could be heard clicking along the corridor in rhythm with the loud sobs that were now beginning to erupt. The remaining upper servants studiously avoided each other's eyes. No Greeves. Now no Mrs Hankey. Authority was temporarily mislaid.

Ernest Hobbs, the new power in the land as Greeves' acting successor, was the first to break the silence. 'Mr Didier, hrumph, the time.'

Five pairs of eyes went to the small French clock on Mrs Hankey's mantelpiece. Their owners took in its message simultaneously. Ten minutes to seven.

Five people reached the door almost at the same time. May Fawcett, hastily scrubbing at her face with a handkerchief, was marginally first. 'Her dress,' she shrieked. 'The bath. If that little hussy's forgotten the water again –' Her scurrying steps echoed down the corridor, hotly pursued by John Cricket in the pursuit of similar sartorial duties for His Grace.

Auguste Didier was shaken. He had all but forgotten for the first time in his life.

Dinner. It was time for *le Diner*.

Adjusting his apron and his cap, Auguste paused at the entrance to the vast kitchen to survey his kingdom. He was tall for a Frenchman, five foot nine inches, and slim for a cook. To his staff he was a god and to the females on it a double god, for his dark, warm French eyes breathed an exoticism into their humdrum lives. Today this god would have news of The Murder, for such the lower servants were now convinced it must be. They had not seen him yet, his assistants. They were moving without that air of total dedication, so necessary for perfection. He frowned. The familiar blast of warmth from the ranges and gas stoves hit him, acting as a stimulant, and pushing to the back of his mind all thoughts of murder. There they could marinate, he told himself, like the fish of the Mediterranean with their provençal herbs. His mind must be clear for the important matter – dinner. Only one hour left. The sense of power surged over him again. He was a maître. Had not Auguste Escoffier himself bestowed the accolade on him? And this was his kingdom.

He sniffed. That was good. The smell of the roasts

slowly browning in the range, the fowls on their spits.

'Gladys, *ma petite*!'

She looked up; instantly the stocky figure in its brown print dress seemed to gain new purpose as she scurried over to the Black Beauty gas stove where sauce-making was about to commence. Some chefs left the sauces completely to their underlings; even the vegetables. Ah, they knew nothing, those ones. The slightest overcooking and – tragedy could strike. Why, a chef he knew in Paris had shot himself when the *brandade* separated, whilst the Comte de Paris was waiting. The thought of sudden death brought Auguste's mind back disagreeably to Greeves but, ignoring it, he set out on his 'Cook's Tour', as the girls disrespectfully called it. What else could you expect from girls not yet eighteen? They did not appreciate that food was an art – for them it was something to fill their bellies, something they could not get enough of at home. But give them another year with him and then they would know. Yet probably before then they would be married. They were forbidden followers, but they always found a way. And who could blame them? There were few Rosa Lewises amongst them.

'Ah, *la soupe*.'

He lifted the ladle to his lips. Gladys' eyes were fixed on him in trepidation. The *potage à la Reine* was light – perhaps a *soupçon* too much cream, but no matter. He smiled at her and her day was made. Annie was not so lucky. The *consommé* – he frowned. It would not be noticeable to any but Auguste, but he could detect a bouillon rushed, brought to the boil too quickly; it was without finesse. It was on his mind to tell her to throw it away, to shame her, but today – yes, today had been difficult, he conceded.

'But next time, *petite* Annie, you . . .'

The tour continued: roasts inspected, pies approved, a

17

sauce for an *entremet*, the turbot kettle prepared, the *carpes farcies* ready, the brandy junket setting nicely in the marble-shelved larder. The final stir for the sorbet in the icebox. Her Grace was particularly fond of sorbets, and would often have them served between courses. To Auguste's mind this was a mistake – *une petite salade*, perhaps, but a sorbet was too extreme. It frightened, not eased the stomach.

Ten minutes to eight: the Freds, as they were known even to the upper servants by now, gathered in the kitchen to take the tureens of soup to the servery. Normally they stood impassively. Tonight was different. They were animated beyond their station.

'Is it true, Mr Didier, that someone's cut old Greeves' gizzard?'

'Where's Mrs Hankey, Mr Didier? She 'asn't really taken poison and fallen senseless over 'is body, 'as she?' This romantic interpretation on the part of Gladys.

'*Non*, Gladys, Mrs Hankey is –'

'I 'eard, 'e did it 'imself –'

'John, the soup,' said Auguste firmly as the first tureen was handed over. Nothing, not even a death in the upper servants' ranks, must disturb the ritual. The Freds returned, their mission this time the roasts. Now Auguste's apprentice, William Tucker, came into his own. The cold roasts were already displayed along the long oak sideboards, where they would remain all evening, in the remote chance that a guest might still possess an unsatiated appetite after ten courses. The hot roasts were borne up to the servery to stand for their ritual fifteen minutes, steaming and tenderising inside their crusty shells, ready for the Duke's easier carving.

'*Attention*, Michael,' came Auguste's anxious shout as the newest of the Freds wavered uncertainly, laden salver in hand.

Next the fish, always Auguste's most troublesome course.

18

He cast an agonised glance at the St Pierre as it whisked by him in the charge of John, the oldest of the Freds. That rhubarb sauce – was it perhaps a little too bitter for the English palate? The salmon, that could look after itself safely in the huge chafing dishes in the servery, but the soles, perhaps today they had lingered a trifle too long in their *ravigote* sauce?

Finally the last of the courses had been dispatched, tired labourers began to contemplate their own suppers, and the whole mighty kingdom paused. Two hundred feet away nine spoons were lifted to busy chattering mouths, murder safely distanced by the green baize door. Tonight Ernest Hobbs, as acting steward, would be standing behind the Duke's chair, Auguste reflected: what more could life hold? A man of sixty, bullied and harassed by the smiling villainous Greeves for ten years, was at last now in a position of power. How would it affect him? If he were Hobbs, he'd be openly jubilant. No more petty criticisms over the state of the plate, no endless callings to account after sudden descents to the cellar to check stock. No, Hobbs could have little cause to regret Greeves' passing. Especially with that business of his daughter. Auguste had not then come to the Towers, but the gossip still persisted.

'Mr Didier, you've been in my still-room,' came the accusing voice of Mrs Hankey, sweeping into the kitchen to interrupt his thoughts. 'Now that I won't have . . .' Clearly she was determined not to allow any diminution of her rights, despite her publicly displayed weakness. She had risen, unable to sleep, unable to see anything but Archibald's contorted face.

'Ah, Madame Hankey, what could I do? The *charlotte* – it needed just a touch – a *je ne sais quoi*.' Auguste, deliberately at his most French, spread his hands expressively. 'Why, only *la belle* Madame Hankey's rosehip jelly would suffice.'

Mollified, though suspicious, Mrs Hankey sniffed. It was

19

true her rosehip jelly was widely known for its purity of texture. Though that did not excuse an unauthorised raid on her still-room, while her back was turned in such tragic circumstances.

In fact Auguste had had another mission in that still-room. He had seen someone die with symptoms like Greeves' before and, in the still-room were the jealously guarded medicaments with which Mrs Hankey treated the sick of the household against all minor ills, among them a sixpenny bottle of extract of aconite bought from Harrods, in small drops the basis for Dr Parkes' recommended cough and cold remedy, but in large doses swift and lethal. The bottle had still been there when he had looked. It was half empty but that told him nothing.

'Very well, Mr Didier, but don't let it happen again. The loss of my Archibald,' Edith Hankey lowered her voice, 'has been a bitter blow to me, Mr Didier; but I'm still the housekeeper here. I shall Go On.'

Auguste grimaced. Why did the English always have to Go On? She'd have felt much better if she'd simply howled and screamed like a Marseilles fishwife. After this burst of confidentiality, Mrs Hankey resumed her professional dignity. 'Supper will be in my room, Mr Greeves' room being – ah – not available.'

'Ned Perkins says they *are* treating it as a possible murder, Mr Didier,' one of the Freds commented importantly as he whisked by with a tray of savouries.

'That will do, John,' came Mrs Hankey's glacial voice. 'This is Mr Greeves you're speaking of, remember.'

Cowed, the Fred sped on his way, planning the relating of his news to more receptive ears.

Auguste avoided Mrs Hankey's eyes.

At last she spoke. 'Murder,' she said disbelievingly. 'In Stockbery Towers? Mr Greeves? Archibald?' Her voice rose high and trembled. She spun round abruptly and disappeared down the corridor to her room, leaving Auguste to his own thoughts.

They were a jumble; he needed time to sit down, quietly, methodically to arrange them as he would the ingredients for a receipt, then leave them to simmer quietly in a *pot-au-feu*. That this was necessary, his French logic told him. Necessary for his own protection. Greeves' death in the afternoon pointed to his luncheon being responsible. True, the first part of that luncheon had been spent as usual with the lower servants, but since Greeves was carefully flanked at the table by his fellow upper servants, it was almost impossible that any of the lower servants could have had an opportunity to drop poison into Greeves' food. That meant the poisoning was confined to the second half of the meal in Pug's Parlour. It was an unpleasant thought – and doubtless would not take long to occur to even the most obtuse of the Kent Detective Branch. And who was responsible for the luncheon? Himself, Auguste Didier. A foreigner, and as such the natural target for suspicion by the Kentish men and true.

Who had a motive to murder Archibald Greeves? After this afternoon's outburst perhaps there were undercurrents in the hitherto reasonably untroubled waters of the Upper Ten of which he had not been aware. What if Mrs Hankey had known about May Fawcett? And Ernest Hobbs, he had a motive if it had been Greeves who got his daughter into trouble. Or May Fawcett herself? Perhaps Greeves had really intended to marry Mrs Hankey after all? May wouldn't have liked that. She had shown an interest in Auguste when he first arrived two years before. But she was not his type. Too sharp-faced and thin-bodied; these high necks and tight-fronted skirts did little to flatter the English figure, and May Fawcett looked like a bad-tempered mare

21

much of the time with her long face and scraped-back hair. Yet she was pretty in a way – when she bothered to smile, which seemed to be less and less recently. If ladies'-maids did not marry, it could be a sad and lonely future. No wonder she boasted about Greeves' attentions. She'd have to leave of course. Hanky-panky – he caught himself firmly – Mrs Hankey would never allow her to remain now.

Ethel Gubbins was very different. Twenty years old, soft, warm, the perfect English country girl of which his mother had told him. Brown curls, big grey eyes and a way of looking at him that sometimes almost made him forget his resolution always to be true, in his heart at least, to Tatiana. Yet Ethel could not be quite so soft as she appeared, it occurred to him. She had to keep five under-housemaids in order, and could be as much a martinet as Mrs Hankey when her rules were transgressed.

Then there were the two men: Frederick Chambers and John Cricket. Cricket, a shifty nervous man in his forties, certainly had cause to dislike Greeves. And vice versa. A valet was a potential rival to the steward. He could whisper in his master's ear at quiet moments, running his bath, dressing him, lacing His Grace's boots, performing intimate services that created a bond between them to which a steward, however efficient, could never aspire. Greeves had crushed the competition somehow, for Cricket plainly walked in fear of him. Chambers was more of an enigma, the type of Englishman Auguste found it hard to fathom. A sensuous man, he guessed, with his full lips and cheeks. About his own age, he kept himself to himself and went about his duties formally and efficiently. He wondered what, if anything, was between him and May Fawcett.

And lastly Edward Jackson – and that curious fact that Auguste's brain had noted at the time, while so much else

22

was going on. Why had Edward Jackson been quite so sure that someone had done Greeves in?

At that moment the bell from the dining-room signalled the serving of coffee and Chambers hurried to take it to the ladies now gathered in the large ornate drawing-room while Hobbs hovered round the gentlemen solicitously with decanters of port and brandy. It was the signal for the lower servants to gather in the servants' hall, and for the Upper Ten, now attired in evening dress, to congregate, a trifle self-consciously at this unusual meeting place, in the house-keeper's room. Mrs Hankey, magnificently attired in deep purple satin, black lace fichu covering her ample chest and high neck, held tragic and silent court, centre stage. May Fawcett floated in black chiffon. Ethel had done her best with dark green crêpe. The visiting ladies'-maids, caught out by this unexpected departure from protocol, were bright birds of paradise in reds and blues.

Almost at once a problem arose. The formal procession to the servants' hall for supper should be led by the gentle-man of the highest consequence escorting the highest-ranking visiting lady's-maid. Mr Greeves was dead, Ernest Hobbs still busy about his duties upstairs. That only left –

'Mr Didier, would you?' Edith Hankey bowed to the inevitable, and inclined her head gracefully towards a small dark girl with dancing eyes – 'The Markeys dee Lavalley,' she announced impressively.

Mademoiselle Emilie Levine, lady's-maid, accepting by custom her mistress' rank for the evening, took Auguste's arm which was proffered with alacrity. There were immedi-ate benefits to Greeves' death, it seemed, and the prospect of an evening speaking French pleased him enormously. His grip tightened. Ethel was not so pleased, and a pout crossed her pretty face, as she took Petersfield's arm, a portly fifty-five-year-old. May somewhat nervously acquired the support of the Prince's valet, a fair-haired young man of stiffly correct manners.

Even once the intimacy of the housekeeper's room was again attained, etiquette demanded they should not discuss their private affairs in front of the visitors – who this evening showed a strange reluctance to depart to their beds. Thus it was eleven o'clock before they were alone, to discuss it, over a small late-night supper hastily prepared by the little still-room maid from leftovers from the dining-room.

Already the house was making early preparations for the night. Bedwarmers were being placed in beds that would not welcome their occupants for several hours yet; refreshments were put out for the gentlemen in case they fancied any slight supper, after the exertions of billiards and cards. The lampboy was preparing candles for Chambers to hand out to guests as they went to bed. Stockbery Towers was still old-fashioned in its lighting, with a mixture of oil and gas, but one never knew when a guest might have need of a candle in the dark mysterious corridors of the Towers, or to signal an invitation. Sandwiches were prepared in case guests might suffer night starvation, and occasionally for more romantic purposes: to a lover a plate left outside a door conveyed the information that the lady was abed and waiting. For the morality of the servants' hall, so strict that a kiss snatched in passing might mean instant dismissal, did not apply upstairs – except perhaps in the consensus that one should not be found out.

In Mrs Hankey's room, the temporary Pug's Parlour, the atmosphere lightened, partly because May Fawcett took herself to bed at an early opportunity in a waft of black chiffon and red eyes. Her Grace, having departed early to bed herself, had graciously given her leave to depart. Hobbs too had joined the silent circle, tired but exhilarated by his first taste of power.

'I still say it was an accident,' said Mrs Hankey, opening the discussion as her double right, both as occupant of the room and as the bereaved. 'An accident. Must've bin. I know you think my poor lamb was murdered, Mr Didier, but if so who did it? And why, that's what I would want to know. Why?'

'The police, they will find out,' murmured Auguste soothingly. 'No need for you to upset yourself, Madame Hankey.'

'The police,' she said scathingly. 'It ain't the whole might of Scotland Yard we got outside, you know. It's only that Ned Perkins on the door and Sergeant Bladon. I've known Tommy Bladon since he was knee high. He couldn't find out who pinched a leg of lamb. No,' she said, looking round defiantly, 'it was a tramp.'

There was a silence. Nobody dared to ask how a tramp could have infiltrated the bastions of Stockbery Towers, and why any tramp should have bothered to put a lethal dose of poison into the steward's food.

'It could have been any of us,' ventured Ethel soothingly but untactfully. 'Any of the outdoor servants, any of the lower servants, any of us.'

'No,' said Auguste quietly. 'Not one of the outdoor servants. They couldn't take the risk of being seen inside. The police will think it's one of us.'

'Us?' said Cricket stiffly.

'One of *us*?' echoed Mrs Hankey in awful tones. She regarded him with dislike. 'Mr Didier, do you see Daisy' - pointing at the yawning still-room maid in the adjoining room - 'or that flibbertigibbet scullery maid of yours creeping into Mr Greeves' room and poisoning his food? Might have been the boy, of course. Mr Greeves was a bit hard on him sometimes - that I will allow. After all,' she said, warming to the theme, 'the poison couldn't have been in the lunch – we all eat that. It must heve been some-thing that he had in his room alone – and the boy prepared all that.'

Auguste thought of Edward Jackson, the sharp fifteen-year-old cockney, and dismissed the idea of his tipping a lethal dose of something into Greeves' food, despite the fact he intended to have a talk with young Edward.

'No,' he said slowly. 'It could have been anyone. We don't know the poison worked instantly. Mr Greeves didn't say much all through luncheon; he could have been feeling ill then. It could have been given to him much earlier – before lunch. It could have been anyone in the house.'

'*Anyone*?' said Mrs Hankey, with horror. 'What are you suggesting, Mr Didier?'

Five pairs of eyes fastened on him. There was an awestruck silence.

Then Mrs Hankey drew breath and spoke: 'Are you sug-gesting, Mr Didier, that it could have been One of Them?' She turned her head to look from the uncurtained window across the dark driveway to the brightly lit drawing-room on the far side of the house, where the myriad lights of the huge chandeliers were still shining out.

'One of the Family?'

Chapter Two

Stockbery Towers had been built in the early eighteen-sixties, a monument to mid-Victorian Gothic grandeur. The former country seat of the Dukes of Stockbery had been burned down in the late fifties, its Elizabethan panelling and solid wood furniture having succumbed to fire on New Year's Eve, while the Duke and his lady were stepping out with steward and housekeeper respectively at the Servants' Ball. By the time they returned, flushed and gracious from their exertions on their inferiors' behalf, the fire was too well under way to save the house. Nothing daunted, the Duke, then a stalwart seventy-year-old, set out to build a monument in keeping with the age. Fired in his youth by a nanny who filled his infant head with crusades and troubadours, he tyrannised the unfortunate architect into adding two instead of the one more modest tower planned, and many pleasing (to him) crenellations, more suited to a stage Elsinore than the middle of the Kentish downs.

No expense was spared. The old Duke worked on the principle that if in order to run a family and guests of forty you needed a staff indoors and out of sixty, then it stood to reason that the servants' quarters should be at least as large if not larger than the main house. Not so in advance of his time, however, that he felt that servants should be seen as well as their presence felt, the servants' wing at Stockbery Towers, almost a peninsula of its own, was so carefully

27

camouflaged by a tasteful row of tall plane trees that to the casual eye it did not exist at all. Grateful as they were for the additional comfort that this privacy and comparative luxury compared with older houses afforded them, it posed some problems for its inmates. It was two hundred feet from the kitchen to the dining-room. From the coalhouse to the women servants' stairs and thence to the bedrooms was four hundred and fifty feet. The transport of coal and hot water had not been taken into consideration. The former was a disadvantage since it had the unfortunate effect that a sauce hollandaise would undoubtedly cool 'twixt kitchen and dining-room, a soufflé sink never to rise again, and even the salmi of game could not be guaranteed to reach its destination with quite that peak of bubble and heat as was desirable. A servery was therefore installed next to the dining-room, lined with heated cupboards and with numerous chafing dishes. Unfortunately, having enjoyed his first shoot from the new Stockbery Towers, followed by his first cold partridge and rum lunch, the Duke expired forthwith and was never to taste the exquisite fruits of the huge and expensively equipped kitchen.

His son, the twelfth Duke, succeeded him at the age of thirty-three and was now, in the autumn of 1891, a man of fifty-eight. With his wife Laetitia, he ruled over his estates as had his father before him, and the tenth Duke before him, right back to the first Duke, a highly unpleasant gentleman whose accomplishments leading to the bestowal of the dukedom had fortunately been clouded in the mists of time. English to the bone, George, twelfth Duke of Stockbery, had one day developed a taste for the bizarre, much as had his father in the matter of crenellations. The Duke had, two years before in 1889, with loud protestation, visited Paris, and once there had developed such a fancy for what he had hitherto categorised as 'foreign muck' that he had imported a French chef, in order that his whim for sweetbreads *à la dauphine* or *écrevisses à la provençale* might instantly be gratified.

Unfortunately, in choosing Auguste Didier, he had miscalculated. Auguste, for all his French upbringing and training in the classical cuisine of France, had an English mother who had once worked as a kitchen-maid under Richard Dolby at the Thatched House Tavern. Consequently Auguste asked nothing more than to be allowed to raise a pork pie, produce a celery forcemeat for a plump Aylesbury duckling, a quince sauce for a leg of veal. Of the basic superiority of English food he was firmly convinced, just as he was of the infinite superiority of the Frenchman in cooking it.

Then a tug of war had developed over who should present the menus to Her Grace of a morning – Auguste to whom to some extent Her Grace was in alliance, not for gastronomic reasons but because she had an eye to the gentlemen guests of the Prince of Wales' set, not to mention the Prince himself, who were known to like English food, plain and simply served – or Greeves who would insinuate his way there when His Grace was present. Then, before he knew it, Auguste would be presented with a menu scored out with His Grace's distinctive scrawl and a host of rich creamy sauces substituted for his delicate subtleties. Or even worse be summoned to the Presence: 'Good God man. Salmagundy? Spiced quinces? Ain't Christmas, is it? Ain't the nursery menu you've brought me, is it?'

'But, Your Grace . . .'

'Tell you what, Did'yer. How about a spot of Nymphs' legs again?'

Correctly interpreting this as a demand for yet one more appearance of the *Cuisses des Nymphs d'Aurore*, created out of frogs' legs, *vin d'Alsace*, and cream, a recipe handed

29

to him by the maître last year, Auguste would incline his head in resignation, averting his glance from the triumphant Greeves.

No, Auguste had no reason to like Greeves. Far from it, their feud into which Mrs Hankey would descend with a certain amount of pleasure, though not through dislike of Auguste, was common kitchen knowledge. The other upper servants he could tolerate. Even Mrs Hankey amused him, and May could be fun on occasions. Her discretion was not as absolute as befitted her position as confidential lady's-maid. Ethel? Ah, Ethel was a rose of pure delight. But Greeves – he was a *salaud*. An evil man. To smile and smile and be a villain . . . He remembered Mr Henry Irving saying those words at the Lyceum on that visit to London. Its purpose had been to greet his former maître, Maître Escoffier, newly arrived at the Savoy Hotel. Against all the rules of Stockbery Towers and with considerable organisation, he had taken Ethel with him. He had held her hand for the first time, then kissed her. He remembered with affection her little gasp as his moustache had touched her and her lips so eager and warm. Not like Tatiana's of course. No one was like Tatiana . . .

The three days that followed did nothing to cool speculation; theories grew, swelled, overdid themselves and were dropped, others sprang, fully armed, to take their place. Superficially the ranks held, underneath each looked to himself convinced of his own position, uncertain of his colleagues'. On the Friday morning Auguste was in the morning room discussing the final details for the menu that evening and for the Saturday buffet, when Hobbs entered.

'Chief Constable Herbert, Your Grace.'

Chief Constable? *Eh bien*, thought Auguste. No Chief Constables for an unfortunate accident that could be attributed by officialdom to a careless French cook. *Ah non*. It was certainly murder then. His French side was immediately excited. The Englishman in him thought of the disruption, not least to his kitchen, and of the consequences – for if it were murder, there must be a murderer. And it would be someone he knew. To a keen follower of Inspecteur Eugène Lecoq, it opened lots of intriguing possibilities. But, if he had hoped to stay to hear more of these interesting events, he was doomed to disappointment. A grunt from the Duke signified his dismissal; a small nod from the Duchess indicated he need worry no more about last-moment changes of plans for the buffet. It could proceed.

He passed the Chief Constable, a plump nervous ex-army major, on his way out. It was not usual for Humphrey Herbert, Chief Constable of Kent County Police, to be nervous, but it was not every day that he had to face the irascible Duke of Stockbery with what would undoubtedly constitute Bad News.

The heavy door closed behind him. Out in the deserted ballroom area Hobbs' and Auguste's footsteps halted. A quick glance of accord and they were side by side, ears pressed to the door. After all, whatever his pretensions, Greeves had belonged to the world of Below Stairs. It was *their* murder. Unfortunately the eleventh Duke of Stockbery's architect had done his work well. The door was solid and very little sound escaped from the morning room. Only the Duke's rising anger could be detected and a few words of the Chief Constable's deprecatory shrill tones.

'Murder, man?' shouted the Duke. 'Why, good God, man, who'd want to murder a perfectly good steward? This'll cause an Upset.' An Upset was the worst calamity that could befall the Towers. Placatory noises were offered by Her Grace. The word routine was mentioned by the

Chief Constable. He murmured of post-mortems. Then of discretion. Just a quick word to ascertain if any of the family or guests had seen Greeves shortly before his demise. A mere formality.

'Me guests? Search the house? Good God, man, don't you know we've got a shooting party on? Got dozens of people coming today. Guests in the house besides. Ain't suggestin' any of them would poison a *servant*, are you?'

It appeared such a thought had never entered the Chief Constable's head. There was a pause while they could hear nothing. Then the voices rose again.

'Do you know what the family motto is, my man?'

It was difficult not to know what the Stockbery motto was in Hollingham, or even in Maidstone where the Chief Constable resided. It was emblazoned not only on the lodge gates, but on the school buildings (the eighth Duke, of an intellectual turn of mind), on the sixteenth-century prison house (the sixth Duke, frustrated in a desire to enter the law), on a chapel in the church (the first Duke, in a belated effort to redeem his soul), and on the almshouses (the seventh Duchess, who devoted herself to good works while His Grace devoted himself to his mistress in London).

'*Charity to the Weak*. That don't mean going around killing off the servants with namby-pamby poison. By God, my ancestor had the right answer. The Black Duke – ran through his valet with a sword. That's the way to do it. The man's way. None of this – what d'yer call it? Aconitia?' The Duke was by no means a bloodthirsty man; he was a straightforward one.

Auguste expelled his breath in a sigh of satisfaction. There was a shuffle inside the room, the tension permeating even beyond the heavy door. They could hear stertorous breathing from the Chief Constable, and Auguste imagined a thick red finger being eased round the tight collar.

'So, Mr Hobbs, murder will out, as your Shakespeare says,' whispered Auguste.

'I never thought anything different, Mr Didier,' Hobbs muttered, 'and that's a fact. Whatever them women thought. He'd never have done himself in, and I don't see it being no accident.'

'But –'

'No, I said to meself, Greeves ain't the sort to commit suicide. And when all's said and done, it's hard to get a dose as big as that by accident like. Not when we were all eating the same food. I don't know much about this – what did 'e call it? – aconitia.'

'Extracted from aconite, the herb the Romans refused to allow to be grown in gardens, in the days when Emperors went in fear of their lives.'

'Easy to get now, is it?'

Auguste shrugged. 'Very. It is sold at any druggist. Aconite is the basis of many medicines. For colds, coughs. Not in sufficient strength to kill perhaps, for that you sign the poison book, but even that is easy, yes. The good Madame Hankey has a bottle –' he eyed Hobbs keenly – 'for Dr Parkes' cough remedy. I remember it grew in the garden of the Widow Lamont, and I remember thinking how suddenly old Gaston Lamont had died. Wolfsbane you call it here. Monkshood.'

'So any of us might have got it,' said Hobbs, cutting this reminiscence short. He too was a straightforward man, and believed in getting to the heart of a problem.

Or was he so straightforward? Auguste reflected. He said he knew nothing of aconite, and yet talked of a 'dose as big as that'. Perhaps, after all, Hobbs was not so simple.

He went back to the kitchen thoughtfully, for once his mind not wholly attuned to food and the perfect presentation thereof. He found himself methodically dissecting the fatal luncheon, much as he would fillet a turbot. It could not be the entrée to blame, it could not be the dessert, it had to be something Greeves partook of alone. And that left him with two choices: none of the upper servants, he could swear, went into the pantry themselves while Edward was serving dessert, and so either Edward Jackson or someone else had poisoned the coffee or the savoury or – he had that sudden sense of excitement, the thrill of satisfaction that he always had when distinguishing the final ingredient that made all the difference in the receipt of a maître cook – yes, it was the brandy. It could only be the brandy. After all . . .

The familiar smell of the kitchens wafting towards him distracted him, and he stood at the entrance savouring this moment, so important to him in the day. The moment when the work was done, the meal at its most perfect, ready to be served, awaiting only his accolade of approval. His thoughts were interrupted by William Tucker. He had been reminded at that moment of a particularly fine *civet de lièvre* served in the Café de Boulogne, where his old friend Anton Dumar had challenged him to name the herb. But he had guessed it.

'Who do you think dunnit, Mr Didier?' came Tucker's voice eagerly.

'There is no doubt. It was Dumar. Only he could have thought to have added the –'

Only the sight of Tucker's blank face brought Auguste to reality.

'Mr Greeves, Mr Didier. He *was* done in, wasn't he?'

Auguste was in a dilemma. Admit it now seemed beyond doubt and the whole kitchen staff would forget the luncheon ahead of them. Yet they would have to know sooner or later. 'Yes, William, it appears that the late Mr Greeves was – er – done in.'

Mr Tucker expelled a huge sigh of satisfaction. 'Who by? Weren't young Edward, were it? Wouldn't blame him if he had, mind you. No, it's to our way of thinking it was one of them.'

He gave a jerk of the head whose direction Auguste misunderstood. 'One of the laundry maids?' Auguste said blankly.

'No, not one of us,' said Tucker patiently. 'One of them. One of the Nobs.'

The Lady Jane Tunstall, untroubled by thoughts of murder, waved her fashionable ostrich plume to cool her pretty flushed face. She dared not go into the morning room or to the door of the garden for fear the right man might not be there, and the wrong one would be waiting for her. It was a most awkward dilemma.

'Lady Jane, my dance, I believe.'

Her worst fears were realised. That horrid serious Mr Marshall gathered the billowing folds of rose pink chiffon that encased her pretty body firmly into his arms and swung her on to the floor. She freed herself indignantly.

'Mr Marshall, you are well aware that the one dance I promised you was the waltz and this, if I am not mistaken, is not it.'

He released her hand immediately and stepped back bowing in contrition which also served to hide the slight smile that came to his lips.

'I do apologise, Lady Jane,' he said gravely. 'I feared seeing you unattended that I had been – er – remiss.'

'No you didn't,' she retorted. 'You were going to come and give me another horrible lecture.'

He looked hurt. 'A lecture? I merely said –'

'You merely said it was outrageous of me. I don't see it is outrageous merely to kiss someone you – you –' She broke off as his grey eyes looked amusedly into hers. How could it have been outrageous to grant a kiss to someone so handsome, mature and gentlemanly as Lord Arthur Petersfield? Twenty-year-old Lady Jane found it a great responsibility being a duke's daughter. And with her brother away, he who had disgraced the family name by eschewing the Guards in favour of the infantry, she had no one to confide in. She had been out over two years now, and delightful company though Mother was she could not help noticing a certain insistence on her duty to marry – and marry soon was clearly the unspoken message. Mother was always producing new eligible young men, or not so young. Lord Arthur was a definite improvement on the previous four candidates and, at the August ball at Stockbery House in Mayfair, had been most attentive to her.

'My dear Jane –'

She whisked round, lips consciously slightly parted, her face poised in profile to greet Lord Arthur, who studiously ignored Mr Marshall.

'Our dance,' he smiled, looking down on her from his superior Guards height. As she floated away on his uniformed arm, she gave Mr Marshall one gracious smile of forgiveness over Lord Arthur's shoulder. He wasn't looking.

Her Grace, Laetitia, Duchess of Stockbery, watched her daughter pirouetting with satisfaction. It was of course highly pleasing to have a daughter so beautiful as Jane that she might be complimented on having produced her, to be twitted that they looked like sisters, but less pleasing to have a daughter of marriageable age, and for everyone to be well aware that they were not sisters. True, the charms of a mere girl, however lovely, could bear no comparison with those of a mature beauty. And what did a twenty-year-old girl know of love? Her heart lurched.

'*Meine Röslein.*'

For once the liquid honey tones of Prince Franz of Herzenberg failed to move her. The note in her voice as she greeted her dearest Prince, so perfect a lover, had a distinct edge to it.

'Ah, Your Highness.'

Normally it was a game between them, this formality in public; but now the Duchess was hard put to it to keep her private feelings to herself.

'I quite thought you had forgotten me.' She tried to keep her tone light, but the laugh rang a little false. A point not missed by the Prince as he released her hand from the kiss. His dark eyes narrowed slightly.

'Forgotten you, *Liebchen*? How could that be possible?' he whispered softly.

She kept her eyes on the dancers on the floor lest the sight of his face so close to hers should lead her to say more than she should. It was a vain exercise.

'Quite possible, it seems, when Honoria is around.'

There was a pause. She stole a glance at him to see how he was taking this remark, and was heartened to hear him say: 'I have told you, *Liebchen*, it is for your sake I do this, dance with Mrs Hartham. Your reputation. We have our moments, our very special moments together. Always when dancing with another I think of those moments.'

Her heart melted. Dear Franz, how could she have doubted him? After all, she was Duchess of Stockbery, whereas dearest Honoria, sweet as she was, was merely the wife of a baron's second son. There was no comparison. But all the same she was not completely at ease. And this murder . . . Suppose Franz became difficult and insisted on his diplomatic rights? His pride might well be offended if the policeman carried out his threat to question everyone in the house. It was not as though Greeves had been any loss. Very far from it. She had always disliked him, even before he . . .

She shivered, and forced her mind away from these

37

unpleasant channels. She pulled herself together with great effort, and looked at Franz shyly from under her eyelashes. It rarely failed to charm him.

'Dearest. There, I've called you that. In public too. That's my second crime this evening. But I shall be good now. You can dance with anyone you please. You're quite right. We mustn't be seen too much together.'

No, she couldn't sacrifice Franz. George knew about it, of course, but never mentioned it. It was a matter of discretion. These things were understood in their circles. Provided no one else knew. That was the code. She thought of the Beresford scandal, still the talk of London. Teddy couldn't take another divorce in his circle, even if the idea of becoming Princess attracted her in her wilder moments. They'd be dropped from the Prince of Wales' set if any breath of suspicion tainted herself and George. She watched Franz swirling round the floor in the arms of an unattractive matron – he was a clever man – and took the arm of a particularly shy youth standing forlornly by a potted palm. He was eldest son to one of the richest landowners in Kent, a fortune made, alas, from butchery, which put him out of the running for Jane even in these free and easy days.

'Do take pity on me and ask me to dance, Mr Taylor.' Her Grace was famous for her charm.

In his library George, twelfth Duke of Stockbery, stood morosely in front of the fire, hands behind his back, an ancestor glaring down at him from the full majesty of his Van Dyck portrait. It had been a rum sort of day altogether. Started with a fellow bursting into the morning room before he'd even read *The Times* announcing one of your guests had butchered your butler or as near as dammit. Then old Hobbs had served the fruit before the dessert.

Hobbs wasn't going to be up to Greeves' standard. Things were going to be deuced uncomfortable at the Towers for a while. He'd say that for Greeves, everything ran smoothly. No discrepancies in the accounts, never bothered him with details, just kept things going. The Duke tried to conceive what could have made one of his servants disturb the calm that he assumed existed behind that baize door. In theory he knew that beyond that door lay a whole world of men and women, but as they were devoted, he assumed, to the cause of serving *him* they became an amorphous block of *them*. Now unwillingly he was forced to face the fact that one of them had apparently dropped a dose of something lethal into Greeves' victuals. The thought of there being such hatred tucked away in his domain was disturbing. He turned his mind to pleasanter topics – Honoria. His brows darkened. No, that wasn't pleasant at all. Where the devil was she? And what was she doing dancing with that nancified Prince fellow? Real ladies' man. Why, he'd sometimes thought he had his eye on Laetitia. The door opened.

'Why, George, how silly. Here you are. I've been looking for you all evening.'

He looked at her suspiciously.

'Dammit, Honoria, you knew I was waiting for you. What the devil have you been doing with the Prince fellow?'

Her pretty eyes lit up with surprise. 'Really, George, what language. Why, I was just waiting to see you. We must be careful, you know. We mustn't be seen together too much. After all, you see enough of me when we're alone.' She giggled. She put her head on one side in that way that always made him putty in her hands.

'Trouble is, I never know with you, Honoria,' he grunted. She came close to him and looked up at him with those large appealing eyes.

'Now, George –'

'Tonight, Honoria?' he asked hoarsely. 'You'll give me the usual signal?'

She smiled roguishly. 'Ah, that would be telling, George, wouldn't it?'

Lord Arthur guided Lady Jane through the intricate manoeuvres of his fifth dance with her that evening. He was pleased with himself. She was the best catch in the Home Counties, perhaps in England at the moment. Not much spare money, but couldn't fault the breeding. And he didn't have anything to fear from Walter Marshall.

'What are you smiling at, Arthur?' Lady Jane whispered, closing her eyes in the bliss of being so close again to this fascinating man, who admired everything about her.

'Who wouldn't smile, dancing with you, dear little thing?' he replied, rather pleased with this turn of phrase.

In fact he was smiling with satisfaction at the future prospects of Lord Arthur Petersfield. He had little doubt about why the Duke and Duchess had invited him to join the select number of guests invited to Stockbery Towers for the whole of the three-week shooting party. After all, at forty-two years old, right regiment, right address, not bad-looking, member of the Prince of Wales' set – and that still counted for something despite the Prince of Wales' present unpopularity – he could hardly fail. And that baccarat scandal at Tranby Croft would soon die down, together with the rumours of his own involvement in it. Lucky that Continental trip had cropped up when it did. The smile left his face for a brief moment. Trouble was that once rumours started they spread to other areas. There were pressures, questions asked when you were forty-two and unmarried. It was time he married, and he could manage someone as docile as this little thing. A year or two's attention . . .

'Isn't this murder exciting, Arthur?' Lady Jane was

very young, and she hadn't liked Greeves at all.

He looked at her patronisingly. 'That's servants' business, Jane. Nothing to do with us at all. Don't bother your pretty little head about it.'

He didn't bother his about it much either. For, as yet, murder was contained behind the fastness of that green baize door.

Mrs Honoria Hartham laughed quietly. She was famous for her laugh. It had a chuckling, throaty quality that conjured up fantasies in men's minds and had done so for over twenty years. Her Grace and Mrs Hartham entered a conspiracy of silence about their ages and, if their figures, like trees, bore any clue to their years, these were known only to their intimate ladies'-maids. Drawn to Laetitia in their common defiance of time, a bond hitherto reciprocated by Her Grace in gratitude at being released from wifely duties to His Grace, they were each other's greatest friends.

'Oh, Your Highness, now we mustn't dance together again. It is just the teensiest bit naughty of you to insist on it.' She tapped his wrist playfully with her fan.

Prince Franz was a little put out. He did not like being slapped playfully on the wrist and, moreover, he had not asked Mrs Hartham to dance but had been skilfully manoeuvred into a position where it would have been pointed to refuse. It was not his policy to offend ladies, and he capitulated. Yet he was equally upset at the thought of annoying Laetitia – no light matter, sure though he was of his hold over her. He dreaded warring women around him, a situation he never courted. It was time he married. He was in his late thirties. His Imperial Majesty the Kaiser Wilhelm II liked his envoys to be married, particularly his London envoys whom he was eager to mould into the model domestic pattern established by Albert the Good. This could not fail to find favour with dear Grandmamma, Her Gracious Majesty Victoria. Appointed to the London embassy in 1888, the Prince had fought against marriage for marriage's sake for some time, but the Kaiser had made his views quite plain in Franz's last visit to Berlin. There was enough choice. His figure was stocky but his height made this less noticeable, and his romantic looks, so reminiscent of the Good Albert himself, ensured that there would be no lack of candidates for his hand. But he had this distaste for women squabbling. It was boring. Sex was sex, for children and home; that he accepted. Here in England he found more was expected – social coquetry, in which he found himself unfortunately accomplished – and successful. After all, one must conform.

'Madame, I am the happiest man alive. Who would not steal your time when he knows himself unworthy of being granted it by favour.'

Honoria's heart danced. This was romance indeed. A prince. Just what she needed to take Cecil's most unwarranted suspicions away from her relationship with George. The Honourable Mr Hartham was a strict man of impeccable upbringing, a member of a highly religious and moral family. A family that had strongly disapproved of his marrying Miss Honoria Mossop with her kittenish ways and lack of family or money. They had been somewhat mollified when she obediently produced three impeccable and highly religious boys but scandalised when, duty done, she proceeded to join the fast Prince of Wales' set. Her husband, spending a few weeks at their Scottish estate, inculcating a sense of feudal pride into his sons, had been convinced that no harm could come to his wife under the roof of one of the noblest of English peers, until a strange necklace turned up among Honoria's jewels. She had explained it away and believed herself safe – until Greeves

. . . If only that man hadn't seen George coming from her room that night.

She shivered. The Prince mistook it for excitement and a sense of doom overtook him.

She saw the shadow. 'Come, Your Highness. You need not despair of my favour. You rate yourself too modestly.' She chuckled.

The Marquise de Lavallée's eyes twinkled. She hadn't had such a good evening for a long time. At sixty-two she was forced to be an onlooker at most things – not, thank Heaven, those that mattered. But this evening there was a rare sport of a murder in a ducal house. The Duke and Duchess, whom she liked, had been ruffled and perplexed at this disturbance to the ordered precision of life. She doubted if they really appreciated what had taken place and wondered if, when they did, the tradition of centuries would guide them through this crisis as it had through so many others. Ah, these English. Instead of revelling in it, they would pretend it had not happened, sweep it below stairs, back behind the baize door. In addition to these interesting speculations, she had watched the pretty child Jane's flirtation with the handsome, enigmatic Lord Arthur; and caught the look in that fascinating young man's eye. Now if she were Lady Jane . . .

But no, she was merely an onlooker. Save in one respect. She looked possessively and with affection at François. Her private secretary who accompanied her everywhere, her *very* private secretary. These things were understood in France. But here in England, how shocked Her Grace would be at the thought of a thirty-three-year-old man creeping into the bed of an old woman of sixty-two, long since widowed. She would not think for a moment of her own sin in leaving the bed of her very much alive husband to

43

run to the arms of a lover, only to change him like the season's fashions when the amusement palled. They did not understand in this cold England that the body of a woman was ageless, that it demanded love at seventy as it had at seventeen, that a woman of experience might have something to offer a shy, retiring young man in his thirties.

From his chair next to hers at one end of the ballroom he smiled at her now. That special smile that he used in their secret moments together.

'Madame . . .?'

She sighed. Even in France it was not permitted to make public display. She tapped his hand gently with her ivory fan. 'Monsieur Pradel, *je réfléchis*. This murder, will they suspect us, do you think?'

He turned liquid brown eyes on her in amazement. 'Us, Madame?'

You know, François, to what I refer.'

His eyes were filled with anger. 'To protect you, Madame – *ma vie* . . .'

That serious young man Walter Marshall sat patiently waiting for his waltz. He had spent a dutiful half-hour with his fellow guests (male), partaking of brandy and cigars while the ladies withdrew, and endured the usual ill-informed political discussion – not, as the ladies unfairly assumed, a discussion of the rival merits of Lillie Langtry and Lady Warwick as mistresses, past and present, to the Prince of Wales. It had been somewhat stilted in this house party owing to the presence of the Kaiser's envoy Prince Franz and views about whether or not Germany had aggressive intentions towards England could not be fully aired.

Since then he had circled the floor with a bishop's wife, sat out under the potted palms with young Mrs Herbert, danced in stately manner with the Marquise, and paid exactly the right number of compliments to Her Grace. Her Grace was very charming to him, but he knew steel when he met it. He was not on the Duchess' list of possible sons-in-law. Now he was sitting waiting for Jane. He had thought of her thus for a long time. Ever since he first met her four years ago, when she was still in the schoolroom, still somewhat pudgy, hair all over the place. She had been in a tree at the time, and, finding descent more perilous then ascent, had been compelled to seek help from the first person that passed. It had been he. He had obliged and, taking her for a servant as she was simply dressed in a print gown, had reprimanded her on the dangers of fair young ladies of tender years putting themselves in positions where they were obliged to expose far more of their (undoubtedly shapely) limbs than was modest. On its being pointed out that he was addressing the only daughter of the Duke himself, he replied, not a whit abashed, that in that event the lecture was even more deserved. Since that meeting he had not been in the least doubt that he was going to marry her.

He was twenty-seven, private secretary to Lord Medhurst, destined as Minister of Commerce in a future Liberal government. He was deemed to have a political future. To be an up-and-coming young man, despite the fact he had once been observed talking to that dreadful fellow Keir Hardie. Yet, since he showed no signs of realising the enormity of his actions, it was in time considered rather daring and public-spirited of him to speak with the head of that funny little Scottish Labour party.

He had been invited because Her Grace considered it useful to have a political face present, to counter rumours that she had purely frivolous house parties. She had made private enquiries as to his family and, upon discovering his

45

school had been Shrewsbury and his family insignificant – his grandfather had been a mere baronet – had dismissed him as a contender for Jane's hand. He was unassuming, a good conversationalist and since he was not on her list it had never occurred to Her Grace, until this evening, that he presented any threat at all.

Nor had it occurred to Lady Jane.

'Well, Mr Marshall, after your previous enthusiasm, you appear, if I may say so, a little lackadaisical in your attentions. I believe it time for our dance,' she remarked righteously now, appearing by his side.

He rose to his feet with a start, bowed and led her on to the floor.

'My apologies, Lady Jane. You are very good to seek me out.'

'Yes,' said Jane offhandedly, 'I thought that too.'

'I'm very honoured. Particularly when you are so much in demand.'

Jane looked at him suspiciously, but he seemed to have nothing more on his mind than the negotiation of the corner of the dance floor.

'Did you really forget?' she asked ingenuously. 'Or were you sulking?'

He laughed, not apparently annoyed, which disappointed Jane. 'No, I genuinely forgot.'

'That's not very flattering!'

'The truth is always flattering to an intelligent person.'

She thought about this, but he apparently didn't need a reply for he continued: 'I'd been thinking about your murder.'

'Thank you very much,' said Jane.

He smiled at her. 'That was badly put. I mean, your steward Greeves' murder.'

'That's all a lot of fuss about nothing. He was much

too nasty a man to murder. They'll find it was an accident.'

'I wonder . . .'

In the servants' wing, all but those unfortunates detailed to wait until the last of the guests had disappeared, at least temporarily, into their bedrooms, the servants were preparing for their briefer hours of rest.

In his room on the second floor, Auguste pulled his nightshirt over his head, welcoming the cool feel of the calico after the hot clamminess of his dress suit donned for servants' supper and redolent of kitchen smells. He was more physically tired than he could ever remember, yet his brain was still whirling, a mass of conflicting thoughts.

'*Les ortolans* – too brown. Four minutes only. Five at the most, and tonight they had *six*. Inattention to detail, so essential to a cook – and so essential in a murderer. How carefully Greeves' murderer must have planned . . . The larks were too skinny. Thirteen ounces I said, not twelve. *Les flancs. Diable!*' Had they been edible even? Had Gladys burnt the *crème de cacao* just a little? No, there would have been complaints, and he had heard nothing. The familiar murmur of contented voices had met his ears as he opened the door to the garden for a breath of the sharp night air. The sound of those that had dined well. Where else could people relax, be happy, be sensuous – and it was his food that made them so. They did not know how to enjoy food properly, these English; they thought it wrong. Yet they had the best food in the world if only they would appreciate it. And with the touch of a maître upon it, it was transformed into the ambrosia of the gods. It was his mission to save English cooking from itself. And now Monsieur Escoffier had come to the Savoy Hotel, between the two of them what triumphs they would achieve! Escoffier in London, himself in Kent – at first, but soon he would travel . . . Noble houses the length and breadth of England. This glowing thought died away and grimmer thoughts took its place, a kaleidoscope of *ortolans*, of death, of glasses of brandy, of Greeves and of blackmail, and those policemen rushing around like one of the choruses from those ridiculous Gilbert and Sullivan operas, looking so imposing in their helmets, but with little proceeding underneath them. He thought again of the evening's chaos, policemen mixing with kitchen-maids and footmen as they examined the housekeeper's stores, and sealed off Pug's Parlour while his staff was trying to serve a banquet for over forty people, and make preparations for tomorrow's grand buffet. It had not been easy. And he was tired – oh, so tired. He climbed thankfully into the small iron bed and extinguished the lamp.

There was a quiet knock at the door. Before he could even think who could be knocking at this time of night, the door opened and a dark-clad slim girlish figure slipped in, two long plaits falling behind her pretty head, and with candle in hand.

'Ethel!' Auguste was horrified.

'Oh don't scold me, Mr Didier – Auguste. I had to come.'

'But if you'd been seen!' He was shocked – amongst other emotions. It would be instant dismissal for her, and probably for him too. These things had to be arranged with discretion . . . even by a maître chef.

'I was ever so careful – I didn't come up the men's staircase.' The male servants' quarters on the second floor were reached by a staircase inaccessible to the women on the first floor, who were provided with their own staircase which, needless to say, did not connect with the second floor. 'I came through the main house.'

'You did what?' said Auguste faintly. Was this his little

Ethel, his English dove? He was obliged to regard her with a new admiration.

'That way I could pretend I'd brought something to one of the rooms.'

'But what if Mr Hobbs or Mr Chambers –'

'Well, they didn't,' said Ethel shortly, dismissing the subject. 'And when I go back, I'll be just as careful.'

'But perhaps you had better wait some time, *hein*?' murmured Auguste, his arm reaching out automatically. But Ethel was intent on other matters than love.

'The policeman said it's now certain it was murder, Mr Didier. Who do you think did it?' She turned large hopeful eyes on him.

Auguste was torn between natural pride that he should be regarded as the fount of knowledge, and pique that she had not come to his room through an irresistible desire to be with him.

'No, Estelle' – this was his compromise to the ugly sound of Ethel. 'My star, my little star', he had called her on the first evening they had walked out. Ethel had liked that. No one had called her a little star in the Maidstone house where she'd been brought up. 'But why do you have to come to ask me this now?' he murmured. Naturally it was an excuse. She desired to be with him.

'Oh, Mr Didier.' Her large grey eyes brimmed over with tears, so that it seemed quite natural for Auguste to draw her closer and put his arm round her. 'I'm afraid they'll think I did it.'

'You?' He laughed aloud at the thought, then quickly stifled it, remembering Chambers in the next room. 'Now why, *chérie*, should they think a little English maid like you should be capable of murder?'

'Because I – there was a reason,' she said in a whisper.

'What?' said Auguste, agog with curiosity. Ethel of all people.

'He tried to – I don't like to say . . .'

'What?' said Auguste, grimly.

'He tried to – well – you know, in the parlour on Wednesday. And then when I wouldn't, he said he'd get me dismissed . . . And oh, Mr Didier, what would I have done? What with no reference, I'd get no other job. And me mum needs the money. So you see, Mr Didier, you must find out who done it. They'll think it's me.'

'But no one will know.'

'Yes, he told me he'd spoken to Mrs Hankey. Lied about me . . . And she'll tell the policemen. You won't let them take me away, will you?'

Auguste looked at the weeping girl, felt her shoulders heaving beneath his arm. He watched her breasts rising and falling under the plain black dress. He could stem those tears in the best of all possible ways. But he was French and caution came before passion – and there was the memory of Tatiana's lovely figure . . .

He withdrew his arm and patted her briskly in the best approved English fashion.

'No, my star,' he murmured. 'They will not harm you. I will discover this murderer for you.'

'Edith,' he had whispered, only last Sunday. 'Just you and me, and a little cottage of our own. Think of that, eh?'

'I'd like that, Archibald, yes. I want to be your wife. Look after you.'

'You shall, Edith. Very soon.'

Edith Hankey tossed and turned in her bed in her bedroom on the ground floor, as she had done all that week, remembering how Archibald had held her hand in that very room where he . . . Now she stared into a bleak future, an

50

endless procession of years, holding office until she couldn't run the Towers any more and was pensioned off – if she were lucky – to find a little room somewhere, alone. Then she thought of May Fawcett and her torment began again. She was glad he was dead now. Glad. How could he have deceived her so? That hussy. All those afternoons off when he said he was visiting his sick brother. And he'd been with her. Her. No, she was glad he was dead. He'd made a fool of her.

Directly above, her rival tossed and turned in her smaller bed on the first floor. She had tried counting pins, tried counting Her Grace's hats, but sleep would not come. She kept seeing the dead face of Archibald Greeves staring up at her.

'What would the old Hankey say if she could see us?' she'd giggled in Archibald's arms only a week ago.

'Don't you worry about that old Kentish pudding. She thinks I've got my eye on her, just because I'm a bit sorry for her. But we know what's what, don't we?' And the deceitful old goat had taken her in the parlour then and there, just where . . . And only a day later she caught him fondling the scullery maid! He was no good. It must have been him seduced Hobbs' daughter after all. Well, she was glad he was dead!

'You thinking of telling His Grace that then, Hobbs? Telling him I make your life a misery, eh? Telling him you can't remember how many bottles of Château Margaux you laid down? Telling him how your Rosie ran after me, deliberately got herself in the family way . . .?'

Yes, Ernest Hobbs was a happy man. Greeves was dead. He could sleep easy for the first time in five years knowing

51

he didn't have to stand those sneers and insults, the sudden shout as he was handling the Staffordshire, the jerk of the arm as he was decanting the port. Now he was acting steward and soon he'd be steward. His Grace was a notoriously lazy man, and would not be bothered to train someone new in the ways of the estate. Hobbs can manage, he'd say.

'Well, Mr Chambers, so you had your eye on Miss Fawcett, eh? Think she'd look at you, did you? Know what she told me about you? About what it was like when you kissed her . . .' And Greeves hadn't even stopped there. 'Still, you didn't let it bother you, did you? One woman found you repulsive, so you try the next. Bill Sidder's widow was an easy target, weren't she? Don't think His Grace would like it though. Molesting the maids, then the estate workers. Do you think he'd like it, Chambers?'

Frederick Chambers was asleep, a smile of satisfaction on his lips. May Fawcett might not want him, but at least Greeves wouldn't have her . . .

'Oh, that's unfortunate, John. Very unfortunate, Mr Cricket. I quite thought you'd be able to get me what I wanted. What a pity. I don't think His Grace likes failures around him, do you, Cricket . . .?'

John Cricket lay awake. He was even more twitchy than usual. Greeves was dead. The police were investigating. Suppose they found out about Greeves' extra source of income and wondered where he got his information from? Wondered if he had an informant the other side of the baize door? How could he explain that Greeves had made him do it, that he had held the threat of dismissal over him? He had his invalid mother to think of. She depended on him. He couldn't have risked it. And it wasn't very serious after all, what he did – only gossip. they could never trace it back to him. Or could they?

Thirty yards from the servants' quarters the house party was settling down for the night. Perhaps settling down was not the right phrase. A stone's throw from the enforced virtuous beds of the servants, their betters set a different example, complimenting themselves on bestowing light and happiness upon this dull world. Prearranged signals were given and accepted, silken dresses rustled up the wide stair-cases, swished through chamber doors and, in due and rapid course, fell to the ground with the expert help of ladies'-maids, followed by the subsidence of billowing petti-coats, corset covers, corsets, chemises, stockings and draw-ers to be replaced by the flattering softness of lace-trimmed silk night attire. Her Grace had informed the company that early morning tea was at seven, and that she hoped no one would be disturbed by the longcase moon clock, the mecha-nisms of which were arranged to chime at six o'clock only, thus providing an hour during which even the most somnolent or assiduous lover could return safely to his own room. In due course a number of doors tentatively opened and the long chain of love unwound down the corridors of Stockbery Towers, dispersing into their several rooms.

Only the Marquise, unworried by the chancy arrange-ments of others, already rested peacefully in the arms of her lover, having requested his room adjoin hers, There were some compensations in being deemed past the age for love.

Chapter Three

Sergeant Bladon arrived at nine on the Saturday morning, once more correctly interpreting his proper place to be the tradesmen's entrance in the kitchen courtyard, and propped up his bicycle against the wall of Mrs Hankey's room. Heavy rain the night before had conspired to bespatter his sturdy uniformed legs with mud from the narrow lane that led to Stockbery Towers and that, combined with a consciousness that his method of arrival did not befit a sergeant of the detective force of Kent County Police, did not put him in the best of humours.

His request for use of the force's equipage had been met by a curt refusal from Naseby. On a good day Bladon would have conceded that the short distance from his Hollingham home to the Towers was easily bridgeable by bicycle or even by foot, but this was not a good day. It was a day clouded by Inspector Naseby. A weaselly-featured man of fifty who had come to the top of the detective branch by his fortunate fluke in trapping the infamous Rum Bubber Bill of the Ramsgate smuggling trade, Naseby would play his cards carefully. He'd be out for the glory of solving the Stockbery case, as it was already known, but it boded fair to be a difficult one and it would be on Bladon's shoulders that the blame would be laid if the ducal temper were to be lost.

'Find 'im, Bladon,' was Naseby's admonition to his

subordinate. 'You know these people. You'll handle it best.'

It was true enough. He felt at home amongst the lower servants. He'd known most of them since the Rector had dipped them caterwauling into the ninth-century font. It wasn't the lower servants he was going to face today however, it was the upper lot. They might have started off local, some of them, but they reckoned themselves a cut above that now.

Jackson's face appeared round the door in answer to his summons and a shadow of wariness crept over it. Bladon knew that look well. It belonged to lads with something to hide.

'Police, m'lad. Mrs Hankey's expecting me.'

With his morale somewhat improved, Bladon marched into the corridor conscious of the whole weight of the Kent County Police behind him. His self-importance received a slight setback, however, as he collided with a scurrying housemaid carrying a breakfast tray, and a few moments had to be wasted in removing some of Mrs Hankey's quince jelly from his trouser leg. This surmounted, he was shown into the housekeeper's room where a silent circle of upper servants greeted him, much as a séance might its medium.

'Hey you,' he said to Jackson, sidling out of the door, 'we need you, young feller me lad. Sit down.'

Mrs Hankey's bosom swelled. A lower servant to *sit* in her room! But the law was the law, even if it was only Tommy Bladon, and she grudgingly made room for an equally reluctant Jackson.

Bladon sat down cautiously on the spindly Windsor chair, his bulk overflowing its sides. He was a conscientious man, and the task in front of him was daunting. He had taken great pains in planning this interview. His reading of the doings of one Sherlock Holmes in the *Strand Magazine* should not be in vain.

56

'Well, now,' he announced, clearing his throat self-consciously, 'from our investigations it seems likely that Mr Archibald Greeves, steward of this establishment, died by the administration of poison.' He was disappointed at the unsurprised reception of this news, and continued rapidly, 'We have determined that in all likelihood it were a poison known as aconitia. One of the deadliest poisons known to man. As used by arch-fiend and murderer Dr George Lamson.' This time he got his reaction. The Lamson case was still talked about, and the ripple that ran round his audience was satisfying.

'Not arsenic, then?' enquired Chambers, glancing at Cricket. 'Not an arsenic eater?'

'Our tests say aconitia. From the aconite plant,' he added, determined that his hastily acquired erudition on the subject should be aired.

'But it ain't traceable in the body,' said Cricket quickly. 'So how do you know?'

'The doctor thought it might be – there are signs, you see: swelling at the base of the throat; distinctive taste of pu – vomit, begging your pardon, Mrs Hankey. And he was right. The detective force has ways of finding out for sure. Not fit for the ladies' ears,' Bladon added swiftly, and somewhat inaccurately.

Ethel's eyes grew round as saucers.

'I knew it,' said Mrs Hankey dolorously. 'Didn't I say so? It's that nasty weed grows in the garden, ain't it? Some must have got in his food by mistake. I told you, Mr Didier.'

Auguste gave a strangled gasp at this direct onslaught on his integrity.

She caught the look in his eyes and hastily amended her words: 'I don't say as how it was you yourself, Mr Didier. More like one of those kitchen-maids of yours. That

Gladys, never got her mind on her work. I don't mean intentional. Must have been an accident. Isn't that so, Officer?'

Gratified as he was by this public recognition of his status, Bladon was not to be deflected by Mrs Hankey's majestic forcefulness.

'Not unless the deceased was the only person to partake of the dish, mum.'

'Then it was suicide,' said Mrs Hankey firmly. She avoided the others' astonished eyes, incredulous at this change of mood from yesterday. 'Yes,' she continued, 'suicide it was. He realised he had, well, betrayed someone dear to 'im and this was his way of saying he was sorry.' She swept on in a surge of self-revelation, unheeding of the ill-suppressed fury of May Fawcett.

'Mr Greeves and I had an understanding, if you take my meaning. But others came between us, and poor Mr Greeves, who was only human, was Led Astray.'

'Astray,' muttered Bladon, recording diligently in his book.

'Too late,' intoned Mrs Hankey, 'he realised the error of his ways.' She fixed him with a sorrowful look. 'Others had their eyes on him, Sergeant Bladon, and more than eyes.'

'You wicked old queenie,' shrieked May Fawcett. It was doubtful if Mrs Hankey knew the word save in relation to her monarch, but its intent was unmistakable. The battle began to rage. Sergeant Bladon, totally incapable of recording this interesting exchange, sat nonplussed in its midst.

'Miss May Fawcett – er – lady's-maid to Her Grace,' supplied Auguste helpfully. The sergeant began to write this down; then decided old-fashioned methods might achieve more.

'That's enough,' he bawled. 'I won't have a pack of women making a mockery of The Law.'

Hobbs, Chambers and Cricket perked up. It was a long

time since anybody had classed Mrs Hankey as a member of a pack of women.

The battle stopped instantly, with a few indignant sniffs from Mrs Hankey, and an angry-faced May Fawcett twitching slightly.

'Now then,' said Bladon, adopting a tone of confidentiality, 'there's no denying Mr Greeves could have poisoned his own food. But generally we have a note saying To Whom It May Concern. Last letters to loved ones, that sort of thing. And there weren't none. Then there's the means. There weren't no sign of a bottle, anything like that around. I have to inform you officially we are treating the death as murder.'

Again there was an anticlimactic silence.

'Murder,' repeated Bladon unnecessarily. 'And that being the case, I need statements as to where you all were and what you were doing at the relevant time. That is, this poison being quick doing its job, in the hour before the deceased met his end.'

The upper servants looked at each other, puzzled.

'Us, Inspector?' queried Chambers doubtfully. 'We were all together, of course. Us and the visitors.'

'At dinner,' supplied Ethel helpfully.

Mrs Hankey assumed control. 'Mr Greeves was took bad at ten minutes past one, Sergeant. All of us, and the visitors' valets and maids, even him –' she cast a scathing look at the cowering Jackson – 'had been together since five minutes to twelve for dinner. 'Cept when he went to the pantry to get dessert.'

'And you had your dinner where?'

'We – that is the upper servants – meet in Pug's Parlour.'

'Where?' asked Bladon, puzzled.

'The name given to the steward's room,' explained

Hobbs, as the incumbent elect. 'Whoever the most senior servant is, in this case the steward, his room is referred to as Pug's Parlour, and there the Upper Ten – us top servants that is – foregather and eat part of their meals.'

'At twelve o'clock sharp we walk together to the servants' hall where we join the lower servants for our entrée – the roast, Sergeant Bladon,' Mrs Hankey added helpfully, for one uninitiated in the ways of gentlefolk.

'And this entry was what?' asked the sergeant.

'Roast lamb, purée of spinach and sorrel, roast potatoes with *un garni de champignons*, mushrooms,' recited Auguste automatically. He had an infallible memory for all menus, in particular those of his creation. He could recount even what had been served in those far-off days in Nice as an apprentice under the Maître Escoffier; what he had served in Paris, when Tatiana . . . The *oeufs brouillés aux truffes* for that special luncheon. Ah, she . . .

'And then we left the servants' hall at twelve-thirty to return to poor Mr Greeves' room for our pudding – er – dessert.' Mrs Hankey quickly resumed her starring role.

'Blackberry fool,' supplied Auguste.

'And that's waiting in – er – Pug's Parlour while you're all in the servants' hall?' asked Bladon, wishing that McNaughten of the Yard could hear this flawless questioning.

'It is brought up from the kitchen before dinner begins and left in the adjoining pantry where Edward then serves it.'

'So, it could have been poisoned before it got there,' said Bladon.

'Not unless we have a wholesale murderer, Sergeant. No one could guarantee it would reach Greeves,' put in Chambers dolorously.

'Only the person who serves it,' Cricket pointed out.

Edward Jackson, tried to look as though he were not there, as all eyes turned to him.

'I'll bear that in mind, lad,' said Bladon heavily. 'What happens next?'

'We come to my room, Sergeant, leaving Mr Greeves, as was, to his savoury and brandy, and we has our tea here.'

'Seems a lot of walking about just for a meal,' grunted Bladon, writing furiously.

'It's always been done this way,' said Ethel simply and conclusively.

'Now, who serves this roast up?'

'One of the odd-jobmen,' answered Auguste. 'Whichever is around.'

'And would you have noticed if he tipped a dose of something into Greeves' food?'

'I do not see how it could be arranged, Sergeant,' said Auguste somewhat impatiently. 'No one, least of all the man who served the meal, could add poison on purpose and be sure it reached its right destination. The plates are filled at one of the tables and passed down. The risk would be too great.'

The upper servants stirred uncomfortably. Auguste seemed to be bringing it unnecessarily near home.

'Nor could any of us add anything to the steward's food,' Auguste continued. 'One cannot take the risk of taking out a bottle, emptying something on to another's dish without being seen.' Auguste hesitated. Should he speak now? Or ask to see the sergeant later? It now seemed so obvious how it was done. He decided against, and continued: 'Only Edward had the opportunity and –'

Edward was looking at him with eyes of alarm.

'And,' Auguste went on firmly, 'it is not possible that a mere child would know about aconitia. He is too young to

61

buy it, no druggist would sell it to a child, too young to know how to extract it from a plant. He is a Londoner, *petit Edouard*, not a country lad.'

'That's as maybe,' said Bladon, shortly, fixing him with a suspicious look. These Frenchmen! A lot of hot-heads running about with sabres and moustaches. Not in the Garden of England, or he'd have something to say about it.

'Like Mr Greeves, did you, lad?' he said, rounding on Jackson.

'Weren't bad,' muttered the boy.

Mrs Hankey snorted. Greeves' bullying of Jackson was common knowledge.

'Now tell us, lad, what went on after you was alone with him.'

'I gives him his savoury.'

'His what?'

'His little titbit he liked at the end of his meal,' said Mrs Hankey.

What Sergeant Bladon liked at the end of his meal was a good plateful of Kentish cherry pudding, washed down with a glass of sweet ale, so talk of savouries did not impress him.

'A nice Scotch woodcock,' she went on fondly.

'A bird?' Bladon was puzzled.

'A savoury of anchovy, toast and cream, to which His Grace is particularly partial,' explained Auguste. 'And what His Grace likes, one tended to find Mr Greeves also liked.'

The sergeant glared at him ungratefully. 'And you cooked this – ?'

'I did,' said Edward in a strangled voice.

'I see,' said Bladon meaningfully. 'And then what?'

'Then I gives him the coffee.'

'And you was alone, lad, with him. All alone,' said the sergeant lovingly.

Edward was too frightened to reply this time.

'But, Sergeant –' interrupted Auguste.

'Quiet, Mr – er – Didier. I'll get to you later.'

'But –'

'Anyone besides you, lad,' said the sergeant, ignoring the further exasperated interruption, 'go into this pantry?'

A miserable shake of the head. 'Don't fink so.'

The rest of the upper servants watched Edward's ordeal with mixed feelings; while the spotlight was on Edward, it was not on them; on the other hand, as a lower servant, they felt it their duty to protect him. In public anyway. *Noblesse oblige*.

It was Ethel who spoke out. 'I hardly think, Sergeant, that, as Mr Didier said, this boy would think of poisoning Mr Greeves. He – er – got on quite well with him, didn't you, Edward?' she said firmly. The other upper servants nodded their reluctant agreement.

'Well now, Mr Edward Jackson, who else *could* have come into the pantry? They would have had to come through Greeves' room into the pantry. There ain't no door from the pantry to the corridor.'

Edward began to whimper softly. 'Didn't put nothing in it.'

'We'll see about that, lad.'

'But, Sergeant –' Auguste tried again. And the sergeant once again ignored him.

Fresh from reading *The Mystery of the Hansom Cab* and fired with detective zeal, Cricket put in brightly: 'Wouldn't the plates have remains on them?'

Bladon regarded him sourly. 'By the time my men got here, Mr Cricket, they'd all been cleared up.' It was a sore point. Naseby seemed to regard him as personally responsible.

'The sign of a well-run household, Sergeant Bladon,' said

Mrs Hankey, gratified, mistaking this for a compliment.

'It sets back our investigations. His Grace is not going to like it. He don't want his guests disturbed, and now they've all got to be interviewed.'

The upper servants were shocked. 'I don't see,' said Hobbs heavily, 'why His Grace's guests have to be bothered.' He would undoubtedly be the one to suffer if His Grace was irritated.

'Thoroughness,' said Bladon. 'That's what police work is. We have to make enquiries as to whether any of them could have been in a position to poison Mr Greeves' food.'

Eight pairs of eyes looked shocked. Those beings from another world concerned with murder? Unthinkable. Wasn't it? 'But Greeves was murdered here,' said Chambers, puzzled. 'Our side.'

Almost a sigh of relief that the other world remained inviolate.

'Your side of what?'

'Of the door.'

'And they never visited here?' The sergeant saw a gleam of hope.

The eyes were again full of fascinated horror at this ultimate sacrilege.

Hobbs cleared his throat. 'No, Sergeant. never does His Grace, nor Her Grace, nor any of the family nor guests enter the servants' wing. Once a year only do they enter here, to open the Servants' Ball on New Year's Eve. At our invitation, you understand.'

'It is like your House of Lords and House of Commons,' put in Auguste.

Sergeant Bladon was not interested in the House of Commons. 'So I take it, it would be unusual to see a guest or the family here.'

'Not unusual, Sergeant. Impossible. But consider, Sergeant –'

The sergeant did not wish to consider. This Frenchie was going to be a nuisance. Fancied themselves as great detectives, the French, so he'd heard. He'd see about that.

'I still think he done it himself,' said Mrs Hankey flatly. 'Like I said. Can't have been one of us.'

'He was a popular fellow then?' said Sergeant Bladon, knowing the answer full well but rather enjoying his power to cause discomfiture.

The Upper Ten refrained from looking at each other.

Hobbs spoke carefully. 'He was not well liked, Sergeant.'

A protest from Mrs Hankey was overborne by Auguste's pointing out that that did not mean people go round killing each other.

'Perhaps not,' said the sergeant, hastily dispelling a mental vision of Inspector Naseby lying over his own desk with a dagger in his back. 'And I heard tell, Mr Didier, you didn't have much cause to like this Greeves much?'

'That is true,' said Auguste with dignity. 'He did not appreciate that I am an *artiste*. We had words about a *soufflé grand marnier*, but men do not kill for that, Sergeant.' This was not quite accurate. He recalled a famous establishment in Paris where the chef had killed his underling who had implied that his *timbale* lacked finesse. 'But it seemed to me, Sergeant, that it is important to determine how this poison was used, whether in pure form in a bottle or by gathering in a garden or hedgerow. And there I think I can suggest –'

The sergeant fixed him with a withering look. Who did this Frenchie think he was? Auguste Dupin, Mr Poe's great detective, whose adventures he had so painstakingly read as a boy? 'I'm told that aconite is found in many large gardens.

65

What about here at the Towers? Any in your vegetable gardens?'

'I said so,' said Cricket brightly. 'It was in the greens. Didn't I say so?'

'Monsieur Cricket, your job may leave you time to wander the gardens of Stockbery Towers but mine does not. When I gather sorrel I do not wander into the wilderness garden to pick some wolfsbane and absentmindedly toss it in with the vegetables.'

Cricket was not abashed. 'It could have been done,' he said obstinately.

'Yes,' chimed in May Fawcett vindictively, 'you always make a point of collecting it yourself. And preparing it. I always cook the vegetables myself,' she mimicked.

Auguste exploded. '*Ma foi*, you English idiots. You think I ruin my art for the sake of murdering that *salaud*. It was not the purée – it was in the brandy. That is obvious.'

'Quiet,' shouted the sergeant again. This time unnecessarily, for a complete silence had fallen. The sergeant took in what Auguste had said.

'This is a confession, Mr Didier? What brandy might that be?'

Auguste gaped at him. 'A confession? *Non. Non.*' He spread his hands in despair. 'I try to help. Three times you shout me down when I try to tell you this talk of savouries, this talk of Edward being responsible is wrong. Of course he is not guilty. The poison was in the brandy. He always had a glass of brandy with his coffee. And did he not that day also, Edward?' He turned a slightly puzzled look on Edward.

'Yus,' muttered Edward.

The sergeant, depressed, stared at his notes. He seemed to be going in circles. 'And when he drank the brandy how long was it before he was taken queer . . .?'

'About five, ten minutes I fink,' Edward vouchsafed rather slowly, clearly bent on saying as little as possible on the grounds that anything he said appeared to incriminate him.

'And who looked after the brandy – where was it?'

'I had it in the pantry.' Edward looked as if he was about to cry.

'So there we are, Mr Didier. Why couldn't young Mr Jackson here have poisoned Greeves, whether it was in the savoury, the coffee – or the brandy?' the sergeant shot out triumphantly.

'Because,' said Auguste slowly, 'it was a Monday. And on a Monday the Duke gave Greeves a new bottle for his own use. It was a usual thing. Greeves would go to the morning room where the Duke would have the bottle waiting, would present the accounts and the Duke would give him the bottle. He used to tell us about it. He was proud of it.'

'Well?' said Bladon impatiently.

Hobbs was looking at Auguste with sudden enlightenment and with mixed feelings.

'The bottle's open when the Duke gives it to Greeves, sir. I opens it when I bring it up from the cellar to check it as a good 'un, and leaves it ready for His Grace in the morning room.'

'And there,' said Auguste, triumphantly, '*anyone* could have poisoned it.'

The upper servants almost applauded. The sergeant did not. He looked grey as the implications set in. He was going to have to tell Naseby. *They* were going to have to tell the Duke. *They* were going to interview his guests a little more rigorously. He made one last valiant attempt, for which Naseby should have given him his long overdue promotion.

'And who keeps the medicine chest here?'

Mrs Hankey blinked. 'I do, naturally, Sergeant.'

'Any aconitia?'

She was shaken, but stiffened. 'Naturally I keep some. Aconite liniment and the like, and some as a base for Dr Parkes' cough cure. His Grace –'

'And where is this 'ere medicine kept?'

'In my still-room.' She indicated the small room leading off her parlour.

'I'd like to view this bottle,' he said severely.

Every pound of her quivering resentment, Mrs Hankey led the way. A bottle was triumphantly produced with a sniff.

'Any missing?' the sergeant growled, determined to keep the upper hand.

He lost it.

'Couldn't say, Mr – er – Sergeant Bladon. When people are ill, I give them medicine to cure them. We don't count the cost of that sort of thing at the Towers.'

'I'll be taking this bottle, Mrs Hankey,' Bladon said hastily.

'You may, Sergeant, I've got another.'

'Who can come in here? Bladon asked weakly, defeated now.

And Mrs Hankey knew it.

'Me, Mr Hobbs and Daisy, of course. My maid. And Mr Greeves – poor soul. Things must have got too much for him. 'E knew it was here.'

'Anyone else?' said Bladon, ignoring this dangled herring.

'I'd like to see them try.'

The sergeant looked round. 'There's a door to the hallway,' he pointed out. 'Anyone could've got in.'

She looked at him with amazed tolerance. 'This,' she pointed out, 'is *my* corridor. No one comes down it without my permission.'

'No one?'

'Except the luggage men to collect the guests' luggage. But I'm always here to supervise that.'

'But what if your lovely back were turned, Mrs Hankey?' asked Sergeant Bladon jovially.

'My back,' she said glacially, 'is never turned. I'd know if someone'd been in here, *Mr* Bladon, I'd know. Don't I always know, Mr Didier?'

Auguste inclined his head.

Sergeant Bladon looked unconvinced, and his eyes gleamed with anticipatory pleasure as though the murderer of Archibald Greeves were already within reach of his plump hand. It was a pleasure to be long deferred.

Four carriages with different crests contained such guests as could be dissuaded from the charms of a late breakfast; the servants walked behind. The family was very democratic. They went to the same church as the servants. At the head of the long column of servants was Mrs Hankey escorted by Mr Hobbs, newly elevated to this honour; followed by Miss Fawcett and Mr Cricket, then Ethel and Mr Chambers and the visiting servants. Then followed the lower servants. For them church was compulsory, except of course for those minions whom God excused on the grounds that they were required to assist with ministering to the guests or with the luncheon. God was therefore forced to do without Auguste on most Sundays. His private devotions were rendered in the family chapel, designed by the architect more for convention than from any great conviction that it would be constantly in use. Auguste liked the chapel. Its Victorian pretentiousness, out of all proportion to its size, reminded him of the small Catholic church of his childhood; of hurrying along the Provençal street under the hot sun; of the impatience of *Monsieur le curé*, anxious to be away to his *déjeuner*; the simple trust of the village folk; the centimes spared with such difficulty to light another candle to the Virgin. To him the chapel had a meaning, a faith that the big Norman church at Hollingham failed to inspire in him. But his devotions this Sunday morning were solely to luncheon. The *grand buffet* for the previous evening had passed from his thoughts as completely as the strains of the orchestra hired from Canterbury for the occasion. The next meal was always the sole preoccupation of a maître chef. The roasts were checked; the watercress stuffing prepared for the geese, the pheasants plucked and ready for the ovens. When all was as ready as to satisfy even Auguste, he went once more in search of Edward Jackson, and this time found him easily, fresh from another 'chat' with Sergeant Bladon. He was moodily kicking oil canisters in the lamp-filling room, watching the diminutive lampboy, lowest in the pecking line, trimming wicks with nervous fingers.

A hand fell on his shoulder. 'Monsieur Edouard, a few words more if you please.'

'What yer want?' Edward enquired aggressively. His thin face would have been attractive, almost angelic, had it not had the look of an adult before his time. He had been living with an aunt in Maidstone before he entered the Duke's service eighteen months previously. He had been a telegraph boy and had won the Duke's gratitude for saving one of his hunting dogs' lives when it had incautiously entered a swift-flowing river in search of its quarry. Fifteen minutes after he had started cycling whistling up the drive that morning he found himself promptly transferred from bringing telegraphs in from the post office to Stockbery Towers to taking them out of the Towers. Then the cold winters of the Kentish downs produced a constant cough and the need to transfer to indoor work. What better than to set him to work for that damned useful chap Greeves?

'I take it you did not murder the good Greeves?' asked Auguste quietly.

Edward snorted by way of reply. He only wished he'd thought of it, had the nerve.

'Now of course we know that it is probable someone poisoned the brandy before it reached you –' he saw the flicker of something cross Edward's face, but could not interpret it – 'but all the same the police will wish to blame the servants if they can. So it is necessary we think a little, *hein*? When Dr Lamson poisoned his nephew he inserted the poison in a raisin in a Dundee cake.'

'I didn't give Greeves no cake,' said Edward sullenly.

'No, Edward,' said Auguste laughing. 'I think we must be sure now it was in the brandy. Either in the morning room or while it was in the pantry before we came or while we were there.'

'But no one was there except me, Mr Didier. And we was all together at luncheon before that.'

'Somehow it was done, *mon ami*. Someone disliked Greeves enough to murder him. And I think, pleasant though it is to have the good sergeant investigating the other side of our baize door, the reasons for murdering him are all on this – So what I wish to know, Edward, is *why* you were so sure it was murder right from the beginning. When you came to find Mrs Hankey, you said someone had done him in. *Why?*'

'Dunno.' This short monosyllable abruptly concluded the conversation so far as Edward was concerned, as he ducked under Auguste's arm to make a speedy exit.

But Auguste was used to the ways of boys, and a quick movement quickly prevented the escape of his prey.

'And now, Edward,' he said silkily, 'tell me why.'

'Plenty of folks didn't like him,' said Edward unwillingly, seeing no escape. 'Old Greeves used to laugh about how they'd like him out of the way. Talk about the power he'd got.'

'Power? Over whom? Over Mrs Hankey? Mr Chambers? Mr Hobbs?'

'Yes,' said the boy, glancing slyly at Auguste. 'He used to laugh and say he'd got more power than the Duke himself and knew more about what went on. He didn't mean just us, neither. The others.'

'Others?'

'Over there.' And he jerked his head in the same direction as had Tucker the previous evening. 'I fink 'e meant *them*.'

A rising excitement grasped Auguste. 'What sort of power, *mon brave*?'

'Dunno,' said Edward. 'But that's what he said. I was in the pantry, see, and he didn't know. When I came out he was putting summit away. That big bible he's got. He sort of smirked when he saw me, and said summit like, "This is the good book, Edward. It means power. My power. Plenty of them would like to destroy it, destroy me. But they won't get the chance." He thought I was a kid, so he didn't care what he said to me. Thought I didn't know what he was on about. I was going to take a peek when I got a chance. But I never did. Then he was done in.'

'But, Edward, do you not see how important this is? Perhaps this Greeves was a blackmailer. And would he blackmail me, Mrs Hankey, Mr Chambers? Our Mr Greeves liked a comfortable life, money. We have no money. No, if he was a blackmailer he was blackmailing those who have . . . It must mean the brandy was poisoned in the morning-room.'

This time he did not miss the flicker of reaction on Edward's face. 'What is it, Edouard?' he asked softly.

There was no response.

Not so gently now, Auguste shook him by the shoulders.

72

'Tell me, Edward. You want to go to prison? You want *me* to go?' The boy shook his head. 'Then trust me, and tell me.'

Edward licked his lips nervously. 'Wasn't done in the morning-room, Mr Didier. Can't 've bin.'

'Why not, Edward?'

'Must have been put in after it got to the pantry. When we were all together. Can't have bin before.'

'Why not?' said Auguste, almost shouting now.

Edward shuffled his feet. ' 'Cos I took a swig of it before dinner. Hadn't been feeling too good and when I puts it in the decanter I thought he wouldn't miss a nip. So I took a drop before we goes to the servants' hall. Right as rain, I was.'

Auguste's hands dropped from Edward's shoulders and he stared at the boy. 'Then it must have been one of us after all.'

He needed time to think, to let the content of this conversation marinate for a while, to reflect. There must have been a way. Meanwhile – 'Edward,' he said urgently. '*Écoutes, mon enfant*. Not a word of this to the good Sergeant Bladon. Not for the moment. Yes?'

Edward Jackson needed no urging.

'Oh, Mr Didier, I couldn't.'

'Auguste, dearest Estelle. You must call me Auguste,' he breathed softly into her ear, a little brown curl tickling his nose. 'And yes you could. Why not? It is a simple thing, is it not?'

'But I don't like to.'

'It is to find out who murdered Greeves. You asked me to find out, dearest.'

'But to –' She blushed.

'He is not that unattractive,' said Auguste.

'But not like –' She blushed again and looked modestly down.

'Of course he is not like me, my precious,' Auguste murmured tenderly. 'But just one kiss . . . Like this.'

So it was, just before going off duty from guarding Pug's Parlour, and being relieved by the Maidstone Constable Tomson, that PC Perkins was overwhelmed by Miss Gubbins not only stopping to speak to him but actually moving very close to him. He was given to understand that she would be only too happy to accompany him to the village dance on her next evening off. Were PC Perkins any more experienced than Ethel herself, he would have recognised Ethel's brave efforts at flirtation as singularly amateur, but, as he was not, he was gratified indeed to find her pretty face looking up at him admiringly and her lips so close to his, it seemed not so very daring to cover them firmly with his own. Ethel was surprised to find it not the ordeal she had feared, while Constable Perkins was oblivious to all but the wonder of Miss Gubbins.

Auguste had entered the sash window of Greeves' room with dexterity. It took but a moment to reach the bookcase and to extract the large family bible. He dared not strike a lucifer match and therefore it was by touch he identified the large shape cut out in the middle of the book which accommodated a small notebook comfortably. He slipped it into his hand, and put the bible back on the shelf. As he straightened up, a hand fell on his shoulder. A hand that belonged to a zealous reader of stories of detection, as the path to the distant horizon of promotion.

'Well, well, well, if it isn't Hawkshaw the Great Detective,' said Sergeant Bladon smugly.

*   *   *

'Just a look, Monsieur *le Sergeant*, I implore . . .'

'Now why should I give you a look, Mr Didier?' said Bladon heavily. He was seated importantly behind the desk specially allotted to him at Kent County Police HQ in Maidstone, flushed with the success of his capture. 'Trying to divert suspicion, that it? It wasn't no book you was after, were it? It was the bottle,' he shot out.

'Bottle?' echoed Auguste in puzzlement.

'The poison container – the aconite bottle,' explained the sergeant, unknowingly sending his reputation with Auguste down to the bottom again. 'Revisiting the scene of the crime, retrieving it. You knew we'd be on to Mrs Hankey's supply of aconitia, so you thought you'd be clever. You had your own bottle, and you hid it after you poisoned the brandy. So then you had to get it back.' Good thing he'd come up to the Towers to see Perkins before he left.

'*Non*,' said Auguste. He glanced at the sergeant and decided his method of approach. 'Monsieur *le Sergeant*, you English are so logical, so clear-thinking. You must see that it is illogical. To a man of reason like yourself –' Bladon's neck grew pink above his uniform collar. 'You must see that had I wished to poison Mr Greeves I did not need a bottle. I grate some root of wolfsbane into the horse-radish with which it can so easily be confused. I mash the leaves into the sorrel, I put the sap in his gravy – I am the cook, it would be simple. No need of bottles from Madame Hankey's storecupboard or anywhere else.'

He held the sergeant's eye, praying he would not see the flaw in this argument. Apparently he did not, for the sergeant went on: 'Then what was you after, then, eh?'

Auguste eyed the book lying under the sergeant's large palm.

'The book, Monsieur *le Sergeant*. I think the departed

75

Greeves practised the *chantage* – blackmail – and this is the book, if I'm right, where he kept the details.'

The sergeant drew a deep breath. This couldn't be happening to him, Mr Tommy Bladon. Blackmail, murder, dukes, duchesses. Why, this was better than the novels of Mr Hawley Smart, whose *The Great Tontine* he had just been reading. Though, mind you, it was his racing mysteries he liked best. Took him back to that day out he and Mrs Bladon had taken, down to the Folkestone Races . . . He pulled himself back from this happy reverie of times spent away from Inspector Naseby and reasserted his native Kent common sense. 'Who'd he have wanted to blackmail among you lot?' he said scornfully. 'The servants ain't got two pennies to rub together.'

Auguste looked at him. 'Not us, not the servants. The other side of that door. The family, the guests . . .'

Bladon's eyes bulged. 'Do you mean – gorlimy, not *him*?'

Auguste shrugged. 'Perhaps. Why not? It will be in the book.' Their eyes riveted on the object between them.

The sergeant, however, made no move to open it.

'If you will allow me to glance at it,' offered Auguste cunningly, 'I will suggest another possibility that might not have occurred to you.'

The sergeant snorted. Then he veered towards caution. Just in case this Frenchie had something to offer . . . 'I can't let it out of my hands, mind,' he warned.

'It is understood. Now, Sergeant, this bottle of brandy left in the morning-room – you will undoubtedly be testing it for the poison –' The sergeant regarded him sourly. 'Does it not perhaps suggest that someone unfamiliar with the ways of the household might think it intended for the Duke . . .?'

Auguste watched as the sergeant's face betrayed that he

76

had taken in the full implications of this statement. He prayed that the crime of sending the police off with a – what did they say? – *hareng rouge* was not a crime punishable by death in England.

Awful chasms of possibility opened up in front of the sergeant. He hardly noticed as Auguste reached gently across for the little notebook.

The Duke was not a good interviewee, particularly as he seemed to be under the impression that Inspector Naseby and Bladon only wanted full details of last Monday's bag.

'Good God, man, how can I remember? Had several shoots since then. Look in the game book, if you like. Write it up every evening.' Once this misunderstanding was cleared out of the way, the Duke turned somewhat mollified to the question of last Monday's luncheon. 'Luncheon was in the house that day. Laetitia'll remember. Came back to the gunroom just before twelve – talked to old Jebbins there. Then over to the bootroom, boots off, change, luncheon at one. Always do. Always is.'

'This bootroom, sir, is just by the servants' quarters, isn't it? Did you notice anything untoward?'

The Duke's irritation broke forth once more. 'Untoward? Mean to say did we see a damned tramp creeping around with a dose of poison in his hand? Got more important things to do than poke our noses into the servants' quarters. Door's there for a purpose, you know. Let them get on with it. No, get the scores out for the game book, make sure all in agreement, ready for the afternoon shoot, that's what we were doing. Never got it, of course, what with all the Upset,' he grumbled.

'Yes, yes, sir. But nothing untoward,' said Naseby soothingly.

Mollified, the Duke rumbled on. 'Everything slipshod

nowadays. It's the servant problem. Above themselves. Running about all over the place getting themselves poisoned. Housemaids here, housemaids there. Me father wouldn't have stood for it. Sacked any woman he saw round the place after twelve o'clock. There have to be rules you know. Freds in dress livery before luncheon. Butlers hopping about upsetting the port. What the place is coming to, I don't know. Servants – treat 'em well and what thanks do you get? Go and get themselves murdered right in the middle of the shooting season.'

The inspector broke into this monologue.

'Brandy, sir. I understand you gave Greeves a bottle of brandy personally, every Monday morning.'

'What of it?'

'That's where we think the poison was, sir.'

The Duke's face grew purple. 'My brandy? Hell's fire! May not have been my best Napoleon, but you calling it poison?'

The inspector broke in again hastily. 'No, sir, not the brandy itself. We think someone may have added poison to it. When exactly did you give it to him, sir?'

'Same time I always do. Before we set out on the shoot. After going through the affairs of the day. Ten o'clock, thereabouts.'

'And it was left in the room unattended?'

'So anyone could have put poison in it,' contributed Bladon, eagerly but incautiously.

The Duke eyed him sharply. 'Anyone? That mean me guests? Me family?'

'Would your guests know it was for Greeves, sir, if they saw it there?'

The Duke's face was a picture, as he contemplated this for a moment. 'Are you saying one of me guests would want to poison *me*?' His Grace was by no means slow on the uptake.

78

'Not necessarily, sir. A servant, perhaps.'

'Nonsense. All devoted to me. Anyway, servants knew it was for Greeves. The poison was meant for him all right.' There was a note of finality in his voice.

Just as Bladon's future in the Kent Police looked precarious in the extreme, the Duke saw the humorous side. The red face spluttered into mirth. His Grace roared. 'Why not *me*, eh Bladon? Always fancied the silken rope. Tried by his peers, eh? That what's in your mind?'

'I'll tell Teddy when I see him next. His Royal Highness will be very amused to hear I'm being investigated.' Lord Arther Petersfield laughed lightly.

Relieved that His Lordship was taking the interview in such good part, Naseby ploughed on. Had he seen a bottle of brandy in the morning-room on Monday morning? Had he known Greeves well? Had he had conversations with Greeves?

'I really could not say, Inspector. I do not keep a diary of encounters with the lower classes.'

Naseby might have felt put down, but His Lordship was smiling amiably if a trifle aloofly. 'Did you know about His Grace's custom of giving a bottle of brandy to the steward every Monday morning?'

'No, Inspector, I did not. I'm a guest, you know. Ain't done to take a close interest in your host's household running.'

Again the smile.

Where had he been that Monday morning?

'My dear fellow, where should I have been?' he enquired of Naseby. 'Shooting of course. Shooting at Stockbery Towers is too damned good to miss just to murder a servant.' He laughed easily, adjusting the elegant sleeve of his Norfolk jacket. With luck he could get another hour's shooting in before tea. That still left two hours before dinner for the seduction of Lady Jane. Not physical of course – that chore could be postponed, but her emotional conquest.

'And what time did you return for din – er – luncheon, sir?'

Lord Arthur considered. 'I really cannot recall for sure, Inspector. At twelve, I believe. We walked back to the gun-room together of course, and then returned to the bootroom as and when we were ready. I went almost immediately.'

'Alone, My Lord?'

Lord Arthur paused. 'I believe so. His Grace and then Marshall came into the bootroom while I was there. Fellow doesn't shoot, you know. Odd sort of chap. I went to change as Marshall came in. So yes, Inspector, I returned alone. Leaving me ample time to rush behind the door to the servants' quarters, enter the steward's room, tip arsenic into the food and return to enjoy my luncheon.'

'You knew Greeves' room was there, sir?'

Lord Arthur frowned. 'Yes, Inspector. I believe so. Regular visitors to this house, and I have the honour to count myself among their number, are aware of the position of the steward's room, owing to our patronage of the Servants' Ball on New Year's Eve, since we gathered there to be escorted to the ball by Greeves. That, however, is a different matter from entering the servants' quarters at any other time of year. I fear I should be a reckless murderer indeed to plan a murder in such a way.'

'And when you returned for luncheon, you noticed nothing untoward?' said Naseby unctuously, anxious to move to safer and more indefinite ground.

One handsome eyebrow flickered. 'Untoward? Ah yes, Inspector, I did notice something.'

The inspector and his subordinate leaned forward eagerly.

'The pheasant was just a fraction overdone. Not Didier's best.'

'Good morning, gentlemen.'

The Prince's manner was more friendly. Despite his thick accent, Naseby felt more at ease with him than with that elegant man about town Petersfield. True royalty, he said to himself, knowingly.

'I do not see how I can assist you, gentlemen.' The Prince reclined at ease in the Duke's leatherbound armchair. 'But His Imperial Majesty would wish me to help you if I can, but I do not see how. It is a servant that is killed, yes?'

'Yes,' said Naseby hesitating, but there was something about the Prince's manner that made him expand. 'But there's some doubt about whether he was the intended victim.' The Prince looked politely interested. 'It's been suggested that His Grace –'

'*Was*? *Was ist das*?' The Prince was startled out of his phlegm. 'But why is this? He died in his room, this servant, yes?'

'But we think the poison might have been in the brandy. And the brandy bottle was left unattended in the morning-room that morning until His Grace gave it to Greeves. It – er – puts us in a difficult position, Your – er – Highness,' said Naseby, suddenly remembering to whom he was speaking. 'Did you see it there, Your Highness?'

This was not as diplomatic as it might have been.

The Prince was a little offended. That was clear. '*Nein*, Inspector, I did not see a brandy bottle in the morning-room. Nor,' his tone was mild, but cold, 'if I had would I have poisoned it. In Germany it is not considered polite to poison one's host. In your country I am a guest, as well as in

81

this house. I would remind you of that, Inspector.'

The inspector was profuse in a flurry of apologies and denials. The Prince had not understood, had misunderstood, it was only he might assist –

'Might have noticed a few details,' put in Bladon helpfully, but earning a glare from his superior. The Prince accepted the apologies graciously with a smile, but they were still aware of an undercurrent of displeasure. Nevertheless he consented to continue.

'My movements that morning, Inspector? I go to the shoot at ten-fifteen. the first drive is at ten forty-five. You see, I have a good memory, *ja*? You can check with my loader, but I think I took twelve pheasants and two brace of partridge. This is not a bad score, gentlemen.'

There were hasty murmurs of approval.

'The second drive was at eleven-twenty. After the drive I compare the score with my loader, and return with the others to the gunroom. In the gunroom I discuss one of the guns which does not shoot well. I return to the house. I remove my boots. I go to change. I attend luncheon.'

There seemed little more to be said.

François was not so precise or so informative. Particularly as the inspector saw no need to be particularly gentle with someone who was both French and a sort of servant.

'*Non, Inspecteur*, I did not see the bottle of brandy.' His voice was almost a whisper.

'Did you know it was there, sir?' Naseby was congratulating himself on his masterly control of the situation.

'I – er – yes, *oui*, knew. I have been to the Towers before, and I was there for the New Year when the Duke invited Madame la Marquise to the ball –' His voice tailed off.

François, unhappily wondering whether honesty were the

best policy, recounted his somewhat vague movements in returning from the shoot. He made such a confusion of it that Naseby saw a gleam of hope. The Stockbery case might soon be solved.

The trouble was, he could not, for the life of him, see why a French secretary should want to poison either the Duke or his steward.

The ladies were even less precise in recollection of their movements. Honoria and Laetitia smiled sweetly and vouchsafed that they were only conscious of its being time to dress for luncheon – their second outfit of the day, or third if they had accompanied the shoot. In fact that Monday none had. Her Grace had spent the time in the morning-room, and no, she informed Naseby frostily, she had not noticed a bottle of brandy. Mrs Hartham had been in her room, the Marquise in the library. Lady Jane was even more circumspect, a faint flush of annoyance on her cheeks. When pressed nervously by the inspector, she said shortly that she had been walking in the grounds – it was such a nice day. Had she met anybody? It transpired she had met Mr Marshall. Mr Marshall had left the shoot. She had been intending to go to watch the drive, but Mr Marshall had detained her. A certain grimness entered her voice.

By Monday evening only the Prince, Mrs Hartham, Lord Arthur, the Marquise and François and Walter Marshall remained. The Friday to Monday visitors had departed in a frou-frou of baggage and carriages for Hollingham Halt station, whence the train would bear them exhausted back to London for a few more days of energetic social life, before another quiet two days in the countryside. On this occasion they were torn between reluctance at leaving the scene of such excitement and anticipation of the delightful tales they could tell in London. Left behind, the resident shooting party – requested to remain for the inquest thus removing their freedom of choice – settled down uneasily. An inquest, summoned for the Tuesday in order not to inconvenience the Duke's guests longer than was essential, offered both diversion and uncertainty. The death had, at first, been the subject of superior banter but the intrusion of the investigation, however apologetically, to their side of the dividing door suggested an unwelcome note of reality.

As one batch of guests departed, another arrived, to enter by different doors. His Grace had given orders that Greeves' relatives – it had been news to the staff that he had a family – should be shown every consideration. As the donkey carts brought their passengers up to the kitchen court entrance, the upper servants lined up with due ceremony and respect to greet them. In Mrs Hankey's room a special tea was laid out. The guest rooms in the servants' quarters were now to be filled with aliens who would be unaccustomed to the etiquette of the servants' wing. The upper servants therefore waited uneasily. Auguste need not have been there, but he was curious to see evidence of Greeves' other life. Few upper servants had one. Servants at their level were not expected to have sexual requirements, or if they did they should be sublimated in their job. Yet somehow, he was amazed to see, Greeves had managed to collect two cartloads of family mourners.

First to step down and sweep into the hall, handkerchief at her eyes, was a woman in her mid-forties with sharp black eyes and a firm fat figure that spoke of determination rather than pliability.

'I want to know what's been going on here,' she stated without demur, disregarding the carefully rehearsed speeches of condolence.

Mrs Hankey attempted to regain the initiative. 'And you are?'

The woman stared at her scornfully, eyeing her up and down. 'Mrs Greeves. Mrs Archibald Greeves. Widow.'

Widow! There was a strangled screech from May Fawcett. Mrs Hankey paled. Auguste laughed. Edith Hankey heard him. With common silent assent, she and May Fawcett moved closer together. The ranks had closed.

Chapter Four

'Raise the coffin.'

Slowly, with infinite care and two pairs of eyes fixed in devotion, they placed their hands upon it. There was a small gasp from the scullery maid, her mind still on the murder, not on her work.

Auguste held his breath. Even now, after all this time, a simple thing like this had the power to move him. It was a work of art, in which he and his assistants had striven together to produce something that would disappear without trace within twenty-four hours, without a moment's thought for the labour and the love its creation had entailed.

'Now, Joseph.'

Slowly, nervously, Joseph Benson extracted the large earthenware jar that filled the coffin-crust, one of a long line of similar crusty products awaiting his attention on the scrubbed deal table. The pie could now be filled. Pork, partridge, pheasant – the stuffings had already been carefully prepared, seasoned with all the subtleties of an English herb garden.

The Duke, to the annoyance of his gamekeeper – and his kitchen staff – had decreed another shooting party, with a picnic lunch, in the interests of keeping his guests diverted. A simple picnic, attended, of course, by ten servants in full regalia, could be guaranteed to amuse the ladies also. Even the Marquise seemed disposed to attend. By such divertissements, when Tuesday arrived, the inquest itself appeared merely another entertainment laid on for their benefit.

The private room of the Drivers Arms, the largest room that could be disposed, for inquests were few and far between in Hollingham, took on an unaccustomed sombreness for the occasion. The last inquest with a jury had been over the old bones found in Amos Pickering's Three Hump Field and that had been an anticlimax when it was discovered they were a cow's after all. This one boded more excitement for onlookers. Even the familiar sight of Bill Bunch, the landlord, torn between his desire to make the most of the additional trade and his curiosity in the proceedings failed to still the nervousness in the upper servants as they took their specified places ten minutes before the appointed hour of eleven.

The arrival of the Duke's party partly dispelled the gloom. Gone were the severe dark walking suits donned by the ladies for accompanying their menfolk to the shoot. The ladies had decided this was a social occasion. Set off by furs, feathers and daring hats, silks and velvets replaced their tweeds and wafts of scent as alien to the Drivers Arms as mint to a Frenchman's garden. Though their sense of occasion did not permit the gentry to smile, not a heart present but was not lightened by the sight of the ladies' soft lovely faces. Impossible to imagine that any would sully those lily-white hands with murder.

The array of hats bobbing above the aristocratic faces further unnerved the coroner. A Maidstone solicitor, Jacob Pegrim was more used to Maidstone Gaol and petty town crimes than to the fairyland of Stockbery Towers and he covered up his awkwardness by an excess of sternness. He glared at the four disparate ranks of those facing him: the family, the servants, the relatives – and the merely curious.

To his left ten good men and true sat, stiff in their high white collars buttoning with difficulty round unaccustomed chins, and set beneath red faces conscious of the importance of their duty. The interesting task of viewing the body now over, they were waiting for the questioning to begin.

The sight of British justice in action fascinated Auguste. It was impressive. In this room at a public alehouse, presided over by a man he would not notice twice in the street, there was a sense of timelessness and inexorable seeking after truth that was more impressive than the florid impassioned pleas of the courts of Albi. Ethel sat nervously by his side, decorously clad in her Sunday best, shifting uneasily on the hard bench requisitioned from the local schoolroom. His hand crept down reassuringly to press her thigh where it was warm against his. A slight blush on her cheek registered the fact.

Coroner Pegrim seemed to have a fixation on food. Details of Greeves' last meal were gone through time and time again, with Mrs Hankey, with Jackson, with Hobbs and – finally – with Auguste. All eyes, and notably the coroner's, were fixed on this foreigner who cooked the food served to The Unfortunate, as the coroner referred to him. There was a marked atmosphere of mistrust. He was French, wasn't he? No knowing what foreign rubbish he might be putting in the food. The jury therefore listened with great attention to his answering of questions about The Unfortunate's last meal.

'Are you aware, Mr – er – Didier, that this aconitia,' pursued the coroner weightily, 'is obtainable in wolfsbane, a common garden weed?'

'Yes, monsieur.'

'And is it true that you gathered some sorrel for this luncheon, some of which was given to the deceased?'

Ma foi, not again! thought Auguste. He patiently explained that there was no way that wolfsbane could be mistaken for sorrel, that there was no way in which aconitia could reach The Unfortunate's plate alone, except by design. This last he perceived to have been a mistake, for he was led to confirm also that it was unusual for the maître to gather his own vegetables for a mere servants' luncheon, and to explain that the sorrel, as were the herbs, was his own special domain. He was glad now he had not told the police about Edward having drunk from the poisoned bottle. It would have set the final seal on his doom.

Wearying at last of the details of food preparations, most of them alien to his jury, who dined on treacle pudding and good Kentish steak and kidney pie with a pint of ale made of the local hops, the coroner turned to The Unfortunate's family.

'Twenty-three years married, we was, sir,' sniffed Mrs Greeves.

'But you did not live together?' questioned the coroner disapprovingly. It was a situation entirely alien to him and his faithful Dora.

He was rewarded this time not with a sniff but a glare. 'Archibald was always concerned to give me a good home. He came to see me regular, Wednesday afternoons.'

Mrs Hankey's eyes hardened, and she stole a glance at May Fawcett. Her lips were tightly pressed together.

'And do you have progeny, Mrs Greeves?' This question had to be reworded before Mrs Greeves could vouchsafe that the progeny consisted of one son, presently, it transpired, in gaol. Auguste smiled. He could not see the point of these questions. But it was amusing none the less to note the rapt attention given to the testimony by May Fawcett and Mrs Hankey, side by side for mutual support.

With the arrival of the police for questioning, Auguste sank back in relief. No more veiled accusations now about the purity of his sorrel purée. He listened complacently while Bladon pontificated on poison discovered in a bottle of brandy, the poison now identified as aconitia.

The coroner's summing up was brief, suggesting to his jury that a fatal dose of aconitia had arrived in Greeves' mouth probably through the demon spirit brandy, and the jury retired to the landlord's parlour for their deliberations. Not for long. They returned to ask a question.

'Could the poison in this bottle have been added afterwards – to mislead like?'

Sergeant Bladon slowly took in its significance. 'Could be,' he said, turning his head to look at Auguste.

Full of self-importance the jury once again retreated, and when they reappeared it was to announce that they found the deceased met with his death by the hand of persons unknown.

Jacob Pegrim, thankful that it had passed off so uncontroversially and that in the excess of enthusiasm his jury had not indicted the Duke, began to repeat the verdict; but the foreman had something to add. 'Furthermore,' he added ponderously, 'we the jury wish to say the cook should be more careful how he prepares his food.'

A definite smirk crossed Sergeant Bladon's face at this unjury-like pronouncement. Auguste half rose from the seat. Did his ears betray him? By his side Ethel cried out, Auguste already dangling at the end of a rope in her vivid imagination. Her worse fears realised as she saw Sergeant Bladon making his way towards Auguste, she burst out crying, and flung her arms round her loved one. 'You shan't take him,' she cried. 'Don't let them take you away, Mr Didier.'

A certain tightening of Mrs Hankey's lips boded ill for Ethel, and the look on Sergeant Bladon's face even less well for Auguste.

*   *   *

91

However his inevitable interview did not go along the lines he expected. For a start, neither Naseby nor the Chief Constable was present. A hopeful sign that he was not immediately for the death cell. He had reasoned, protested, explained it was impossible for food to be polluted by him; pleaded he was not an incompetent fool who went to the garden to seek sorrel and came back with wolfsbane, and then suddenly found the intelligence to conceal his guilt by adding poison to the brandy – in a different form of course, since the addition of leaves would be noticed – in order to cover his tracks more thoroughly.

'Oh we know that, Mr Didier,' said Bladon cheerily.

'You know that?' echoed Auguste faintly.

' 'Course you might have, no denying that. Might have been what you was doing when I caught you that night. That book being a red herring, as they say.'

Auguste closed his eyes in momentary despair. Then opened them quickly when Bladon continued: 'But we don't think you did. Leastways for the moment, that is,' he added cautiously. 'After all, you pointed out about the brandy and how it might've been meant for the Duke. 'Course, we'd've found out anyway. So that might have bin cleverness on your part. But that, I doubt. Takes an Englishman to think that clever.'

Auguste compressed his lips. 'But the inquest . . .?'

'Ah yes,' said Bladon heavily. 'Fortunate that. It gives us a freer hand, you see.'

Auguste eyed him indignantly. '*Et moi*? What of my reputation?'

It seemed that the Kent County Police were unmoved by thoughts of Auguste's reputation. 'You've been very helpful to us, Mr Didier,' said Bladon kindly. 'Very helpful.'

'I am delighted to have been of service,' he murmured. The sarcasm passed Bladon by. 'So now it is not the poor silly cook who had the little accident with the sorrel. It is the blackmailer from the other side of the green baize door. Yes?'

Bladon looked cunning. 'Not blackmail, no. We can't necessarily go along with that.'

Auguste stared. 'But you saw the book, this Greeves, he is blackmailing –'

'All we saw was a list of figures and initials, Mr Didier. It might have been blackmail, it might not.'

'You also think someone wanted to poison the Duke then? For what? An affair of the heart?'

Bladon was shocked. In his view His Grace was married to his affair of the heart.

'There's other motives for getting rid of Greeves besides blackmail, *and* without bringing His Grace into it,' said Bladon severely, saying more than he had meant. He turned red. Naseby would have his scalp if he could hear.

'What?' asked Auguste. 'Inspector, these are *my* colleagues.'

'Now you know I can't tell you anything of the sort,' said Bladon uneasily. 'I said too much already. I'll tell you this though. There's jealousy.'

'Mrs Hankey?' asked Auguste. 'Ah but, Inspector, she would not kill Greeves. He was her one hope for the future.' Unless, of course, he thought to himself, she had found out about the real Mrs Greeves.

'I didn't say Mrs Hankey.'

'But May wasn't jealous of Mrs Hankey –'

'I didn't say –'

'Who then?' Could he mean Chambers? Jealous of Greeves over May Fawcett. But how could Bladon have known? And the problem remained – how could they have done it?

'Of course,' said Bladon, annoyed at this dismissal of his

revelation, 'there still ain't nothing to show you didn't put the poison in the bottle of brandy yourself, Mr Didier.'

'Hrumph,' commented the Duke, in traditional pose, warming his hands before the drawing-room fire.

'My husband means to say, Monsieur Didier,' chimed in the Duchess sweetly, 'that we have every confidence in you. We are quite, quite sure that this is all a dreadful misunderstanding. That it could not possibly have occurred through any fault of yours.'

'Thank you, Your Grace,' said Auguste quietly. He had been shaken. Not so much by the revelations of Sergeant Bladon, but at perhaps what he imagined were odd glances thrown at him by the lower servants when he returned to Stockbery Towers in the afternoon. The upper servants were outwardly punctilious in their loyalty naturally, though he detected a slight gleam of malicious pleasure in Cricket's eyes. Ill news travels fast. The scullery maid was daughter to Joseph Turner, number nine on the jury, the hallboy was second cousin to Matthew Binden up at Roundtree Farm who was brother-in-law to Terence Makepiece, saddlemaker, number six on the jury.

Publicly, at least, the ranks closed round Auguste, now that the trouble had come. Frenchman or not, he was one of them.

Yet the unity that Auguste perceived was a superficial one. No sooner had the jury returned their verdict than the upper servants' deep unease broke out once more. United they might be together, but individually their hopes, fears and torments surfaced.

May Fawcett, returning from dressing Her Grace for luncheon, was accosted by Frederick Chambers in the front hall, who drew her into the anteroom.

Chambers looked at her ungenerous, selfish face. However could he have thought her beautiful? He gripped her by the shoulder. 'You told him, didn't you? You told him about you and me. Laughed about me with him?'

She freed herself and rubbed her shoulder indignantly. 'No, I didn't. And what if I did? There ain't no you and me anyway. As though I'd consider you!'

'You liked me all right last Servants' Ball,' said Chambers hoarsely.

'No, I –' May stopped to consider. Archibald was gone now. And she was twenty-eight years old. 'Yes,' she said unwillingly, 'yes, I did, I s'pose.'

'You knew he was married, didn't you?' said Chambers. 'You found out, didn't you?' He was triumphant.

She looked at him in fear. 'How did you know?'

'I heard him telling you, May. Laughing at you. I overheard, you see. Did you do him in, May? I wouldn't have blamed you.'

She looked at him. He was no great catch, but – she put out a hand towards him and large tears began to form in her eyes . . .

It was Hobbs who suffered from the frustration resulting from her need to appeal to hitherto scorned admirers. She always picked an easy target: 'I don't expect Mr Greeves liked being told what you thought of him, Mr Hobbs. Did he get time to go to His Grace, like he threatened? Or did he die first? You had a cold, didn't you, Mr Hobbs . . . Did you use Dr Parkes' remedy? Make some up . . .?'

'What are you doing in here, Mr Chambers? Mrs Hankey wouldn't like it, would she?'

Cricket had stolen up behind him as he stood in front of the medicine cupboard in Mrs Hankey's storeroom.

Chambers whirled round, his face red. 'I was just

looking, Mr Cricket. Just looking to see how easy it would have been for anyone to come in . . .'

'Oh yes? Not you yourself was it, looking to see whether the police had taken the bottle away? After all, you had good reason to get rid of him, didn't you?'

It would give John Cricket great pleasure if the murderer of Mr Greeves could be discovered amongst his colleagues. It was unlikely then that his own link between Greeves and the Duke's side of the house would emerge.

'Miss Gubbins, I want a word with you.'

Mrs Hankey bore down upon her, a ship in full sail. 'I just remembered something Mr Greeves said to me. He said he was going to speak to me about you. Something very serious. What was it, Miss Gubbins? He never got a chance to tell me, poor lamb.' Her voice was heavy with meaning.

Ethel turned pink, then red. 'I'm sure I don't know, Mrs Hankey. And if you're implying . . .'

'I'm not implying anything, miss. I just want to know who murdered my Archibald. And it seems to me –'

'It seems to me that you knew him best, Mrs Hankey. You should know who murdered him.'

Mrs Hankey's mouth fell open at this assault from unexpected quarter. 'Me? Know who murdered Mr Greeves?'

Oblivious to these fiery developments, and now dismissed from the Gracious presence, Auguste was returning to the kitchens when he was stopped by Walter Marshall.

'May I ask a moment of your time?'

Auguste followed him into the library, seldom used at Stockbery Towers for its rightful function. The beautifully bound volumes, including a first edition of Lambarde on Kent, remained pristine and acquired value through their mint condition. Lady Jane was the only member of the family to disturb the tranquillity of their lives and her excursions were more confined to the lighter end of the bookcases containing the novels and bound copies of *The Theatre*.

'We have met before, Mr Didier, have we not?'

Auguste smiled. He had not thought Walter Marshall would remember.

'At the Savoy last year, monsieur. When I was visiting Monsieur Escoffier.' Newly arrived to run the kitchens of the new Savoy Hotel, his old maître and dearly beloved mentor Auguste Escoffier had received him. While he was there Walter Marshall had visited the chef's room, also to renew an acquaintance begun in Nice. It had surprised Auguste at the time for this serious young politician had not struck him as the sort of Englishman who admired French cooking. He had proved to be wrong. Walter Marshall did, and he had liked Auguste. He admired the French willingness to accord honour where it was due, and not to halt at the boundaries of class. He himself found a gate through those boundaries whenever he could; and if there were no gate, he leapt the wall. He was a determined young man.

'It's all nonsense of course,' declared Walter Marshall roundly now. 'These bumpkins don't know what they're talking about.'

After a moment's surprise at being spoken to as a human being and not as a cog, however vital, in an inferior hierarchy, Auguste shrugged.

'It is natural,' he replied. 'No Englishman, they think, would be so unsporting as to put poison in a man's victuals; no English lady would even consider such a thing, so it had to be a foreigner. That leaves the Prince Franz, the Marquise, her secretary – and myself. And who is best placed to poison food? Me. The cook. *Voilà*. The case is solved.'

'But it is simple enough to prove you had nothing to do

with it; or rather, to be accurate, impossible to prove you did –'

Auguste bristled.

'My dear fellow,' said Walter, 'no offence. I see absolutely no reason that you should have wanted to send the steward off to an untimely death even if you were at daggers drawn –'

'How did you – ?'

'Not too difficult,' said Walter drily. 'Archibald Greeves was not above dropping remarks here and there about his colleagues – those that were a threat to his sovereignty. Fortunately the Duke is too – er – unintellectually inclined to notice.

'It seems to me, Didier,' Walter Marshall continued, 'that on today's showing the local detective force is not likely to come up with the right answer. This is a problem that you and I, irrespective of our respective positions as guest and – er – servant, being the most logically minded people present have to solve.'

Auguste's chest swelled. His eyes gleamed. He saw the point. Were not the French the most logical nation in the world? Then he put that logic to work. Why should Walter Marshall be so interested in a mere chef's plight? It could not be pure devotion to the cult of gastronomy, in saving Auguste for the nation.

'Why?' he asked simply.

'You would agree, Didier, that someone in this house murdered Greeves? And that being so, would you not agree there remains a dangerous situation?'

'You mean,' Auguste thought carefully, 'that it may happen again. This time for less cause, if it is presented, since the first time it was not detected. It is possible, yes.'

'I shall not feel happy,' said Marshall with difficulty, 'about leaving this house while those still here might be in danger.'

Auguste noted his deliberately offhand manner.

'And you, my dear Didier, are the prime suspect at the moment, are you not? It must be to your advantage to help solve this case.'

Auguste shook his head. '*Non*, monsieur, I ask you to believe me. The police are not interested in me. They tell me so and indeed were it so in truth, I should be in Maidstone gaol, not free in the kitchens of Stockbery Towers.'

'Then I ask you to consider, Monsieur Didier, that your pretty little friend who was so concerned at the verdict might be next,' said Walter firmly.

Estelle? His Estelle? Impossible to think of his pretty Ethel the next victim of a poisoner. Unlikely . . .

'Very well, Monsieur Marshall. *Écoutez*.' Realising the advantages of an ally on the far side of the green baize door, Auguste spoke. Fifteen minutes later Walter Marshall was in full possession of the blackmail theory, of the black book so interesting in prospect and apparently so disappointing in reality. He was also in possession of the 'police' theory of the Duke as intended victim. But Auguste did not tell Walter Marshall about Edward's drinking from the brandy bottle. He was not yet confident enough to present such cast-iron evidence that the murderer belonged to his side of the baize door. He would tell him soon perhaps. The flavours were permeating, the marinade was working, instinct told him; soon some solution would occur to him.

'So you feel one of the guests is responsible?' said Marshall frowning slightly.

'It is more likely Greeves was blackmailing them or the family,' Auguste pointed out daringly.

'Unless he took his goods in kind,' replied Walter. 'After all, he had to get his information from somewhere. The family or guests wouldn't come right out and tell him.'

'That would only apply to the family,' pointed out Auguste.

'Then the guests are ruled out anyway,' said Walter.

'No,' said Auguste slowly. 'Not necessarily. The guests at the moment are all regular guests. They have been here before. You all know how things are done. And,' his eyes quickened, 'Greeves' duties took him to London to Stockbery House with His Grace to oversee the accounts. We do not know what opportunities he might have had there. A gentleman's valet is sometimes his weak point and Greeves would have had ample occasion to talk to them, hand them a *pourboire* in return for information.'

'At Stockbery House, yes –' said Marshall, considering. There was a ball there, in August for instance, we were all there. And other times – earlier in the summer. Ascot in June, for example. A big house party at Chivers, Lord Brasserby's place. Greeves would have been there also. There, too, he'd have had ample opportunity to bribe the servants.' He broke off as an idea came to him, one he could not yet divulge to Auguste. Instead, he said hesitantly, 'I may trust you, Monsieur Didier, may I not?'

Auguste drew himself up. 'I am a man of honour, monsieur,' he said with dignity.

'Very well. It is not beyond the bounds of possibility that there was scope for blackmail among the guests – there or here –' Walter said diffidently, 'should Greeves have acquired proof by whatever means.'

Man of honour or not, Auguste was diverted to learn of the intrigues of the Honourable Mrs Hartham, of the suspected liaison between the Prince and the Duchess.

'But these are affairs of the heart? One does not murder for that? In England?'

Walter thought of the rules of the society in which he moved. Of the irredeemable disgrace if affairs were

100

dragged into the public eye, especially for those in the Prince of Wales' set, with the Prince still embroiled in the Beresford divorce scandal. 'Oh yes,' he said slowly, 'I think to some murder might be a very easy price.'

'And what of Lord Arthur?' asked Auguste unthinkingly. Gossip travelled speedily in their servants' kingdom. 'An affair of the heart also?'

'No,' said Walter shortly. 'But the rumours are that he has heavy gambling debts – baccarat. He treasures his friendship with the Prince of Wales, and the Prince is in enough trouble over baccarat with Tranby Croft and the Gordon Cumming scandal in everybody's mind.'

Auguste shook his head in wonder. A Prince being called on to witness whether a friend cheated at cards. All a matter of honour, it was said. Honour, yes. All men had their idea of honour. But that it should rest in cards! Strange, these gentlefolk.

'There are other rumours too about Petersfield,' said Marshall, slowly. 'Unsubstantiated. They always float about.' He hesitated. 'Reasons that he is not married.' His knuckles were white, and he put Jane out of his mind with difficulty.

'Ah,' said Auguste with interest. The English crime his countrymen called it. Then he realised the reason for Marshall's hesitancy and hastily changed the subject. 'And this German prince? What of him? Could the *salaud* Greeves have obtained bad information on him through his valet?'

'There we are in deep waters, my friend. Not only deep but serious. I must be careful, because much of this concerns my job. But I can tell you this. There are some who say that Gladstone is too old, that the Liberals will be out of power for many years yet. Yet I believe that when the General Election is held next year, it will be not Lord Salisbury who is returned but Gladstone. And my colleagues think the same. Lord Salisbury is a great man, Didier, but he does not, in his colleagues' view, see far enough. He sees, forgive me, our enemies as being France and Russia. And that, under Bismarck, might well have been true, cunning devil. But Bismarck has gone, and the Kaiser cannot determine whether to love or hate England. While Victoria lives, we are perhaps safe. But if she were to die . . . Moreover there is a Machiavelli in Germany who wields much influence behind the scenes, who stirs the pudding – von Holstein – is he friend or foe? We only know he perverts everything he comes across.'

'Like Greeves,' said Auguste, interested.

'Very like your Mr Greeves. When I see the Prince, I remember that he is a diplomat in the embassy, and therefore probably the personal choice of von Holstein and von Holstein is the *eminence grise* of Germany. Early in his career, von Holstein was the chief witness in the case against Arnim, accused of spying in the Paris embassy. But some say now that von Holstein himself masterminds all spying in German embassies abroad. It is a wild point, and one I should not be making perhaps, but if this Greeves had come across something through the Prince's valet perhaps that put his diplomatic mission in jeopardy . . . It is a thought.'

Ten minutes later Walter Marshall was in possession of the motives of such of the upper servants as Auguste knew, or guessed, including, after some hesitation, Ethel's own. He had felt badly about this, yet if Ethel were to be safe, Greeves' murderer had to be found, quickly.

'And your own motive, Didier?' asked Marshall quietly.

'Mine?' asked Auguste indignantly.

A slight smile crossed Marshall's face. 'I have to say that a new parlour game incurring much mirth has been invented for after-dinner recreation – that of guessing motives for the demise of Archibald Greeves, not those from our side of the door of course.'

'And what was attributed to me?' asked Auguste grimly.

'Oh, you would approve, Monsieur Didier. So far as I recall it was that Greeves had caught you boiling the sauce for a salmi of game.' He laughed as he saw Auguste's expression. 'Now,' he continued, 'let me get this straight, Didier. You say it is impossible for the upper servants to have poisoned the brandy during the dinner, but is it not possible they too had access to the morning-room while the bottle awaited the Duke?'

Auguste considered and nodded. 'But they could not *know* the Duke would not drink it himself?' he added quickly.

'Ernest Hobbs would,' said Marshall softly. 'But let us continue to the end of this argument. For logic's sake. You also say it is impossible for any of us to have infiltrated beyond the servants' door to have poisoned it while you were all at lunch. The ladies, perhaps? Myself even? I did not stay at the shoot that day.'

'No, monsieur, the risk. Too great.'

'Nor the men, when they returned from shooting, and before you returned from the servants' hall? The door to the servants' quarters is near the door where the men return from shooting. It would be easy enough to slip through; all of us know the layout of the place well enough. I've stepped out at the Servants' Ball myself and know Greeves' room. And servants' luncheon is known to be at twelve o'clock.'

'No time, monsieur. Again there is the risk of being seen going through the door by the footman on duty in the front house. Or the gentlemen returning from the shoot. They take their boots off, and chat. At half past twelve we come back to Pug's Parlour, and the footmen change into their livery in their little room the other side of the door –'

'So it seems the bottle was most probably poisoned in the morning-room,' said Marshall slowly. 'Yet it seems to me there is one thing you have overlooked, Didier.'

'Monsieur?'

'If this book you tell me of is in truth Greeves' blackmailing accounts, where is his proof? And what did he do with all the money? He had to be paid in cash. And you don't blackmail someone without concrete evidence. He could not walk up to, say, Petersfield and say, "Aha, do you know what I know, my lord?" So where is it?'

Auguste made a moue of disgust. 'So, Mr Marshall, my dreams of being the great detective are shattered. I did not think of this. You are right, of course. It cannot be in Greeves' room or the police would have found it, and there would be no more talk of sorrel purée. Besides it was too risky. As for the money – I think this wife, yes? His afternoons off?'

'Now my turn to forget. So we go a-hunting you and I, Didier. I on my side of the door, you on yours. And, Didier – remember just one thing. The Lady Jane has no motive,' Walter said firmly.

Auguste smiled. '*Je comprends*. Nor in that case, monsieur, has Miss Gubbins. It is understood?'

'Understood,' said Walter Marshall, and laughed.

The funeral of Archibald Greeves was a strange affair. It turned the natural order of hierarchy upside down. The relatives, having been entertained luxuriously if not warmly by the Upper Ten for two full days and one evening, were at the forefront of the church, a weeping Mrs Greeves heaving impressively behind a thick black veil, followed by the upper servants; at the back of the church the family and guests, there to show a presence. The coffin was taken from the carriage, its horses dressed in their rich black plumes, by three estate workers and, surprisingly, by the Duke himself, who maintained gruffly to Lord Arthur that Greeves had been a damned fine steward, whatever else he'd done. It was perhaps the one word of praise for the deceased voiced that day.

A tight-lipped May Fawcett watched the coffin borne past. By her side Edith Hankey, their faces wet with tears less for Greeves than for themselves. Next to Auguste stood Ethel, a juxtaposition strictly forbidden under usual circumstances. But these were not usual circumstances and Mrs Hankey was too preoccupied and Ernest Hobbs too overcome with the dignity of his new position to raise objection. Auguste was touched by the girl's devotion, seeing himself as a chevalier of old riding to arms to protect the damsel he loved. Ethel would be very easy to love. She would make a good wife – make *someone* a good wife, he thought hastily. He must be careful. Ethel was not one he could love lightly. Ethel would expect marriage. And even if there had been no Tatiana, a good maître should be married to his art, not a home-loving little wife. He should be celibate – well, in mind at least. Nevertheless, as he glanced at Ethel, her chin silhouetted as she stared ahead in solemn devotions for the good of the soul of a man who had never meant well towards her, Tatiana and celibacy seemed a long way away.

What would it be like to have a wife? Marriage was a funny thing from a bachelor's point of view. His eye was drawn to Mrs Greeves. Had that old devil once been passionately in love with that stout determined dragon?

He tackled the dragon on the way back to the Towers.

'Permit me to offer you, madame, my sincere condolences.'

She glanced up at him through the thick black veil and even through that he could see malevolent eyes.

105

'You're that cook, ain't you?' she said. 'The jury think you killed him. Why you're not locked up, I don't know,' she added vindictively.

He flinched. 'I am not locked up, madame, because I did not poison your husband.'

'You mean they can't prove it yet.'

'Madame, you are an Englishwoman and Englishwomen are always fair-minded. It is not proved I am guilty and until then I am innocent. This is not France, madame.'

Perhaps something about his face convinced her, for her tone was less harsh when she said: 'That's as maybe. But the end's the same. He's dead. And where's my money coming from now now –'

'I am sure His Grace will –'

She laughed scornfully. 'That pittance – after what my Archibald –' She glanced at him. 'He was a generous man.'

'Might I call on you, madame? I wish to discuss –'

She looked up at him. 'Think I'm going to tell you where I live? I'd be murdered in me bed.'

Auguste noted her expensive hat, he was a connoisseur of women's dress. It was not bought out of a steward's wages, that. Either Archibald Greeves brought home the takings of his blackmailing activities every Wednesday afternoon, or else she was a *poule de luxe*. And that, looking at her, seemed extremely unlikely.

Chapter Five

'She's gone, Mr Didier.'

Five pairs of eyes regarded Auguste with shock and distress, confident that he would produce the remedy for this calamity. Mr Didier was their maître, despite what the jury said. He would know.

He looked at his minions in despair. Was there no one? After all his training? Was tragedy to strike again without let or hindrance?

'Quickly, Gladys. Cold water, *vite, vite.*'

In blind obedience, Gladys scuttled to the scullery, pitcher in hand, and returned, still quivering, lest the reponsibility for the catastrophe fall solely on her skimpy shoulders.

Auguste seized the pitcher, and gently, but oh so gently, dripped it on to the corpse. Slowly with gentle manipulation the egg yolks bound together and unified. Disaster had been averted. The hollandaise was secure. Time enough to apportion blame hereafter. Auguste sighed. Perhaps he was wrong ever to imagine he might leave even the simplest part of a sauce to a junior. He thought of Monsieur Escoffier who would never delegate any part of *la sauce* to an apprentice, no matter how promising. Yet how were they to learn if never entrusted with real responsibility?

A quick check of the stuffed pike, the port and chicken pie, the turkey in aspic, the truffle-filled pheasants, the poached soles and Auguste's mind was eased. It was, after all, only a light Friday luncheon, and the roasts he knew could safely be left to William Tucker, the pastry to Joseph Benson. They would never be maîtres, of course, but they had promise, yes, great promise. Tucker had a rapport with spits and ovens, knew precisely the effect of each change of position, each increase of heat. It was a pity his facility went more to old-fashioned ranges than to gas ovens, which he eschewed. Strange for a young man, but there it was. Progress had its drawbacks, he said, and give him the old ovens.

Yes, Auguste could safely leave luncheon for the moment, in pursuit of an equally if not more pressing problem. Miss Gubbins was flustered at being thus interrupted in the middle of her routine, even by so welcome a visitor as Mr Didier, and felt her need to impress him by her control of the small bevy of print-gowned underlings before dismissing them and turning, heart fluttering delightfully, to Auguste.

'My Estelle, the affair becomes serious, yes?'

Ethel nodded fervently. She had been scared by the inquest, not knowing whether at any moment Sergeant Bladon might descend with the full majesty of the Law, handcuff her beloved Auguste and remove him where she would never see him again. Ethel was a sensible girl, but young, and she too was influenced by the awful adventures of Peggy in the latest issue of her *Girls' Companion*.

'We have to think for both our sakes, yes?'

Ethel nodded even more enthusiastically. That little word 'both' gave her young heart a thrill. She was not to know that Auguste had simply been thinking that Sergeant Bladon's foolish hand might yet be laid on her as well as Auguste. If he were to discover that Edward had drunk from the brandy bottle, then the Kent County Police would look no further than the inmates of Pug's Parlour for their villain. As yet, Auguste could not think, despite application

108

of his French logic, of any solution to the problem of how the family or guests might be implicated, but still he clung with all his English mother's obstinacy to the theory of blackmail.

'My dove, listen carefully.'

Ethel listened. Her round innocent face grew flushed and pink. 'Oh, I couldn't, Mr Didier.'

'*Ma petite crème*, you can, and you must.'

Ethel halfheartedly looked for a means of escape, but there was none. Auguste was holding her by the shoulders pinned against the blanket-room door, in a manner that would be most satisfactory under other circumstances. She began to whisper so softly he was forced to put his face a great deal closer to hers to hear.

'And these plates of sandwiches, my dove. Outside whose doors?'

She understood immediately. All upper servants realised the reason for those nocturnal plates as a signal to the enthusiastic – or not so enthusiastic – lovers.

There followed a long list of names, but Auguste shook his head impatiently. 'No, last Tuesday night. The day the guests arrived. Can you remember?'

Ethel looked doubtful. 'The usual, Mr Didier.'

'And that is?'

'Mrs Hartham.'

'And who is the guest that comes creeping in the night?'

Ethel looked prim. 'I don't *know*, Mr Didier, but –' She hesitated then shut her eyes. 'His Grace,' she said firmly.

Auguste continued remorselessly. 'And who else?'

'Her Grace's door,' said Ethel, more forthcomingly. She had no liking for Her Grace who had once criticised the polishing of her boudoir Sheraton table.

'The Prince –'

Ethel blushed.

So Walter Marshall was right.

'And Lord Arthur, Mr Marshall?'

'Keep to their own rooms in the bachelors' tower. So they say.'

'And what think you, my Ethel, of these nocturnal walks?' She blushed, suddenly remembering her own recent walk by night, it occurring to her for the first time what Auguste must have thought. As if she'd ever . . . but then, Mr Auguste was a gentleman.

'They're gentry . . .' she replied, wonderingly. Auguste bent the extra five inches necessary from his five feet nine to plant a kiss on her lips, musing again on the morality of the servants' hall that never judged its masters by the standards they were forced to impose on themselves.

Auguste returned to give his attention to the final details of luncheon. Somehow even the excitement of spitch-cooked eels and chartreuse of partridge lacked its usual lustre. He had a problem almost more interesting. The murder of Archibald Greeves. As he stirred, seasoned, tasted, it occurred to him that perhaps the life of a detective was much like that of a cook, the experiments, the deduction, the co-ordination of elements, the basic routine . . . He checked the garnish for the cutlets, the dressing for the St Pierre. The fish with the thumbprint of God, or that of the devil; the John Dory the English called it. He covered the fish with the sauce, then garnished the sauce. Something stirred in his mind. He grasped at it, but it would not come. Something Walter Marshall had said? Something the Duke had said? It would not come. He must leave it there to simmer . . .

Luncheon concluded satisfactorily – and Auguste never failed, despite his experience, to enjoy a sense of relief that all had passed without disaster – he made his way to the library where he had arranged to meet Walter Marshall. But it was not Mr Marshall whom he discovered enjoying the

110

purlieus of the Stockbery Towers storehouse of learning. It was the Lady Jane and Lord Arthur interrupted in the middle of a kiss. Lady Jane sprang back, stepping accidentally on the silk train of her muslin teagown, embarrassment changing to indignation as she realised who the intruder was. Lord Arthur remained cool, though there was a glint in his eye that did not bode well for Auguste should they meet at a time when he was not required to preserve appearances before a prospective bride.

'Kindly withdraw at once, Didier,' said Lady Jane coldly. 'How dare you come in here?'

'I beg your pardon, My Lady,' said Auguste, endeavouring to look contrite. 'I was expecting to find Mr Marshall.'

It was the wrong thing to say to Lady Jane. The ice in her eyes grew harder. 'Mr Marshall, as you can see, is not here,' she informed him loftily.

'I can see that, My Lady.'

'Then get out, fellow,' drawled Lord Arthur. His words were quiet, his face remained pleasant, but there was something about him that made Auguste decide to take his advice quickly. As he closed the door thoughtfully behind him, Walter Marshall was walking across the ballroom floor. He nodded to Auguste and made to enter the library.

'It's occupied, sir,' Auguste said apologetically.

The tone of his voice made Marshall look at him sharply. 'Her Grace?'

'No, sir.'

'Ah.'

Marshall stood, hand on knob for a moment, looking down at it intently. Then he let it go. 'Reason as well as conscience doth make cowards of us all . . .' he murmured. Then instantly he recovered himself and said briskly: 'The morning-room then. It won't be in use now.'

Auguste looked on him with respect. This was the French approach. He was not accustomed to finding it in Englishmen. Reserve, yes, the stiff upper lip, but the ability to use the brain when under emotion . . .

Auguste found it strange to be invited to sit down in the morning-room – to him it was the place where he stood respectfully waiting for orders.

'Well now, my friend, what news?'

Auguste hesitated for a moment. But he had decided that he could tell Walter about Edward Jackson, now that his brain was simmering with that elusive idea. 'For us, not good, not good at all.' He proceeded to explain about the brandy, and the so important little sip taken by Edward.

'Then tell me, Didier,' said Marshall, 'why are the police still so interested in *this* side of your famous door?'

'The police do not know,' said Auguste unwillingly.

Walter's eyebrows shot up. 'You have not told them –'

'No,' said Auguste with dignity. 'I wished to reflect, before I tell him to tell them.'

'You took a risk, my friend, and another in telling me. Suppose I tell the good sergeant?'

Auguste shrugged. 'That is your decision, monsieur. But I believe strongly that the murderer is *not* one of us. I had an idea, but it will not come. It will, soon, however. It is there. Inside my head.'

Walter smiled. 'And I'm to assist this painful birth?'

'*Alors*, Mr Marshall,' Auguste replied with dignity. 'Only you can. I am thinking . . . the shoot on the day of Greeves' murder. You attended?'

'Of course,' said Walter. 'We all did that day. Even the women were enthusiastic since it was the first day. The sun was out and the Duchess dragooned us all into coming. I even had to take a gun myself for a few minutes.'

'And how did you all come back?'

112

'Ah,' said Walter, glancing at him. 'That I cannot tell you. I – um – left early and took a stroll through the gardens. But, Monsieur Didier, before you write me down as a suspected person, I do confess, I was not alone. However,' he said hurrying over this, 'I gather from the talk recently that the gentlemen returned to the gunroom together about twelve. The ladies come first normally – it takes Her Grace some time to repair the ravages of the morning in order to appear at luncheon. Why do you ask?'

'In which order though, Monsieur Marshall?' Auguste insisted.

'I don't see – well, as far as I can recall, Her Grace, Mrs Hartham and the Marquise came back first, then His Grace. When I returned with Lady Jane –' he paused, frowning – 'I found His Grace in the bootroom and Petersfield just leaving. I think Francois Pradel came in next, and then the Prince.'

'And what order did you leave the bootroom in?'

Walter raised his hands helplessly. 'I've no idea. We all were ready for luncheon, I recall that, though it was a scramble. It usually is.'

'And what time does the shooting party normally return to the house?'

'Oh, the same time as today roughly. We leave the field about a quarter to twelve, and are usually in the bootroom about a quarter past.'

'And which field was that?'

Walter shot him an amused look. 'You 'ave ze theory, already, Inspector Didier?' he mocked gently.

'No,' said Auguste sadly. 'The watched pot does not boil.'

'And suppose it does boil, what then? Have you proof? Proof of blackmail yet?'

'No,' said Auguste glumly. 'But the Mrs Greeves, a

113

plump pigeon, is she not, with expensive plumage? I think she does not live in fear of the workhouse that one. Her home, I would like to see it, know what it is like, but she believes me a murderer.'

'Easily accomplished,' said Walter. 'I'll drive there tomorrow. But do you think she has the evidence there? Is that where you think it is?' An idea came to Walter, but he said nothing. He, too, would let it simmer.

'No, I do not think so. This Greeves would want to gloat over his evidence. Here at the Towers he had a rich river in which to tickle many trout,' commented Auguste, 'if all our rumours are fact.'

'And I another trout, messieurs?'

The Marquise de Lavellée had entered the room unnoticed, and stood imperious and commanding at the door. They hastily rose to their feet. Her eyebrows lifted as she took in Auguste's presence. No teagowns for the Marquise. As strictly corseted as she would be all day, her heavy blue satin dress was plain by current fashions, subtly so, to draw attention to the magnificent pearls, round the high collar, which set off her white hair. Her lively dark eyes looked from one to the other with interest.

'Gentlemen, be seated,' she said softly.

Auguste remained standing uncertainly.

'Monsieur Didier, I believe. Pray be seated,' she commanded.

Auguste sat down, his respect growing. She had accorded him the monsieur; she knew a maître from a chef. She did not sit herself, but advanced into the middle of the room beautifully poised, hands held as only a Frenchwoman could hold them. 'So it is *la chantage*, the blackmail, of which you speak? And our good departed steward.'

'You guessed, Madame la Marquise?' said Marshall astonished.

114

'But of course. This Greeves, he tried to blackmail me. Me,' she swelled indignantly. 'So it is probable he blackmail others also. *Pas difficile*.'

'And did he succeed in blackmailing you, madame?' asked Marshall calmly.

'No, Monsieur Marshall, he did not. I told him to tell everyone. To tell the Duchess, tell the Duke, tell the stableboy. I tell him to go to the devil.' She paused and a smile of great sweetness came over her face. 'So now you are wondering what this man Greeves could blackmail an old woman like me about, *hein*?'

They made deprecating noises.

'Aha!' said she, sitting down on a chair. 'I will tell you. For I cannot be accused of murdering this man, if I tell you I am prepared to tell you what it was he knew about me. So, gentlemen, I tell you. Monsieur Didier, you are a Frenchman, you will not be shocked, I think.' Yet she paused a little before she spoke, and the beringed fingers tightened in her lap. 'Monsieur François, my secretary. This Greeves found out that François is more than a secretary. Much more.'

'He is a lucky man,' said Auguste rallying quickly and gallantly.

'Thank you, Monsieur Didier.' She inclined her head, then immediately rose to her feet. 'And now, gentlemen, I shall leave the two detectives –' she mocked them gently – 'to their investigations.' She hesitated and turned to Marshall. 'As a gentleman, Mr Marshall . . .'

'Of course, madame.' Walter's face was grave, perhaps, Auguste thought, a trifle shocked.

'*Et* Monsieur Didier? A Frenchwoman's honour is in your hands.'

'Madame.' For an instant as he bowed over her hand he was reminded of Tatiana – something in the smile, in the way she held her head. Then it was gone.

'Ethel, my dearest, it is not simply to pick the grapes that I ask you to accompany me to the kitchen-garden conservatory,' said Auguste firmly.

'No?' asked Ethel, her hopes rising. They were quickly to be dashed.

It had been Marshall who had pointed it out, and Auguste was amazed for not having asked Ethel himself before.

'How is it, Estelle, that you know who visits during the night when good little girls like you – are you not? – are tucked up in bed? You leave the sandwiches, but how do you know for whom the signal is meant?'

'I don't,' said Ethel, her brow puckered. 'I suppose it's the gossip.'

'But this gossip. How do you hear it?'

Ethel considered. 'From Mr Cricket,' she said at last, 'or Miss Fawcett, sometimes Mr Chambers. But mostly Mr Cricket.'

'Ah,' said Auguste. And doubtless this too was how Greeves got his information.

To see Hobbs was his next task. Now the police had abandoned their guard on Pug's Parlour, Hobbs had moved in, taken loving possession of its leather chair and marble fireplace, and obliterated all signs of its previous owner. True, his possessions were not so good as those of his predecessor, removed now by the sorrowing widow, but they pleased Hobbs, who seemed remarkably unaffected by the fact that his feet now rested where the late steward's remains had been only a week previously.

With some unspoken sense of decorum the upper servants were still taking their meals in Mrs Hankey's room, but

116

Hobbs obsessively occupied his own room at every conceivable spare moment.

Auguste found him there. He had always liked Hobbs, whom everyone else found rather colourless. Auguste did not.

'So, Mr Hobbs, your own Pug's Parlour at last,' he remarked banally, looking round the familiar room, now suddenly strange.

'Yes, Mr Didier,' the habit of ages dying hard. The steward's privilege was to omit the title, but Mr Hobbs was not yet so bold with his position.

'We must start having meals again here – I've missed them,' said Auguste with less than truth. For Mrs Hankey's room was a great deal warmer for all its exposed position. Perhaps it had something to do with its occupier's own generous curves. 'You're not nervous of my meals, despite what the inquest said?' asked Auguste in jest.

'I don't hold with foreign food,' said Hobbs heavily, 'but I will say this. For a foreigner you cook all right, and there's no one going to believe you made a mess of things, Mr Didier.'

'The police think so,' murmured Auguste. 'Yet I had no reason to kill him. But you did, didn't you, Mr Hobbs? Every reason. So it's important you help find who really did it.'

There was a silence. Then: 'Tell the police about Rosie, did you?'

'No,' said Auguste.

'It wasn't her fault,' said Hobbs, staring at some point far beyond Auguste. 'She was a good girl up to the time he got hold of her. Ruined her.'

'*La pauvre.*'

'And so she drowned herself – best thing really.'

Auguste shivered. The best thing? He began to look at Hobbs in quite a new light.

Saturday began early for the staff of Stockbery Towers and in particular for Auguste Didier, chef. Tonight there was another ball. When Stockbery Towers had a ball, Merrie England was reborn. This one had been arranged at short notice and tempers in the kitchens were higher than the heat thrown out by the ranges and ovens, already at full blast to cope with the number of expected guests. It was only a small ball; merely sixty people to be entertained. The refrigerators shook with ices; the cool larders burgeoned with raised pies, galantines and cooked hams. At eight o'clock the delivery men were coming in a continuous trail to the kitchen door. Already Auguste was moving as nimbly as Jacques le Jongleur, juggling tasks dexterously and fielding disaster before it occurred. The garnishes were prepared, all organised for the last-minute adding to the aspic jelly: the truffles, the plovers' eggs, the quail eggs, the *entremets*, the jellies, the charlottes – Auguste ticked them off methodically in his mind's eye on the system he had taught himself. The apprentice learns from his master, he learns his way, his methods, he learns the basic craft, the tricks, the finesse. But a maître is born, not created. After he leaves the master, he is on his own, and upon his own genius he imposes his own discipline. Auguste made a face at the boar's head, staring at him unblinkingly from amidst its aspic garnish. Not a real *sanglier*, of course. This was not *La France*. But it would do. A head of a bacon hog, cut deep and carefully boned, the bristles singed off, and inside his own special forcemeat of tongue, bacon and truffles, moistened with a mirepoix of wine. For ten days it had been marinating in its brine before cooking, intended for a grand picnic but snatched two days before its time for this ball. He would ask

Gladys to produce some chrysanthemums from the gardens to finish the decoration; last time he had applied gum paste in the Continental fashion and there had almost been a disaster, with the heat of the room. A boar's head that apparently wept tears of sorrow. Even a maître can err.

In the steward's room meanwhile a reluctant Edward Jackson was being coaxed into a footman's livery.

'We need all the help we can get up there,' said Hobbs firmly. 'Just keep an eye on me, and I'll tell you what to do.'

'But I ain't never been up with the swells before,' wailed Edward as he was forced into stockings and breeches; he only fell silent as the wig was placed upon his head. Traditional to the last, the Duke insisted that full dress livery meant just that. For formal occasions their own hair brushed with violet powder was not enough for his footmen. Wigs were to be worn.

Edward peered at himself in the mirror.

Two cherubic cheeks peeped out from under an all-but snowy white wig giving his over-mature young face an innocence that was largely foreign to him.

'Lucky we had this spare livery,' remarked Hobbs complacently. 'Off you go and give Mr Chambers a hand, young Edward, and remember don't speak to no one if you can help it. Don't you open your cockney little mouth more than you have to. You'll look like all the others unless you speak.'

The boy obstinately remained, gazing in disgust at his reflection in the servants' hall mirror. 'I look just like a Fred,' he muttered beneath his breath. 'I don't wanna go, Mr 'Obbs.'

Hobbs' voice rose menacingly. 'Out, Edward. Up there this instant.'

God had spoken. It wasn't Greeves, true, but another

God seemed to have taken his place. Edward cast him one scared look and ran.

Walter returned in the governess-cart from a day's outing just in time to change for dinner, in thoughtful mood. It had not taken long to find the establishment of Mrs Greeves, fifteen miles away. It was a Queen Anne villa of generous proportions. She was known as the Widow Greeves, visited once a week by her brother. Walter thought carefully about Greeves and his character and the idea simmering at the back of his mind firmed up. Tomorrow he would act on it. He would see the Duke.

But much was to happen before that Sunday morning dawned.

Behind the baize door a seething mass of frustration was prevented from explosion only by the limitations inposed by the duties of the evening ahead. Nevertheless certain events took place.

Frederick Chambers kissed May Fawcett and received a slapped face for his pains. May Fawcett then informed Mrs Hankey, who had surprised them, that she was a jealous old biddy. Mrs Hankey forthwith burst into tears, simultaneously informing Miss Fawcett she was dismissed. Miss Fawcett pointed out only Mr Hobbs and Her Grace could dismiss her. Ernest Hobbs appealed to their better natures. He was disregarded. Ethel sided with May Fawcett, Mrs Hankey informed her she was dismissed. Mr Cricket for once in his life played the hero and defended the rights of Miss Ethel Gubbins; Mrs Hankey threw a sugar loaf at Mr Cricket. It missed and caught Auguste entering Pug's Parlour to place the evening dessert in the pantry a glancing blow in the left shoulder, causing him to drop a large blueberry pie upside down on the floor. French imprecations flew through the air.

'You are mad, you English. Mesdames, messieurs. *The ball*. Remember, if you please.'

Carriages drew up and disgorged rustling, silken-cloaked ladies, their fragile arms held possessively by top-silk-hatted gentlemen. Equipages softly and silently vanished away, while their owners ascended the six white steps of Stockbery Towers, so painstakingly blancoed daily by Ethel's minions, and on this day twice so manicured. Bevies of beauties swept through the porticos, a kaleidoscope of rich-coloured gowns peeping beneath their cloaks, waiting to be shaken out and fussily arranged in the privacy of the Duchess' suite, lace fichus carefully swirled to display what they were intended to conceal; it was necessary to ascertain immediately who was present, to mark prey for the evening, to ensure that only those people whom one wished were given the opportunity to fill their names on your card and that only *the* person should be allowed the supper dance.

Only a dozen servants in full dress livery, six imported from the village, betrayed the fact that there was another world within Stockbery Towers, wherein a vast army slaved with dedication and, in some cases, satisfaction, to ensure that the Duke and Duchess of Stockbery's ball should be a success and reflect due credit on their coroneted heads. One platoon of this army applied itself assiduously to the last touches to the buffet. For the titillation of jaded palates they laboured over the finest products of Auguste's art.

'The secret, Joseph,' said Auguste didactically, for he believed in communicating his wisdom whenever possible, 'is that they all look the same.'

He stopped still in the middle of applying a shrimp to the herb mayonnaise on the *darne de saumon*. Thus it was that a

121

mere crustacean was responsible for his realisation of how Archibald Greeves had been murdered.

Down at Kent County Police Headquarters in Maidstone Sergeant Bladon and Inspector Naseby were working late , with two cold mutton pies from Master Tucker's pie shop awaiting their pleasure. What Mrs Bladon would have to say about this would never be recorded; the sergeant, however, was half gratified that his views were of such importance that it warranted his staying late, and half annoyed that he would be missing the company of one Joseph Hopson, and more particularly his plump jolly wife Nancy, invited by Mrs Bladon to share their repast that evening. But be that as it may, the Stockbery case took precedence. For the umpteenth time Inspector Naseby and Sergeant Bladon were trying to figure out just how the Honourable Mrs Honoria Hartham had managed to poison the brandy to give to the Duke.

The players were making their opening gambits now; the band had been playing some while. Lord Arthur strode towards the Lady Jane. To claim her for the first dance showed a certain panache he felt, a masterly handling of the situation to which the Lady Jane did not seem averse. She was discouraged, it was true, because she had not been able to avoid Mr Marshall who had blandly written himself in for the supper dance, showing a blatant disregard for her feelings since any gentleman should have realised from her manner that this was not what she had desired.

'Jane,' said Lord Arthur, as they whirled around to the strains of the music. 'I have something very particular I wish to talk to you about. Shall we take a turn in the orangery?'

Her heart jumped. She closed her eyes. This, then, was it. The moment that all women waited for. When a man – *the*

122

man – would say . . . She looked at his dark handsome face so close to hers, and thought how unbelievably happy she was.

His Grace was very far from being unbelievably happy. He'd been forbidden access to Honoria's arms the night before on the grounds that she had to look her best at the ball, and, dammit, if she wasn't trying to keep him at arm's length tonight, too. Asked her for the supper dance only to be informed that the Prince was taking her in. Damned Prussian. Prince indeed! Everybody who could say Schleswig Holstein boasted of being some kind of prince nowadays.

'Why, George, what a positively miserable expression. Anyone would think you weren't glad to see me.'

Honoria had appeared at last. She was at her most provocative and His Grace had no more chance than a particularly slow-moving fly of avoiding this Venus-trap.

'Hardly been near me all day,' was all he could manage in the way of a protest.

'But I wanted to, George, oh how I wanted to. You don't know how jealous I am seeing you with all those lovely women at the shoot. And knowing that we must be careful.'

'I'm tired of being careful, Honoria. Dammit, I want you – and by God, no damn foreigner's going to have you.'

Honoria looked skittish. There was a time when that look had raised fires in him; now it infuriated him even though it occurred to him that she looked a little silly. For some reason this made him even angrier. Whatever Laetitia was, he thought, looking at his Duchess, she wasn't silly, and by God, no woman like Honoria was going to make a fool of the twelfth Duke of Stockbery.

No, Laetitia certainly was not silly. She was thinking hard. She was scrutinising her best friend, meditating as to what

123

awful revenge she could wreak upon her. At the moment, boiling that pretty body in oil seemed a fate too good for her.

Her Grace, her attention distracted by the welcome sight of her daughter being led in the direction of the orangery by Lord Arthur, had not been pleased to discover a few moments later that the Prince was to escort Honoria to supper; his protestations of the need for discretion this time failed to convince.

'My reputation, I feel, my dear Franz, can stand the occasional assault.' Then, feeling this was a little tart, she managed a light laugh.

'*Liebling*, we will meet later. Much later. When you and I can be alone.'

He caressed her with his dark eyes, but for the first time it seemed to Laetitia that it was perhaps just a little mechanical. Nevertheless she was jealous. Honoria was forgetting her place.

'You take much for granted, Your Highness,' she replied a little coolly. 'Perhaps this evening I do not wish to be alone with you. The cuckoo clock may not sing tonight.' Her own private signal.

'Dearest,' the Prince's eyes clouded, 'have I offended you? Of course you must be alone if you wish, stricken though I shall be.'

This was not what Laetitia had intended. She pouted, and tossed her curls. 'If you don't *want* to be with me tonight . . .'

'But, *Liebchen*, you wished to be alone . . .'

'If Honoria Hartham is so attractive . . .'

These women. These English women. So demanding. He hated warring women.

'Dearest, for tonight perhaps, you are tired after the ball . . .' He kissed her and and, with great relief, fled.

The Duchess, her woman's wiles quite deserting her, tried to restrain her temper.

Jane smiled a beatific smile of assent to Lord Arthur, and indeed led the way to the long orangery that ran the length of the library behind the house. This had been another conceit of the eleventh Duke, who had insisted on its being built incongruously on the back of the house, thus causing the architect of Stockbery Towers to die prematurely of shock and outrage. It was an approved spot for dalliance, the statuary of naked gods and goddesses being classified as art and not as erotic encouragement.

It appeared that the Lady Jane had a speck of dust on her lovely face that entailed close examination by Lord Arthur for its removal. Once that was accomplished, he seemed to find it difficult to distance himself.

'You will marry me, won't you, Jane? You must. I want you to be my wife. All my life I've been waiting for someone like you . . .'

Having heard the words she had been imagining all day, instead of replying as any well-brought-up young lady had been trained to do, Jane merely managed a gulp and said, 'Yes please.'

'You wonderful filly. Can I kiss you, Jane?'

An inarticulate murmur gave him to understand that no objection would be raised, and his lips were placed respectfully on hers. She closed her eyes to savour every moment, and was rather surprised to find she had not fainted – perhaps it was not essential. She tried hard to feel like Evelina when Lord Orville fell to his knees before her, but could only be aware of Lord Arthur's moustache tickling her upper lip. Still, it was all very satisfactory and no doubt she would get better at it in time.

It was at this inopportune moment that Walter Marshall

came storming through the door to claim Jane for the supper dance. His face was angry, his eyes blazing and he bore little resemblance to the cool young politician whose reticence was such an asset to his career.

He planted himself stockily before them both, and in a manner that definitely veered on the truculent, said: 'Our dance, Lady Jane, I believe?'

She drew herself up in a dignified manner.

'Mr Marshall,' she said, 'it must be clear to you that you are intruding.'

'No doubt,' he said briefly, 'but it is still our dance.'

Lord Arthur laughed. He could afford to. 'Run along, dearest, I can wait. Let this young oaf have his dance.'

Walter's hands clenched, but he restrained himself – just.

Lady Jane cast a devoted look at Lord Arthur, and one of an entirely different nature at Walter. She marched out of the orangery by Walter's side to the dance floor. She accepted his arm stiffly, her lips pressed tightly together, baring them in a grimace.

'Mr Marshall,' she hissed, 'I shall never forgive you.'

'For claiming you for our dance?' he asked, equally icily.

'For coming in then. Lord Arthur had just asked me to be his wife.' Even as she spoke, she felt that she had been a little unwise in this precipitate announcement.

Walter Marshall stopped dead in the middle of the floor. He seized her hand and marched her off the floor and into the morning-room.

'Did you accept?' he asked grimly.

'Of course,' she said with dignity. 'I love him.'

'You fool,' he said simply.

She gasped. 'How dare you speak to me like that?'

'Quite easily. He's well over twice your age. He's never been married. There're all kinds of stories floating around, from which he's only protected because he's close to the Prince of Wales. And he's stone broke. He only wants you because you're a duke's daughter.'

A bright spot of anger appeared in each of Jane's cheeks. 'I suppose it's not conceivable that he might want me for myself?'

Deliberately Walter considered. 'No, it's not. I can imagine someone wanting you for yourself. But not him. He can't even kiss you properly.'

This time she flew at him physically as well as verbally. 'You were watching? But that was a – a sacred moment. You shouldn't –'

He caught her hands and pulled her to him. 'This is how you should be kissed.' And proceeded to show her. It was nothing like Lord Arthur's kiss. For a start, there was no moustache to tickle her. And then there were several other interesting sensations that almost made her wish she could continue in this diverting occupation. Then she recollected Arthur.

When she succeeded in breaking away – which took a little while – she marched to the door and said in carefully restrained tones, 'Mr Marshall, you will leave this house,' a dignified statement somewhat marred by the curl hanging over one eye.

'You haven't slapped my face,' he pointed out objectively. 'You're letting me off very lightly.'

She hesitated. Her fingers itched. But he held her gaze. Abruptly she flung herself out of the door and slammed it behind her.

Prince Franz of Herzenberg was pleased. At last a chink, a hope, that he might with grace disentangle himself from the Duchess. He was not at all sure how he had arrived in her toils. The Kaiser led an exemplary home life; he

127

expected his diplomats to do the same. Victoria's court, too, was exemplary. He had not therefore bargained on the machinations of London society and was finding himself hopelessly out of his depth. He lived in fear that word would reach the Kaiser. And in even greater fear of –

'Your Highness,' breathed Honoria, sinking low to the floor with the desired result that her pretty bosom beneath her décolletage was clearly visible. 'Our dance. The supper dance.'

The Honourable Mrs Hartham was drunk. Drunk on champagne and the headiness of female power.

'Your Highness,' she trilled. 'This exquisite buffet. Dear Laetitia. She excels herelf. And yet,' she glanced archly at the Prince, 'I feel I might still be a little hungry at the end of the evening.'

'Indeed, madame?' replied a Prince, a little nonplussed.

'I might ask for a plate of sandwiches,' said Honoria with heavy meaning, tapping him lightly with her fan.

The stiffening of his muscles in annoyance passed her by as did the significance of her statement to him.

'Would you care to share them with me?' She glanced at him coyly, letting her gaze fall modestly.

'That would be delightful,' replied the Prince, entirely at sea now.

'Of course, dear Laetitia . . . She won't mind? She is my dearest friend.'

'I am sure Her Grace would not object to your asking the butler for sandwiches.'

She chuckled. 'What a delightfully witty man you are.'

The Prince could see nothing witty about this statement but smiled and bowed.

'Of course I haven't *decided* yet; no lady could. But I will give you my answer later this evening.'

The Prince gazed at her blankly. Were all Englishwomen mad?

'If I say yes, if, mind you, you naughty man, delightful man, it will be about an hour before I will feel a little hungry. When you see the sandwiches then I will be yours. Yours,' she said in a thrilling undertone, and tapped him archly once more. 'Now go, Your Highness, we will be marked.'

Slowly the awful truth began to dawn upon Prince Franz von Herzenberg.

The gentlemen had retreated to the library, glasses of the best Napoleon in their hands. They were of course discussing the international situation. It was a safe anchorage.

'Salisbury's got it right. Everyone's talking about the navy but it's the army we've got to look to,' rumbled the Duke. 'Say it meself, Cambridge is past the job. Need a new man. Nothing against the Queen, God bless her, but it's time her cousin went. It's the army won us the Empire.'

'And the navy keeps it,' said Walter quietly.

'My dear fellow,' drawled Petersfield, 'what's the navy done since Trafalgar? I believe it fired one gun in the Crimea, though, did it not?'

'Precisely,' said Walter. 'That is its function. Defence.'

'And you Liberals believe that Germany's to be feared. That we should build up the navy even more to guard against her. Doesn't make much sense. France and Russia are the enemies you need to build sea power against, not a land power like Germany,' Petersfield said patronisingly.

'Like the Germans meself,' said the Duke ruminating. 'Don't think much of this new Kaiser though. May be the Queen's grandson, but too clever by half. Now Marshall's right there – the Kaiser's got a bee in his bonnet about our navy and the need to keep up with us. Why, I remember at Cowes –'

'I can assure you, Marshall,' said Arthur, interrupting this reminiscence, 'that Germany has no aggressive intentions. Russia is our common enemy. Why, look at the alliance the Chancellor signed with us last year.'

'There are rumours that he talks of a war to be fought . . .'

'Nonsense, my dear fellow. And if so, it would be against Russia. No, they want to stay friendly with us. Believe me, I know these fellows. Went there with Teddy once. Kaiser wants peace and so do the Foreign Office.'

'Whom did you meet there?' asked Walter.

'Caprivi.'

'Not von Holstein?' asked Walter slowly.

'Von Holstein? Who speaks of von Holstein?'

Prince Franz of Herzenberg had entered the room unnoticed, and his face was white.

Honoria began to contemplate the night ahead. She remembered the touch of the Prince's hand during the waltz, the pressure of his arm as he led her in to supper, the whispered words over the galantine of chicken. The look in Laetitia's eye! Well, all was fair in love. And Laetitia would never hold it against her. The Prince was far too attractive for her not to understand. She turned her thoughts from delights to come to find Lord Arthur handing her a glass of champagne. Honoria did not care for Lord Arthur – he was too suave for her taste and, moreover, was clearly not in love with her, which did not endear her to him – but her drunkenness overcame her dislike. Besides, she had witnessed an interesting little scene earlier. She decided to be arch.

'Arthur, dear, what a lovely evening! Dear Laetitia is so exquisite at organising these little dances. Now do dance with me. Poor me is all alone.'

'Dear Mrs Hartham, I'd be delighted. How kind of you to ask me.'

The sarcasm passed her by. She gathered the train of her pale blue satin dress in one hand, and they took the floor.

'Dear Lord Arthur, do you recall the Marquess of Stevenage's soirée earlier this year? Dear Mr Wilde was there. Dear, dear Oscar.'

Lord Arthur frowned. 'Writes some strange books, that fellow.'

'Nonsense, Lord Arthur. What can you mean? Lovely, lovely little books, about swallows and princes - happy princes.' She gave a slight hiccup. She had been reading *The Happy Prince* to her younger son. She had cried. *Dear* Oscar. Thus she thought of him though she had met him but once. Proud of her association with the arts, she was oblivious to the fact that his reputation had somewhat changed with the decadent *Picture of Dorian Gray* published earlier that year, and was somewhat puzzled, therefore, by Arthur's reaction.

'Hardly know the fellow,' said Arthur shortly. 'Met his wife. Liked her. No friend of his.' Few in Society were now.

That reminded Mrs Hartham of the interesting little scene she had witnessed earlier. 'Come, Lord Arthur. You're too modest. Now we're friends aren't we? After all, I do know your little secret.'

Seeing him for once disconcerted, she tapped him playfully with her fan. 'Come, Lord Arthur, I'm sure you wouldn't want me to be the one to tell dear Laetitia, would you? Or the dear Duke? So just you be nice to me.' She flashed a brilliant little smile at him, as the dance ended.

Lord Arthur did not return it. His face was devoid of any expression at all.

'My dance with you, Honoria,' said the Duke grimly. He had decided enough was enough and arrived to claim his own, even if the lady had made it painfully clear his company would not be required that night.

'Oh George,' Honoria giggled. 'How delightful. I did not see you there. And Mr Marshall too.' He had arrived, clearly anxious for a word with Lord Arthur which His Lordship seemed indisposed to grant.

Honoria held out her glass again. The giddiness of being the cynosure of so many male eyes was as heady as the champagne. 'George, my champagne. I'm *so* thirsty.'

The Duke, disgruntled, was determined mot to give ground, but instead turned rather pointedly to Marshall: 'Who was that chap von Holstein you were talking about?'

'Von Holstein? Possibly the most dangerous man in Europe today,' said Walter grimly. 'He prefers to remain in the background, for the trappings of power do not interest him. The practice of it does. He pulls the strings of Germany's foreign policy but because he remains in the background no one knows what his aims are. He is a Machiavelli. A blackmailer. An intriguer. He builds up dossiers on those that displease him and quietly, catlike, bides his time. A bachelor, a wine-lover – and a very powerful man. He is said to have a hand in the choosing of all Germany's diplomats.'

'Like that fellow Herzenberg?'

Walter nodded. 'Presumably. Possibly the Baron von Elburg too. You've heard of him? Another London diplomat. Is he a Kaiser man? Or the Chancellor's? Or von Holstein's? Who knows how these threads link up?'

Bored from the moment politics were mentioned, Honoria began once more to contemplate the night ahead. It was time to put His Highness out of his torment. To let him know of the bliss in store for him. She, Honoria, would be his. Ah, how happy he would be. Happy, happy Prince. She giggled. He would be the Happy Prince of Herzenberg.

132

She emitted a soft champagne giggle to herself. She summoned the nearest footman to her side. He was just a footman to her, a person in livery. She did not see the boy's round face, eyes goggle-eyed at the chatter, the perfume, the swish of silks and satin. It was Edward Jackson's first ball.

'You,' said Honoria Hartham imperiously, daringly, in case George's attention was drawn to her, and half hoping it would be. 'I want you to take this to His Highness.' She plucked a flower from her corsage.

'What 'Ighness?' Edward managed to stutter, glancing round fearfully for Mr Hobbs in case he was overheard opening his mouth against instructions.

Honoria sighed. Really, the class of servant dear Laetitia was employing nowadays was quite impossible.

'The Prince von Herzenberg.' She turned and pointed him out to Edward. He grinned, as Honoria said: 'Tell him to think on Mr Wilde's story and wear this flower for me.'

Edward had long since come to the conclusion that while gentlemen were stupid ladies were even stupider, but set off obediently clutching the yellow carnation in his now slightly grubby Berlin-gloved hands.

Honoria turned to find the Duke's eyes riveted on her. Had he heard? He stepped in front of Lord Arthur and took her arm, none too gently. Just as an excited Edward Jackson returned from his mission.

'Prince says to tell you 'e understands, mum.'

She smiled at him. 'Thank you, my man. Thank you so much.'

The Duke glared and Lord Arthur stared in some puzzlement at Edward Jackson, still hovering uncertainly, until the boy blushed and began to back away.

'What did that boy mean?' said the Duke slowly. 'Tell you he understands.'

'Nothing, you naughty man. Just a lady's secret. And I

133

can keep a secret. I can keep everyone's secret. Yours, and yours – and yours!' She chuckled, tapping each flirtatiously with her fan.

It was well after one o'clock in the morning that the last guest departed and the house party crept wearily to their beds. It was thus almost two when the last footman climbed wearily to his second-floor pigeonhole, too tired even to ponder the delights of the first-floor women's quarters that he was so strictly forbidden to savour. Auguste, his duties finished an hour since, was already slumbering fitfully, dreaming of a presentation of crawfish *à la provençale*, with a smiling Escoffier standing by in approval. The crawfish grew and grew in size, their claws stronger and stronger, engulfing him in their embrace; then suddenly it was Ethel that embraced him – alas, only in his dreams.

Slumber had not yet come to many of the guests and family bedrooms. In her bed Lady Jane lay awake and thought starry-eyed, not of marriage but of weddings; thirty feet away in the bachelors' tower Walter Marshall tossed and turned, calling himself every kind of a fool and remembering the touch of Jane's lips. The Duke and Duchess were each in their dressing-rooms, contemplating an unfamiliar night of connubial bliss. Lord Arthur dwelt with satisfaction on the future so carefully organised for himself. In her chamber the Honourable Honoria Hartham, clad in decorous white satin, awaited the arrival of her new lover. And at two o'clock, the door of Prince von Herzenberg's chamber opened and he began to creep stealthily along the corridor.

Chapter Six

In the fastnesses of her room, Edith Hankey, half roused from sleep by the sound of the bell, rolled over again in her bed, thankful that her days of answering such summonses were past. It was not unusual for the night bell to ring in the women servants' corridor on the first floor, nor for it to ring so persistently. What was unusual, however, was the scream that ensued when the unfortunate housemaid arrived at the source of the summons.

It did not, from the second-floor guest rooms, permeate to Mrs Hankey, but Auguste Didier, in his tiny room above, and the twenty occupants of that corridor sat bolt upright in their celibate beds. By osmosis their alarm spread to the first floor, and thence to Mrs Hankey, who became gradually conscious that something unusual was afoot. In less chaste beds in the main house occupants hovered uncertainly. The social code did not provide for this eventuality.

Ethel was the first present on the scene. What she saw made her white to her lips and, for the second time in ten days, Mrs Hankey was greeted by a peremptory summons, this one delivered amidst the sobs of an underhousemaid.

'It's that Mrs Hartham – she's – looking funny –'

Mrs Hankey rose without a word, donned her decent woollen dressing gown, seized her ipecacuanha and the nux vomica and hurried up the women's backstairs. On reaching the second storey she collided with Auguste who had investigated the source of the noise and found his Ethel white-faced but bravely coping with an obviously dying Mrs Hartham, and was on the quickest route back to seek Ernest Hobbs.

'Mr Didier, what are you doing on the women's stairs, might I enquire?'

'There is no time for such nonsenses, Mrs Hankey. It is, I think, the same as Mr Greeves – the doctor must be fetched. His Grace is being notified.' He brushed by her with no more ado.

Undecided for the moment whether to defend the inviolacy of the women's stairs, but impressed by his face as well as his words that something was indeed amiss, Mrs Hankey let him pass. Stockbery Towers was not yet advanced enough to have invested in a telephone, and thus the groom was once more summoned to take the brougham to the village for Dr Parkes.

'Oh my Gawd,' said Mrs Hankey, as for the second time in ten days she was faced by a near corpse. Mrs Hartham lay half on her bed, half on the floor, surrounded by vomit. Her girlish face was contorted into a grimace of surprise as if in protest that her life, for which she had not ordained this end, should have played this cruel trick on her.

Mrs Hankey approached her cautiously and lifted one arm. 'She's going to die,' she whispered flatly to Ethel who, now that responsibility had been taken from her hands, was weeping quietly. Mrs Hankey's main thought was not sorrow for a woman she did not know even by sight, but by the certain knowledge that this did not bode well for Stockbery Towers, and with the good of Stockbery Towers she identified herself completely.

Ethel was weeping for Mrs Hartham. A woman she'd seen yesterday, laughing and smelling deliciously, wearing a pale blue satin dress with real rosebuds down its side and long blue gloves to match, and satin slippers, slippers that would dance no more.

They could hear footsteps now: the ponderous ones of Hobbs, conscious of his position as steward; further off a pattering. Like little mice the lower servants were gathering at the door to the main house, determined not to miss what seemed likely to be an exciting event. Doors were cautiously opening across the way. Up the staircase from the first floor came the Duke, regally clad in a dark red Paisley silk dressing gown, followed by his Duchess, irritated beyond measure that she was obliged to reveal herself *en déshabille*, which, as it was her husband she was spending the night with, was by no means as elegant as it might have been in other circumstances.

His Grace was faced by Mrs Hankey at the door of the closed room.

'What the devil's going on?' he grunted furiously. 'Mrs Hartham not well? What's everyone rushing around for? It's the middle of the night, dammit.'

Mrs Hankey adopted suitably low tones. 'Took, sir.'

'Took?' The Duke looked blank. 'Ill, you mean?'

'Dying, I fear, sir.'

The Duke gave a muffled exclamation, his face grew red and he pushed Mrs Hankey unceremoniously out of the way. Her Grace, her mind working speedily and mindful of the proprieties, pressed in quickly after him. Mrs Hankey's lips closed in a tight line. She could hardly order His Grace out, but all the same . . . Visions of Mrs Hartham lying there – well, at least she was decently covered, but in her nightdress!

The Duke stopped still, as he took in the scene. 'Honoria,' he said in a strangled voice. He crossed over to her, and bent over her, his face white. Then he looked at the bedside table. His hand went out towards a plate of sandwiches lying on it.

137

'Sir, I don't think,' faltered Ethel, 'you should do that.'

The Duchess looked round, taking in her presence. Then: 'The girl's right, George. Leave her as she is. The police will want to . . .' Her voice was unusually gentle. It was Honoria lying there convulsed in agony, Honoria, her greatest friend, with whom she'd shared so many secrets, so many confidences. Yet at the moment it might have been a stranger. Her concern was for her husband. She was the stronger of the two, and now he would need her.

'Police?'

'Well, George, it might not have been an accident.'

The Duke straightened up and turned to look at his wife. A look passed between them. Then he buried his head on her shoulder and, turning, she led him out of the room.

Dr Parkes' examination was brief. By the time he arrived Honoria Hartham was dead. He had seen those symptoms in the same house ten days before, the contorted body, the agonised face. His face was grim as he stood up, the effort making him gasp a little. His Grace having left the scene, the doctor was obliged to make do with Hobbs, who speedily organised the dispatch of groom and donkey cart to the village to rouse Sergeant Bladon.

Then the doctor took Mrs Hankey back into the room. 'Now, my good woman,' he said.

She glared at him. She had never liked Dr Parkes.

'These sandwiches.' He pointed to the plate of wafer-thin sandwiches. 'When were they made?'

'Naturally,' she said haughtily, 'they would've been fresh made, just before the poor lady came to bed. When she asked for them. Naturally.'

He took the matter no further; that was for the police. It seemed clear enough that one of them had been the means of another speedy death. Save for the water flask and glass by the lady's bed, there was nothing else by which poison could have been administered.

When Sergeant Bladon arrived, Mrs Hankey felt on safer ground. She had his measure. PC Perkins was posted on the door, a job less to his liking than before. Before, he was amongst his own kind and had the occasional glimpse of Miss Gubbins to sustain him; now he was standing on thick carpet, staring at a window that looked out across the roof of the ballroom; along the corridor there were doors with gold-painted handles, and painted decorations which opened and shut, disgorging occupants like his mum's treasured weatherhouse she'd won at a fair. Feminine draperies, the like of which PC Perkins had never seen before, floated by. Blushing, he kept his eyes on the floor. It had not been so when he arrived. There, to his delight, had been Miss Gubbins and though he tried to avert his eyes he could not help noticing she was wearing night attire under a thick blue dressing gown, with her hair down in plaits like it used to be when they played in the hayfields all those years ago. To his impotent fury that Frenchie fellow had his arm on, if not around, her possessive-like and was leading her back to the servants' wing. It quite took his mind off what was going on in *there*.

In *there* Sergeant Bladon and Dr Parkes were doing their best to quell Mrs Hankey, with His Grace standing grimly by, dressed now and determined to stay. He saw it as his duty. Honoria had been a guest under his roof – quite apart from other considerations. Bladon was writing laborious notes, watched with eagle eye by Mrs Hankey. He walked around to examine the plate of sandwiches several times.

'It was in those sandwiches, of course,' Parkes remarked gravely and importantly. 'You'll need to find out who made them.'

139

Bladon was annoyed. He cast a look at the doctor who had crossed his path more than once. He played golf with Naseby, and that was enough for Bladon. They had satisfactorily proved how Mrs Hartham could have poisoned the brandy, and it was galling to find the lady had escaped the consequences of this revelation to which Bladon had devoted so much time.

'This 'ere water jug,' he said to the doctor. 'Poison – if that *is* how the lady passed over – get in that, could it?'

The doctor shook his head. 'She could not have taken that much of the poison to kill her so quickly in water without noticing the taste. It could not so have killed her. Unless she chose to take it, of course.' Bladon looked up quickly. 'No, it had to be the sandwiches.'

Bladon obstinately bent down to examine the glass. ' 'Ere,' he said in excitement. 'Come and look at this. That's not water in that glass, it it?'

The remnants of a pale liquid lurked round the bottom. The doctor sniffed it cautiously. 'No,' he said slowly, 'it's not water.'

Bladon was triumphant.

'It's wine, or champagne, perhaps,' continued Parkes.

Dampened, the sergeant looked around. 'No bottles here, ' he grunted.

'Probably brought it with her from the ballroom,' offered the Duke.

Mrs Hankey looked as scathing as she dared. 'Not in the glass, Your Grace,' she said. 'That's a *night* drinking glass.'

His Grace thought over the implications. He scowled. So there was somebody with her, he was right, dammit. And he knew who it was. The minx. Saying she was tired. Now what was he to do? If that Prince fellow poisoned Honoria he'd blast him with his own Purdey. Yet how could he let

Honoria down by speaking out. She still had a reputation, dammit. No, Laetitia was worth ten of her . . .

It was a short night. By the time Mrs Hankey reached her bed again, the housemaids were already up and stirring, yawning even more than was their wont. Ethel had not slept, and found it easier to rise with them than to exercise her prerogative and take that extra half-hour. Better to be busy than to think again of that white convulsed face, and turn her mind to pleasanter things such as how kind Mr Didier had been, how he'd understood how she felt about Mrs Hartham, how he had put his arm round her to comfort her – when they were out of sight of everyone, of course – and kissed her; he didn't seem to mind that her hair was all down and she was in the ugly old dressing gown. It wasn't his usual kind of kiss at all . . . He'd only kissed her like that once before, when on that never to be forgotten day he had taken her to London to the matinée of Mr Irving, and then to the Savoy to meet Mr Escoffier and they'd come home quite late, so that it was quite dark as they walked up from Hollingham Halt . . . quite dark.

Yet, as she got up and washed in her basin with the tepid water that one of the housemaids had placed outside her door, such pleasant thoughts faded, as she brought to mind what had been worrying her. The sandwiches. The doctor had asked about the sandwiches. And she had made them.

'These sandwiches, miss. You usually make sandwiches?'

Sergeant Bladon was looking less like the fatherly figure she had always taken him for, partly because he had been up all night.

'No, I –'

'Can't hear you, miss.'

She forced herself to speak. She was innocent. She

had nothing to hide. 'No,' was all she could manage.

Auguste was protective. 'No, Sergeant Bladon, but everyone else had gone to bed. So when Mrs Hartham rang for some sandwiches, Ethel was the only one still up.'

Sergeant Bladon turned purringly to Auguste. 'Ah, Mr Didier, so how come you know so much about it?'

'Because I was there,' said Auguste. 'I gave Miss Gubbins the duck to place in the sandwiches.'

'Oh did you, Mr Didier?' Bladon beamed. 'Unfortunate really. *Very* unfortunate, you might say. You being so - ah - closely connected with the demise of poor Mr Greeves.'

Auguste controlled himself with an effort. 'Monsieur *le Sergeant*, you know very well that the poison that poisoned Mr Greeves was in the brandy bottle, not in the luncheon.'

'Oh I know that, do I, Mr Didier? Well, you may think I know it, but what I know ain't going to count much longer. It's the new man you'll have to convince. First thing His Grace insisted on this morning is that this fellow from Scotland Yard comes down. He's going to be attached to us for a while.' Bladon was torn between relief that responsibility was now to be lifted from his shoulders, and irritation at this reflection on the Kent Police's competence, even though it was one in the eye for Naseby. 'He'll want to see you, Mr Didier. You too, Miss Gubbins.'

'Me?' Ethel looked frightened.

'You made the sandwiches, see.'

'But, Sergeant,' said Auguste impatiently, as to a child, 'Miss Gubbins was alone in Mrs Hartham's bedroom - why could she not have removed the sandwiches if they were full of poison which she had put there?'

'Could have been a trick,' said Bladon portentously. 'To throw us off the track.'

Ethel dissolved into tears as the enormity of her position hit her.

Bladon was taken aback. 'There, there,' he said uneasily. 'Don't take it hard. I daresay they won't be too hard on you.'

Strangely, this failed to calm Ethel's fears.

Auguste was perplexed. It had seemed so simple over the mayonnaise. He knew just how Greeves had been murdered and guessed why. Blackmail. But why then Mrs Hartham? Was it accident perhaps? No, no accident. So Marshall was right – there was danger for all in Stockbery Towers till this murderer was discovered. And now Scotland Yard. Auguste had a high opinion of *La Sûreté*, but of Scotland Yard . . . they made mistakes. That he knew. They had good men there; they had found Charlie Peace, many other murderers too, but of the application of logic, of patient reasoning? That was a French gift. Not English. They would be prejudiced. They were used to what they classified as the hot-headed émigrés who flocked to London's Bohemia. In their way they would be as prejudiced as Bladon. A Frenchman present? Let us blame the Frenchman.

Directly he entered Pug's Parlour he knew something was wrong. There was a silence as they saw him, a heavy silence and Ethel was in the midst of it. She jumped up when he entered and regardless of decorum threw herself into his arms. May Fawcett's lips grew thinner, Mrs Hankey's bosom swelled.

'Mr Didier,' she gulped, 'they think, they're saying –' and she broke into a torrent of weeping.

'Ah yes, what are they saying?' he replied steadily, keeping his arm round her defiantly while she searched for a handkerchief.

Nobody enlightened him. A few feet shuffled uneasily.

May Fawcett, braver than the rest, finally ventured: 'Remarkable, isn't it, Mr Didier, that it was you prepared the sandwiches, you two together, that is?'

'So that makes me the murderer, *hein*?' enquired Auguste mildly. 'First I kill Greeves, then I go out and kill a woman I do not know.'

'Not murder, no,' said Mrs Hankey eagerly, pacifyingly. 'Accident was what we thought.'

'They said you might be one of those people just likes killing people for the fun of it,' said Ethel, noisily snuffling. 'Like that Dr Palmer.'

'Did they indeed?' Auguste regarded his colleagues with fascinated horror.

'Say what you like, Mr Didier, the poison was in the food and you prepared it,' said Cricket, eyes flickering malevolently.

Five pairs of eyes regarded Auguste, not giving an inch. No longer one of them now. Their former united front was giving way. And he was the outsider. He must hurry to find this murderer. The sands were running through the egg glass rapidly.

Inspector Rose of Scotland Yard sat in his second-class compartment on the branch line to Hollingham Halt and gloomily considered his immediate future. Unless this case was solved and double quick, and in the manner least upsetting to the Duke, his position was likely to be awkward. He was under no illusions after reading the notes rushed up by special courier the night before as to why he had been detailed to this assignment. The Men of Kent were neatly bypassing the possibility of failure by acquiescing in the Duke's request to the commissioner on the tenuous grounds that the crime might well have had its genesis in

London. Walter Marshall's sudden interest in the August ball at Stockbery House, Mayfair, had not escaped the Duke's attention.

Nor was Rose under any illusions as to why he, Rose, had been selected. Too low-ranking an officer could not be sent to Stockbery Towers; too high-ranking an officer and they would fear to fall. Rose was not a man who regarded the world through rose-coloured spectacles – they tended to be distinctly grey. Nor was he possessed of much humour, fortunate in view of his name, which had he been conscious of its unsuitability for a ferocious senior officer of the Yard would have been a drawback indeed. Instead, it was a strength. The villains knew when Rose was coming. Some of his gloom was inherent, but much due to his delicate stomach, not eased by the culinary skills, or lack of them, possessed by Mrs Rose. A vicar's son, brought up in close contact with the East End, he had a way of handling villains, as he called them, that inspired healthy respect for Egbert Rose and in turn gave him an understanding of the criminal mind that stood him in good stead at the Yard.

Stockbery Towers was not going to be his milieu, however; he felt it in his bones. What did he know of Dukes and Duchesses and Honourables? Give him a mobsman, a cracksman, a bit faker and he knew where he was. But these swells – it was an alien world.

Morosely he threw down the window to survey the Kentish landscape and a cloud of sooty smoke blew in his face, making him gasp and reach for his handkerchief. Thus half blinded and eyes streaming he arrived at Hollingham Halt.

'Hum ha,' commented Rose gloomily. He had been listening to Naseby with the occasional interruption from Bladon for an hour, closeted in the Duke's writing-room. A high

145

honour this and, coupled with the presence of the ducal carriage at Hollingham Halt to await his arrival, a sure sign that His Grace had recognised that murder had entered the front portals of the Towers.

'What do you – um – think?' asked Naseby ingratiatingly.

Rose was staring out of the window. What he was thinking was that all those gardens out there must need a tidy bit of upkeep; not so many flowers of course as in his little house in Highbury, more naked statues, in fact. He wondered if they had to be scrubbed, and if so, who . . .? He pushed this thought away and tried to concentrate. He had in fact already reached certain conclusions about this case. One was that he didn't like Naseby.

Sergeant Bladon regarded his long lean face respectfully, trying to suppress the improper thought that this Scotland Yard chap looked somewhat like a mournful bloodhound pup. He pushed this rare flurry of imagination away. Rose wasn't that young anyway, must be forty, forty-five perhaps.

'The cook,' Rose said abruptly. 'I want to see the cook.'

Naseby stared. 'But, surely, His Grace, you'll want to see His Grace?'

Rose considered. 'No,' he said at last, 'the cook.'

'But you must say how do ye do to the Duke first.' Naseby was shocked.

Rose reluctantly ceded ground. 'The Duke then.'

His Grace was somewhat mystified to find himself alone after a mere five minutes, inveigled into feeling it better their discussion were postponed; much of the information, he understood, Rose could glean from other people, thus causing the least upset to His Grace. A sudden unexpected smile from Rose found His Grace agreeing this would indeed be best, and Rose had gone.

* * *

'You're the cook,' said Rose. It was more of a statement than a question, as he waved Auguste to a chair in the writing-room. His Grace had suggested the servants might more suitably be interviewed elsewhere, but Rose had pointed out the upset to the routine of the kitchens and thence to the Duke's dinner.

Auguste took his time. Always sum up one's opponent. He saw a man with a noncommittal face but with intelligent, darting eyes. No Bladon this, or a Naseby either. 'I am the maître chef.'

'French for cook, I know that,' said Rose, calculatingly dismissive.

'Maître chef - it is not the same thing.'

They eyed each other carefully, prowling round each other in mental duel.

'The inquest jury added a caution against you,' said Rose abruptly.

'The jury were fools - they do not understand the preparation of food.'

Nor did Rose, but he let that pass.

'Nor the purpose of logic,' added Auguste.

'Good men and true,' murmured Rose.

'That is right,' agreed Auguste. 'Their verdict was correct, but they do not know how they get to it. The logic is not for them. It is for you - and for me.'

Rose put down the pen he had been pretending to make notes with - always a useful distraction for his victims. 'And what does logic tell you, Mr Didier?' It was impossible to guess his thoughts.

'That we have two murders, one on one side of the green baize door, one on the other. But that most probably unless we have two murderers at large in one house, they were done by the same person. And that while Mr Greeves could have been murdered by someone from the main house, it is

147

out of the question Mrs Hartham could have been murdered by someone from the servants' quarters.'

Rose regarded Auguste in silence. He twiddled the pen, paying scant respect to its George III pedigree. 'A convenient theory, Mr Didier,' he said drily. 'Since I understand –' he pretended to inspect some notes by his side, 'ah yes, you prepared the duck for the sandwich that killed Mrs Hartham.'

Auguste waved this aside. 'Physically, yes, *we* could have poisoned the sandwiches; Gladys the scullery maid could have crept from her bed in the midst of the night and poisoned the sandwiches, but she would not, Monsieur *l'Inspecteur*.'

'Would not?'

Auguste tried to explain. 'The main house, it is another world, m'sieur. What reason would a servant have to kill Mrs Hartham? Discovery, you will say. They killed Greeves because he had driven them beyond endurance, Mrs Hartham somehow knew about it and so she too was killed. Ah, *Inspecteur*, it is not likely. They are beings from another world to most of those in the servants' hall; and to us upper servants even, they are scarcely human – we do not think of death in connection with them. We would run from them, flee from them, but not kill. No,' he went on, 'it is the blackmail you must look for.'

Ignoring this tempting carrot which had already been put to him by Naseby as an irrelevance, Rose remarked: 'Your French logic we hear so much about, Mr Didier. But my superiors like facts. No use to talk to them about flighty fancies and such like. It wasn't fancies that caught Charlie Peace, just years of patient footslogging. Just give me a nice fact, Mr Didier.'

'Very well, Inspector,' replied Auguste quietly. 'I will give you your fact. It is beyond question, is it not, that the poison for Mr Greeves was in the brandy bottle?'

Rose regarded him thoughtfully. 'Don't let that Frenchie fellow think he's home and dry,' Naseby had said warningly only half an hour before. But Rose was made of sterner stuff than Naseby. 'That seems to be the way of it,' he said carefully.

'And you think it might have been poisoned in the Duke's morning-room? Well, I will tell you that it cannot. Because Edward Jackson, the steward's boy, drank from that bottle while it was in the pantry next to Pug's Parlour.'

'It don't seem to me, Mr Didier, that your French logic is working the right way round at all,' said Rose mildly. 'Very unfortunate, you might say, for you and your colleagues.'

'Now, I go on to show you –'

'No, Mr Didier, I'm a plodding sort of chap. One step after another. Let's have a word with this 'ere boy, see what he says.'

Rose did not look a plodding sort of chap at all, decided Auguste, looking at his sharp eyes.

'Pull the bell, Inspector.'

Rose looked at the ornate bell rope, and with a smile of satisfaction pulled it. He glanced at Auguste. 'Often wondered what it was like to do that,' he offered mildly. A footman was dispatched in search of Edward Jackson who appeared, mulishly reluctant, some minutes later. He shot a look at Rose, then kept his eyes downcast.

'True is it, lad, what Mr Didier says? You took a swig of brandy before you joined the others at dinner?'

'Yus,' he muttered, scuffing at the Wilton in a way which would have brought instant dismissal had Hobbs caught sight of this foul deed.

'And that was in your pantry, by the side of Mr Greeves' room?'

'Yus. Ole – Mr Greeves put the bottle there before dinner.'

'And this dinner. Was it in Mr Greeves' room?'

'Nah,' said Jackson with scorn for such ignorance of the ways of the gentry. 'It were in the servants' hall like it always is. Then old Greeves and the rest came in 'ere for their dessert. I serves that,' he added, not without pride.

'Why didn't you tell the police about drinking from the bottle?'

Edward stole a glance at Auguste, and clearly decided he had more to lose by alienating Auguste than the police.

'Forgot about it,' he pronounced.

'Did you need, my lad, did you indeed? Sure you haven't just remembered it, like?' Though what he would have to gain by this, Rose could not see.

'Nah.'

Rose was looking at the boy in a puzzled way. 'Ain't I seen you somewhere before, lad?'

'Nah,' muttered Jackson shortly.

'Got a good memory for faces,' said Rose thoughtfully. 'Have to, at the Yard. Lot of villains about nowadays. All right, lad, off you go. Not you,' he added to Auguste who showed signs of retreat also. He looked at him heavily. 'Why me?' He made it sound like an accusation. 'Not Naseby or Bladon. Ain't because of my friendly face, is it?'

'No,' said Auguste untactfully. 'Because I am certain, monsieur, that one of His Grace's guests killed Greeves – and now this lady – and I wish to explain to you how he could have done so. And so it is necessary I tell you everything. You see, if Edward speaks the truth, then no one could have poisoned the brandy after he drank from it because we were all at lunch in the servants' hall. And no one but Edward entered the servery after we returned.'

'As I understand it,' said Rose, frowning, 'you said no one could have entered the servants' quarters from the main house without being recognised – the risk would be too great. And everyone agreed with you.'

150

'No,' said Auguste histrionically. 'I say that, yes I do. But what, Inspector, if he were or she were dressed like a servant, like a footman, and creeps in quietly – he would be taken for a footman returning from front-hall duty.'

Rose laughed, not the reaction Auguste had intended. 'Touch of the Lecoq in you, eh, Didier? No, my friend, murder ain't like that, all dressing up and creeping along corridors; it's knives in the dark, and jealousy and hands round throats. None of this fancy stuff. Not like the *Strand Magazine*, you know.'

Auguste was indignant. 'Monsieur, you do not realise. It *is* possible; there is no other solution. Let me tell you, now. The afternoon of the murder,' he went on eagerly, 'I presented the menus to Her Grace as is customary. His Grace was also present. He made a remark about the routine of the house having been upset . . . and one of the things he mentioned was that footmen were leaping about in full livery before luncheon.'

'What of it?'

Auguste looked pained. 'You would not understand, Inspector.'

'Naturally not,' murmured Rose.

Auguste swept on. 'That is a crime. Dress is as important for a servant as for the ladies and gentlemen. You must not transgress the rules. The housemaids wear their print dresses until luncheon; in the afternoons they must wear black; no housemaid must show her face above stairs after twelve o'clock. And the footmen do not wear their livery until after luncheon. In the mornings they wear informal dress, except the two on duty in the hall who wear what is called undress livery –' Rose looked puzzled. 'That is to say, dark coat and trousers. In the afternoons they put on their dress livery but *never* till after luncheon. Only for very formal occasions do they wear wigs, and that makes it full dress livery. Normally they sprinkle violet powder over their own hair to get the white effect.'

'So?' asked Rose, suspicious that this rigmarole was some kind of leg-pulling.

'So, where did His Grace see a footman in full dress livery *before* luncheon?'

'In the front hall?' suggested Rose laconically. 'Someone's got to be on duty there.'

'No,' said Auguste. 'Not in *full* livery. It would stand out like a black olive in a *purée de marrons*. And furthermore, His Grace would not go through the front hall before luncheon. He would go to the bootroom, then to the bedroom to prepare for luncheon, and for that he would go up the backstairs, not the principal staircase by the front entrance.'

'If,' said the inspector, frowning, 'I follow your drift, Mr Didier, you're implying he saw this fellow somewhere between the bootroom and the staircase –'

'Perhaps even coming out of the servants' quarters,' said Auguste.

'But the risk, man. At close quarters the Duke would recognise his own family, or a guest, whatever high falutin' stuff he was wearing.'

'But it was a reasonable risk,' said Auguste, excited. 'He was unlucky in running into the Duke, but one footman looks like another – with a wig on. Just a footman. They are all Freds to His Grace. He calls them all Fred because he does not know one from the other.'

Rose turned this over in his mind. 'He'd have to know a lot about your movements,' said Rose warningly. 'The Duke might not know one footman from another. But you would – wig or no wig.'

Auguste shrugged. 'Our movements are well known, monsieur. He would have half an hour before the upper servants returned to Pug's Parlour, and the footmen on luncheon duty went to change. In all great houses it is the same. Servants' dinner at twelve o'clock. And all the guests have their servants with them – easy enough to discover the layout of the house. And these guests here, they have visited many times, including last New Year, when they attended the Servants' Ball and came through the baize door to our side of Stockbery Towers.'

'The family would know how you work, of course,' said Rose ruminatively. He lit a pipe, a rare sign that he was relaxed yet alert. Mrs Rose did not like a pipe. But it was a wonderful aid to concentration. He puffed away in silence.

Then: 'There's a flaw, Mr Didier, in this fairy story of yours.'

'That is?'

'Tain't usual, I imagine, for family or guests to have a spare footman's uniform handy to put on.'

Auguste explained: 'The footmen's changing-room is by the backstairs, only yards from the entrance used on return from the shoot. And it is on the *far* side of the baize door. That is where their livery is kept, and where they change into it at twelve-thirty, and dust in their violet powder. And there are always spare liveries there, in case extra help is needed at dinner. Monsieur, the murderer would come back from the gunroom; slip in and put on the livery, make sure no one was around, check through the window that no one was about to enter the garden door, and come out and into the servants' quarters. If by bad luck he is spotted, no one will give a second glance at him. He will be invisible. He is a Fred. Then, after he had added the poison, he would emerge through the baize door and into the livery-room again; he would have about twenty-five minutes from start to finish before the footmen would come to change there. Then he would climb out of the window when no one was in sight and enter the garden door as though he had come straight back from the shoot.'

Two heavy draws on the pipe were the only evidence that Rose was listening. 'Tell you what,' he said conclusively, after a long pause, 'I'll think about it, Didier. Yes, I'll think about it.'

'Honoria was a friend, dear friend,' explained the Duke gruffly, bewildered. His world was crumbling around him.

Rose's instinct told him something was amiss; the Duke was avoiding his eyes, but nothing in Rose's previous experience had acquainted him with the possibilities of clandestine passions amongst the aristocracy, whom he had been reared by his mother, a hard-working village school-teacher, to regard as irreproachable as the dear Queen herself.

The Duke's not inconsiderable brain was working unusually hard. Torn between his simple code not to reveal the Prince's rendezvous, and his anxiety to avenge Honoria, he grappled with the thought that there was no earthly reason that the Prince would want to poison her. All too keen on keeping her alive, so far as he could see.

'Your Grace' – now that Rose was in his stride he found the Duke fitted comfortably into one of his seven categories of witnesses. Having thus pigeonholed him, he felt happier. He was category four: 'something to hide'; he'd play him along like he had Archie Wilson, a pawnbroker and trafficker of stolen goods. In fact they had a fair bit in common . . . 'I heard tell you were talking to Mrs Hartham with several other gentlemen not long before the ball finished. Now what would that have been about?'

His Grace brightened. Now that was something he *could* talk about. And did.

'And I also heard tell,' went on Rose carefully, 'that on

154

the day in question, when Mr Greeves met his demise, you saw a footman in full livery before dinner.'

His Grace gaped at this abrupt change of subject. Patiently Rose repeated the question.

'Footman? Dammit, man, you're here to catch a murderer, not to investigate the running of me household.'

'If you could remember, sir.'

His Grace frowned. 'No discipline nowadays. Freds getting above themselves. How the devil d'yer expect me to remember a footman?' Yet he thought, then his brow cleared. 'Not dinner, man. Luncheon. Damned fellow. Full wig. Shouted at him, took no notice. Couldn't chase him behind the door. That's where I saw him. Going through that servants' door.'

The Duchess, her immediate job over, was now in tears as the reality of Honoria's death sank in. Not that these tears would show in front of Rose who was, after all, a kind of superior servant. A dangerous one though, and one that must undoubtedly be charmed. Yet she was terrified. What if Franz had visited Honoria that night and – ? She played with the thought that he had poisoned Honoria for love of her, Laetitia, but dismissed the idea. She was a woman who could face reality. But she could hardly ask dear Franz . . . She would have to remain in torment.

'*Oui*, monsieur.' François' answers were almost inaudible.

Had he known he was cast as one of only four possible suspects for Greeves' death, and thus Mrs Hartham's – the women had been discounted as unlikely wearers of footmen's apparel – he would be even more terrified.

When did he come back to the bootroom? It transpired that François could not remember exactly.

Had he spoken to Mrs Hartham at the ball?

155

He had not. He was with Madame la Marquise. She would speak for him.

The Prince von Herzenberg breathed deeply. It had not been a pleasant night and now today looked as if it boded as badly. This inspector was prying a great deal too closely. Almost as though he knew Mrs Hartham had not been alone. Yet that was impossible. He had removed the champagne and the glass. There was nothing left to show Mrs Hartham had had a companion. It did not cross his mind that someone might have mentioned the possibility that he was a visitor. If you told no one, no one knew. That was the code.

'So you did not know the lady well, er – er, Your Highness,' asked Rose solidly.

'She was a guest here, as I am. I knew her as a delightful lady, a charming acquaintance.'

'And at what time did you retire to bed?'

'About twelve.'

'And you did not see the lady after that?'

The Prince sat up stiffly. '*Nein*,' he said forcefully. 'I am not the lady's husband.' Mentally he relived the horror. All so terrible. He had seen the plate of sandwiches lying outside the room – their signal that all was ready. He had taken them in, and found her in playful mood. She had been flirtatious – a shared glass of champagne. Then her nibble at the dainty sandwich, another glass of champagne, an interval of love . . . and he shuddered. It had happened so quickly. First she was there, then convulsed on the floor. He had automatically pulled the bell rope and then fled. He had no choice. Had the Kaiser learned that one of his followers had been attending the bedroom of a lady to whom he was not married and moreover one who was married to someone else, let alone a lady who had died, he would most certainly have been withdrawn from his English assignment. Back to Germany, back to von Holstein's web . . .

'You danced with the lady at the ball, I understand. And she sent you a message. Now what would that be, I wonder, Your Highness?'

The Prince stiffened. He must take care. Great care. 'Merely an arrangement to share the last dance together, Inspector. She sent me a flower.'

Petersfield gazed at the inspector for some time before replying. If he hoped to put Rose off by this technique he was mistaken in his man. Rose was immune to it, as he was to the blusterings of Bill Perkins, the costermonger whom he had hauled in for information.

'The order we returned to the bootroom? It's two *weeks* ago, my dear Inspector. However, as I told the sergeant, I believe I was the first to arrive, followed by His Grace. Then came Marshall. After that, I cannot say. I left on Marshall's arrival.'

'At the ball, I believe you were talking to Mrs Hartham?'

'I spent some time with her, we – er – danced together. We spoke of mere trifles, Inspector, as you will be aware one does at such times.' If he hoped to discompose Rose this time by such tactics, he was again disappointed.

'So, if I told you it was reported she talked of giving away your secret, I'd be wrong,' Rose went on doggedly.

A nerve twitched in Petersfield's face. Then he laughed lightly. 'My secret, Inspector? Oh, a very nefarious secret indeed. She spoke of my engagement to Lady Jane; she had just accepted my hand. Mrs Hartham spoke of revealing it to His Grace before I did, that is all. Now this unfortunate business means I cannot speak to His Grace until after the funeral. So I must ask you, Inspector, to respect my confidence. Your word as a – um – gentleman.' His eyes flicked over the ill-tailored suit and large brown boots, and he took a satisfied puff of cheroot.

Old Jebbins who was in charge of the gunroom was inclined to the truculent. He pointed out to the inspector that he was not going to leave off his counting of the ammunition just to talk about a shoot over and done with these two weeks. Once the majesty of the law had been impressed upon him, he reluctantly left his task and gave part of his attention to this 'Lunnon' fellow.

'No,' he said, with some satisfaction, 'I can't remember who were here, when they was here and when they left. 'Specially two weeks since. Why, bless you, there's been a dozen shoots since then. I got better things to be doing. What kind of gunroom would I be keeping if I kept spotting who left when 'stead of counting the guns and ammunition now, you tell me that?'

To this even Inspector Rose had no answer and, for once in his career, retired vanquished.

'To the bootroom.' Walter paused. 'I returned to the house about twelve-fifteen. I left the shoot shortly after it began. Lady Jane was kind enough to accompany me on a walk around the gardens –' a slight exaggeration of the truth, but it would do. 'We returned to the house together. She will vouch for me. But why? Ah, the maître has been talking to you, I see.'

'The cook?'

Walter smiled. 'Yes, the cook, though he would not appreciate the terminology. I hope, Inspector, you do not look in his direction?'

Rose sighed. 'Everyone seems very keen to arrest the cook. Don't see any reason to myself. Despite his cock-and-bull stories. Livery, pah!'

He watched Walter carefully and seemed satisfied by what he saw. 'Fellow's got a theory – one of you might have slipped on a footman's livery, popped inside the door, poisoned the brandy and out again.'

'Indeed?' said Walter slowly, considering. 'And you, Inspector? What do you think?'

'Oh, I don't say it's not possible,' said Rose carefully. ''Course if Lady Jane will back you up that puts you out of the picture. Wouldn't risk it, stands to reason.'

Walter's lips twitched. He considered. 'But if Didier's theory is true, only a certain number of people could have done it, Inspector, allowing it to be unlikely a woman could accomplish the necessary déshabille in the time available. There are the Prince, François, Petersfield, and –' He stopped.

'His Grace,' supplied Rose, matter-of-factly.

Walter rose to his feet angrily. 'I do not feel, Inspector, I can sit here and discuss the possibility of my host being implicated.'

'Sit down, sit down,' waved Rose. Then, as Walter showed no sign of complying, more peremptorily, 'Sit down. Cook keeps raising the question of blackmail. Do you believe him?'

'Do you?' rejoined Walter.

Rose almost smiled. 'Let's get him here,' he said abruptly.

Auguste arrived, annoyed at being interrupted in the midst of a complicated *farce normande*, but was mollified by Walter's presence.

'Sergeant Bladon tells me, Mr Didier,' said Rose slowly, 'that you handed over the black book in somewhat unusual circumstances. Now, Sergeant Bladon, not being used to the wicked ways of villains the way I am, did not see the obvious – perhaps you wrote this blackmail book yourself, Mr Didier?'

'Me?' Auguste blinked at him, bereft of speech at the barefaced accusation.

Rose looked at him dourly. 'Why not? You seem very enthusiastic about this blackmail; you gave the sergeant the book.'

Steel against steel. For the first time, Auguste felt a tinge of fear. He was well enough aware that it would suit everybody, except the servants, if the crime could be blamed on them, and preferably on the foreigner, and this man, he felt, might even be able to do it. He had the brain, unlike the others. He subdued his panic, glanced at Walter and set his reason in motion. He answered quietly. 'I tell you this man Greeves was a blackmailer. Mr Marshall will confirm that his widow lives in great comfort. But what I cannot tell you, Inspector, is where his proof was kept. Mr Marshall says where did Greeves keep his evidence? I do not know, but I tell you this, Inspector Rose, if it exists and I believe it must, it will not be in a tree in the grounds, underneath floorboards, tucked under a mattress, no. He was a cunning man, a bold man, and it will be hidden in a safe place, but an obvious place, so that he could laugh at his victims. He was like that. He would laugh; not outwardly but inside himself.'

Inspector Rose nodded slowly, seeming to be satisfied at Anguste's answer.

'We have given it a lot of thought,' said Walter, 'Mr Didier and I. He would want his evidence near, not at his wife's house, but where, we have no idea.'

'Oh, I've an idea all right,' said Rose. 'Yes, I've a fair idea.'

It was almost seven by the time Rose was ready. By this time His Grace was nowhere to be found. Ten minutes elapsed before he was tracked down to the billiard-room whither he

160

had repaired with Walter Marshall. Marshall made as if to go as Rose made known his wishes but His Grace asked him to stay.

'Won't be long, will you, Rose? Deuced good game, want to finish it, what? Give you five minutes, finish the game and then I'll have to change for dinner.'

If Rose was disconcerted he did not display it. If His Grace was prepared to have a third party present at the discussion of his private affairs he was either a fool – or a very clever man.

But whatever, if anything, the Duke had feared, did not materialise. Rose did not ask him again about Honoria Hartham. He seemed much more interested in Archibald Greeves.

'Was he what you might call a nice man, Your Grace?'

His Grace's eyebrows shot up. 'Nice? He was my steward. Don't ask me if he was nice or not. Popular enough. Knew how to behave. Let him stay to drinks sometimes. Some sense of breeding.'

A glance shot at Rose should have warned him that he too was being judged on this score and failing.

'A clever man, would you say, Your Grace?'

'Did the accounts all right. Nothing wrong that I could see.'

Walter Marshall, sitting in the corner, glanced from one to the other. He tried to judge where Rose was leading, but it was difficult to assess. 'A rich man, would you say?'

The Duke blinked. 'Rich? Paid him well enough. Got a few valuables though. Asked me to look after them for him. Waiting to give them to this lawyer chap the widow is sending.'

'Ah!' breathed Rose. A smile of quiet satisfaction crossed his lips fleetingly.

The Duke looked surprised. 'Show you tomorrow if you like.'

'Now, please, Your Grace.'

His Grace frowned, ostentatiously took out his pocket

watch and regarded it. Then he glanced at Rose and gave in. 'In the safe, morning-room.'

Walter Marshall, keenly interested, followed.

His Grace swung out a rather bad oil painting of the eighth Duke to reveal a wall safe. Out of it he took a large packet.

They opened it up.

'That's my wife's handwriting, dammit,' said the Duke, staring.

But Rose was quicker than he. 'I'll take these, Your Grace.'

'Yes, but wait a minute,' said His Grace, puzzled. His brow was furrowed with the strain of thought. Laetitia's handwriting?

Now His Grace was quite definitely upset. Dinner had to be put back half an hour. It was a gloomy gathering. Lord Arthur Petersfield, the Marquise, Walter Marshall and the Prince all seemed resigned to spending the rest of their lives at Stockbery Towers. Tempting as the thought would have been when they were first invited for the three-week shooting party, now that they were not free to return to the lure of London for the odd day or two, its delight was rapidly losing its allure. But the police had been adamant. Walter, who had managed to get leave of absence from Lord Medhurst, who was fortunately engaged in Newcastle on party business, was the most sanguine of the guests; Lord Arthur was impatient to leave the delights of Stockbery Towers for the fleshpots of London now that his goal had been achieved; the Marquise wished to return to her own country and the comforts of her own bed, despite the amenities she had brought with her. The Prince, his life complicated by a superfluity of women, thought longingly of his embassy behind its iron gates.

Supper was equally sombre in the servants' hall. An atmosphere of uncertainty reigned over it. No one had told them anything. Even PC Perkins was no longer a source of information. Would the hand of the law fall on them and sweep them off? Were they even now sitting side by side with a double murderer? Eating his cooking? They pecked at their food, and one of the best barons of beef that the Home Farm could produce, and a soufflé specially concocted by Auguste to soothe their minds, passed for nothing.

Equally glum, Inspector Rose sat down to his solitary supper. His presence had caused great concern for the protocol of Stockbery Towers. Was he servant or guest? Should he dine with the family or with the servants? Mrs Hankey had come up with the solution. The old school-room was quickly converted to a working-room and dining-room, the old nursery for sleeping quarters. And there sat Egbert Rose, gloomily inspecting a rocking horse with a faded blue saddle that mocked him from the shadows.

'Just a plain bit of fish,' he had told Auguste, on being questioned as to what he would like for his supper. 'Nothing too rich, mind,' he said warningly. It was the cry of his life. Not that Mrs Rose produced rich food, but such were the unfortunate results of her repasts that Egbert laboured under the delusion that she did.

Auguste had returned to the kitchen, seeing this as a direct insult to his cooking, not the desperate cry of a man tortured too long by inefficient cuisine. 'Nothing too rich,' he muttered in disdain, as he laboured. The results he took up himself and set the tray with dignity in front of Egbert Rose.

Before him lay shining cutlery and napkins, a rose in a silver vase, provided by Ethel, and an array of gleaming silver dishes.

163

Inside them was nothing that was instantly recognisable to Inspector Rose as anything, let alone fish.

'It looks rich,' he said forebodingly.

Auguste stood in front of him, arms akimbo. 'Monsieur, it is *not rich*.' He held his eye firmly, until Rose's fell, and reluctantly the inspector began to spoon some food on to his plate. Not till he had taken the first mouthful, did Auguste feel free to depart.

When an hour later Edward Jackson went to collect the dirty dishes, the inspector was sitting in front of the nursery fire, an unusually restful expression on his face, hands across his stomach.

The silver salvers were all but empty.

'He ate it all, Monsieur Didier,' whined Edward. 'There ain't enough left for me.'

'Edward, if you still desire the *sole au chablis*, you must wait till the leftovers come down from the main hall,' said Auguste firmly.

'Yes, Mr Auguste. 'Course, I could slip on me footman's get-up and go up there and get some now,' said Edward daringly. 'If I wait for the Freds to come down I'll be starving to death. Go on, Mr Didier, let me. They'll never recognise me, I'll just be a footman, like I was at the party – it'd be a laugh.'

'Edward,' said Auguste warningly, 'if Mr Greeves were still alive, you'd never dare do it. You do as you wish, but I do not know anything, do you hear, *anything*, if you are caught. You can plead your case with Mr Hobbs yourself. I wash my hands of you.'

164

Chapter Seven

Edward Jackson, resplendent in full dress livery, walked somewhat warily into the dining-room. Fortunately, for his confidence was not as great as he had made out to Auguste, it was empty – of everything in fact, since all signs of the sumptuous repast which had taken place had vanished. From the drawing-room came sounds of soft, cooing conversation, from the billiards-room the sharp cracks of cue on ball, and the murmur of brandy-thickened voices. Edward considered. Not all the food had been brought back to the kitchens – the cold plates must still be in the servery, in case some were speedily required to prevent the sudden starvation of any of the guests. Perhaps there'd still be some of that sole-shabblee there as well in a chafing dish. With this cheering thought, Jackson turned down the corridor towards the servery entrance. The corridor, however, was no longer empty. Coming from the ballroom was a familiar figure.

Edward Jackson grinned. 'Wotcher,' he carolled cheerily, perkily.

The recipient of the greeting did not respond, but turned away.

Edward, taken aback, turned to matters of more immediate moment. In the servery lay the forlorn remains of Auguste's genius. The company had apparently appreciated the *sole au chablis* as much as had the inspector for none remained, but enough galantine, chicken in aspic, and Yorkshire pie were left to fill the hungriest belly. The galantine was a particularly fine one, and Edward Jackson was intent on appreciating it to the full. So intent was he that he was not aware of the door of the servery quietly opening behind him, and was taken completely by surprise as the heavy bronze lamp crashed down on his head.

There was something troubling him. Was it the ingredients for the kidneys for tomorrow's devilled kidneys, something omitted? His late-night checking of the luncheon preparations? No, it was less tangible than that . . . It was something to do with Edward. And livery. That was it. Mrs Hartham had been murdered, and Edward had been at the ball in livery. Now Edward had gone to the main house once again in livery – and Auguste had not seen him since. With a sudden rush of panic Auguste began rapidly to dress once more, and rushed downstairs. The kitchen was still active with the routines of late evening. William Tucker was still up with two yawning girls, and two Freds were waiting for Hobbs' signal to clear food from the main house.

'Edward, Mr Didier?' asked Gladys. 'No, why do you want Edward?' She was aggrieved, for she had a sneaking suspicion that her god did not rate her own abilities highly. But Auguste had not waited.

He tried the servants' hall – empty. Pug's Parlour was in darkness. With a growing sense of alarm he checked the cubbyhole of a room that Edward Jackson shared with Percy Parsons. Percy lay snoring stertorously, mouth open as wide as the Moffat lamps he so industriously tended. Of Edward there was no sign.

Regardless of his hastily donned attire, Auguste rushed towards the baize door. Thus it was he found Edward Jackson lying on the floor of the servery, surrounded with

166

blood and the splattered remains of the galantine.

An enormous rage grew inside Auguste that anyone could do this to Edward, who was little more than a child, coupled with a heavy feeling of guilt that he had condoned this stupid prank. Trembling, he lifted the boy's arm and was relieved to find it warm; once his own fear had subsided he managed to detect a gentle pulse.

Within ten minutes Mrs Hankey was again in command, and the donkey cart once more setting out on the now familiar journey to Dr Parkes.

Egbert Rose, roused from the most peaceful postprandial slumbers for many a day, picked up the bronze lamp, turning it over and over in his hands, thoughtfully. What a story it could tell. There was someone new at the Yard working on a theory that people left fingerprints every time they touched something, and that soon you'd be able to indentify your villain by them. Maybe, but not yet. With a sigh he put the lamp down on the sideboard and turned to Auguste.

'This is a sorry business. Only a lad. It seems, Mr Didier, that you have quite a habit of being around when anything goes on. Bob's your uncle, as they say, here we are again. Quite a coincidence.' His tones were jocular, but his eyes watchful.

'Monsieur *l'Inspecteur*, if I had hit this poor child over the head with a lamp, would I be the one to come to tell everybody. "*C'est moi*, this is what I have done"?'

'Now you mustn't take me too seriously, Mr Didier,' said Rose mildly. 'Just making an observation.'

'I came to seek Edward because I was worried about him.'

'Oh? Another bit of the old detective work, eh? Now why might he be in danger, did you think?'

'I was worried because *I* sent him up here. To look for

167

food – he wished for some of the sole that I gave you for dinner, monsieur. That's why he is in the footman's livery. Normally he would not be allowed above stairs, but on Saturday he was at the ball as a footman because they needed extra hands, and that gave him the idea. Put on the livery again and no one would think it strange to see the figure disappearing into the dining-room. And I let him do it.'

'So he was at the ball that night, was he?' said Rose with rising interest. 'Night Mrs Hartham got herself murdered. Now that's interesting, Mr Didier. Considering as how Mrs Hartham was seen talking to a footman just before the ball ended.'

'But what could Mrs Hartham have to say to Edward Jackson?'

'He took a message to someone.'

'A lover?'

Rose's eyebrows rose fractionally. 'Lover?' he said. 'The lady was married.' He knew that only too well. He had spent two hours with a furious Mr Hartham, who had arrived in a temper and a hired brougham as intent apparently on seeking out the perpetrator of the blot and the scandal on the name of Hartham as to mourn for Honoria's death, however ornate the black-edged handkerchief.

'Ah,' said Auguste, embarrassed, 'but the sandwiches . . .'

'That you helped prepare,' Rose reminded him.

'The sandwiches,' went on Auguste disregarding this, 'they are a signal to a lover that the lady is ready to – er – receive.'

Rose looked outraged. He and Mrs Rose had never needed plates of sandwiches. He was only too well aware of the seamier aspects of sexual relationships between men and women, but this delicate soufflé of passion was alien to his world.

'Mr Didier,' he said severely, 'of course, you're a Frenchman – that sort of thing may happen in France but not in England, I assure you.'

'Perhaps not, Inspector,' murmured Auguste diplomatically.

Rose was satisfied, having put Auguste in his place. He had not yet had time to examine the bundle of papers he had taken from the Duke's safe.

Half an hour later a pale, unconscious but living Edward Jackson was tucked up swathed in bandages in Mrs Hankey's bed, a makeshift bed having been made up for the nurse. Mrs Hankey had reluctantly agreed to banishment. Outside the door stood a sleepily reluctant Constable Perkins, dragged from his slumbers yet again, in order to forestall night intruders.

The upper servants sat in armed truce in Pug's Parlour. The thought that Edward was hovering between life and death a few feet away and that this was his territory they were now invading depressed them all. Hobbs did not stand on the same ceremony as Greeves. Indeed he welcomed the company, having been used to it all his working life. They were interrupted by a knock, and one of the Freds put his head round the door.

'Beg pardon, Mr Hobbs, Edward's aunt, Mrs Robins. Bin to see the inspector, sent her down here.'

A timorous woman of about sixty came in, red-eyed from weeping. She seemed overawed by the panoply of people waiting her. Mrs Hankey rose to do the honours, Ethel murmured of a nice cup of tea. They sat round awkwardly, not knowing what to say. At last feeling that effort was called for on her part, Mrs Robins vouchsafed that: ' 'E's a good lad, really.'

There was a chorus of assent.

' 'E's had a hard life, Edward.'

This time the chorus was not so enthusiastic as they took this as an implication that the hardness was inflicted at Stockbery Towers.

She hastily made amends. 'In London that was. Afore 'e came here. You've been good to 'im, I know that. He used to tell me on 'is day off once a month. "That Miss Gubbins, Auntie, she's nice to me".'

Mrs Hankey looked put out. It was *her* privilege to be spoken of kindly by subordinates.

Stepping into the awkward silence Auguste asked politely: 'How long has he lived with you, Mrs Robins?'

' 'Bout two years now. 'E was a telegraph boy, like what he was 'ere before His Grace took him on. Didn't like it though. Right ill 'e was when 'e came to me. White-faced little thing just like 'e is now . . .' And, thinking of the still white figure she had just seen swathed in bandages, she began to weep silent tears as they looked on helplessly.

Word speedily went round Hollingham village. Ten good men and true, already summoned for their second inquest in a week, scratched their heads and dwelt on thoughts of a double inquest. Indignation gradually took over. That Greeves was one thing, and Mrs Hartham was another – up from London, from another world. But Edward Jackson was a different matter. He lived with his aunt Maidstone way, and had done these two years. He was almost a man of Kent. They took it as a personal insult and, for the first time in three centuries, the peaceful village began to mutter against the establishment of the Duke of Stockbery. It was not generally considered that His Grace himself had crept up in the middle of the night and bashed the steward's boy over the head, but nevertheless it was his house and there were some right funny goings-on.

Rose was partaking of a hearty breakfast in the front schoolroom, even if kedgeree and devilled kidneys were not precisely what Mr and Mrs Rose usually began their working days with. Unfortunately their effect was considerably spoiled by Rose's preliminary perusal of the bundle of papers from the Duke's safe.

What he found there was stronger meat for a delicate stomach than anything even Mrs Rose could produce. Taken aback after glancing at the first four letters from the Duchess to the Prince *and* to the Duchess from his predecessor, a well-known explorer of the unknown continent, he set them on one side, and strengthened his resolve by finishing his coffee.

By the time he had done so, Bladon had arrived, eager not to miss anything now that responsibility had passed to another.

'Look at this, Bladon,' said Rose gloomily, abruptly. He tossed across with scant respect the last of the Duchess's letters. Bladon was half fascinated, half thinking it *lèse majesté* to be thus conducted into the inner life of the Duchess of Stockbery.

'Seems to be pretty fond of this Prince fellow,' said the sergeant, considerably understating the case. Both men had been married for many a long year, but the contents brought a blush to both faces as they read on, steadily avoiding each other's eyes.

Rose had first made his name at the Yard by his investigations into one of the goriest murders in London's East End since Jack the Ripper had departed the scene, and the sexual habits of Londoners generally whether in the seamier quarters of Bethnal Green or the riper brothels of Mayfair and St James's; he had broken up a thriving trade that, despite Mr Stead's crusade, still thrived on child sex, including that in the nastier bordellos both heterosexual and homosexual, culminating in the Cleveland Street scandal of 1889. He had not turned a hair throughout that investigation into this homosexual pleasure-ground for rich men and their wretched perverted boys. Nor had he paled at the sight of Mary Kelly, the Ripper's last victim. Those were facts. Part of his job. This was something else. In theory he knew that ladies however apparently respectable might yet harbour distinctly sexual thoughts and even express them. He had once been privileged to read Miss Madeleine Smith's letters to her lover. But even the Dilke political scandal had not convinced him that ladies of high social standing might play an active part in such affairs. To Rose, ladies had hitherto always been ladies, even if gentlemen had occasionally been blackguards.

Sergeant Bladon's thoughts were far less complicated. He was simply shocked.

'Well, that cook fellow was right,' grunted Rose at last. 'The departed was a blackmailer, and that was his blackmailing record book.' He stared at the neatly collated piles of papers in front of him. What fools people were. Seemed the gentry were as stupid as anyone he'd come across up East. Plenty on the folks here at the Towers and quite a bit on some he'd never heard of. He sighed, foreseeing several weeks of work tracking down the people concerned once he got back to the Factory. He thought longingly of his untidy little pigeonhole in Scotland Yard. Funny how the name stuck, even though they'd moved.

There was a scandalised gasp from Sergeant Bladon. He had found a rare scrap from His Grace to Honoria. His Grace was not often given to epistolary effusions.

'Nothing on his fellow servants,' Bladon pointed out.

'Wouldn't need it, Sergeant. If I understand you aright, this man had the power of life and death over them anyway.

172

He could just tell them to go, no reason given. Played around with them. I've met the type. That pretty girl, one who made the sandwiches, she blushed right up when I asked her what she thought of Greeves. Probably made advances to her. And he'd got those two women where he wanted them.'

The contents of the last envelope provided more of a puzzle. Rose stared at the piece of paper.

'Bladon,' he said finally, 'what would you say this was?'

The sergeant looked at it, but reluctantly was forced to admit: 'Couldn't rightly say, sir.' All it looked like was a series of squiggles.

'I think,' said Rose slowly, 'it's part of a ship's plan. Possibly the engine room.' He put down the piece of paper and reached for the little book that Auguste had found in Greeves' bible. He studied the figures inside once more while Bladon gazed at him eagerly, transported into the world of his dreams. Ships' plans, high society, blackmail. For a few heady moments, he saw himself uprooted from the purlieus of Maidstone and swept off to the heady heights of Scotland Yard: 'I must have this man near me, Commissioner.'

Rose, oblivious of these plans for his future working conditions, studied the initials opposite the figures carefully. There could be no doubt now that L might well stand for Laetitia – the use of the Christian name would fit with what he had heard of Greeves. H reflected his use of Honoria Hartham's little notes. A for Arthur Petersfield. He turned to the envelope in front of him that he had not yet opened. A handful of IOUs fell out. Rose thought for a moment. Then he pulled the bell rope. Bladon watched enviously. He could well imagine what would happen if he had pulled it, Maidstone police or no, he wouldn't care to face one of those footmen.

'Ask Mr Marshall to join us,' Rose said abruptly, as though summoning His Grace's footman was of no more import than summoning Betsy, their maid of all work at home. His response was a great deal more efficient than Betsy's.

Typically Rose wasted little time in preliminaries when Walter arrived. 'What do you think this is?' he greeted him, pushing the piece of paper over to him.

Walter studied it and frowned. 'I've no idea, Inspector,' he said evenly. 'No idea at all.'

'Come now,' said Rose cordially. 'None of your "confidential government business" here. I got two murders to solve. Murders, Mr Marshall.'

'I would have to talk to Lord Medhurst, my superior –'

'Murders, Mr Marshall. Want another, do you? You heard a boy's been knocked on the head. Think that has nothing to do with it? If he dies, that's three. How many more do you want?'

'Very well, Inspector,' said Walter at last. He glanced at Sergeant Bladon doubtfully. Rose followed his glance.

'Go and see how that boy's faring, Bladon,' he said kindly.

Bladon, deflated and reluctant, departed.

'You were right to think this paper important,' said Walter. 'Have you heard of the Rivers papers?'

'Ah,' said Rose with satisfaction, 'thought it might be.'

'They went missing, as you know, last June. After Lord Brasserby's house party at Chivers. Thomas Rivers, the designer of our future battleships, had given the papers to Lord Brasserby of the Admiralty for Saturday to Monday because there were rumours of a planned break-in at the Foreign Office and no risks could be taken. They turned out, of course, to be false rumours planted deliberately. The real plan was to take them at Chivers. They have not

174

been seen since. Even this is not the original – you can see it is a copy, it is too poorly executed for anything else. But here, Inspector, is one vital plan for a battleship of the future.'

'And it turns up in His Grace's safe,' said Rose. 'Significant.'

'More significant than you think, Inspector. These weren't just any old state papers – they were *naval* papers. And, as you know, it was remarked on the new Kaiser's last visit to England that he had displayed an over-keen interest in our naval plans. He is jealous of our navy. Some say so long as Queen Victoria rules England will be safe, for he is in awe of her, but the Queen cannot live for ever. It is our Prime Minister's view, and that of most Conservatives, that England has nothing to fear from Germany, for she is anxious to be our ally; that she has signed one alliance and will others; that the Kaiser is the Queen's grandson, the son of her favourite daughter; and that our enemies are still France and Russia, and it is against them we must defend our shores. So it might be that the Rivers papers found their way to Paris or to his Tsarist Majesty – were it not for von Holstein.'

'Baron Friedrich von Holstein?'

'You've heard of him?' Walter eyed Rose with respect.

Rose nodded. 'Did Bismarck's dirty work for him. We get a few history lessons at the Yard.'

'Von Holstein is still behind the strings of German diplomacy, the most dangerous man in Europe, we Liberals think,' said Walter soberly. 'He holds no high office, no obvious pomp, but *he* decides who shall be Germany's allies, who her enemies. All our diplomacy is going towards making sure that Germany and Russia do not enter into an alliance, but for the wrong reasons. For fear of Russia, not Germany. It was rumoured that Bismarck signed such an alliance – and von Holstein started life under Bismarck's instruction. Bismarck still lives, though no longer in office. Perhaps his policy lives also. With Germany and Russia in alliance, the balance of power is gone for ever. The British navy will need every battleship she has. And the reason, my dear Inspector, that the Liberals fear Germany, not Russia, is that there is a Machiavelli behind the scenes – and the Rivers papers disappeared.'

'Very interesting, Mr Marshall, highly interesting. Now, I'll tell you something even more interesting. Equally confidential. When these papers disappeared suspicion fell on Brasserby's guests, and do you know which we decided it was? I'll tell you. It weren't no German. It was a Frenchman, a Monsieur Francois Pradel. And most interested I was to come here and find that same Frenchman a guest.'

Walter gasped. 'François? But no, you must be mistaken. He does not have the –' He stopped, for he realised he did not know what François was like. He was the Marquise's secretary. That was all.

'Father's an admiral, you see. It all fitted. We never proved anything.' And there had been nothing in the book, either, Rose thought regretfully. Not unless the P. F. he'd taken to be Prince Franz was a transposition of F. P.

'Prince Franz is at the German embassy in London. Who more likely to be von Holstein's spy?' said Walter slowly.

'At the Yard,' said Rose, 'it was thought a Baron von Elburg at the London embassy was behind it. Prince Franz's name did not come up.'

'He is answerable to von Elburg,' said Walter. 'His secretary.'

'Ah,' said Rose. 'Now, one other thing I'll show you,' he went on, pushing the other envelope to Walter across His Grace's Georgian desk.

176

Walter looked at the slips of paper that fell out. His face remained impassive.

'Well?' asked Rose.

'Copies of gambling chits,' said Walter slowly. 'Baccarat losses.'

'Read the signature?'

'Petersfield. Arthur Petersfield,' said Walter grimly.

'Baccarat,' said Rose with satisfaction. 'Wouldn't be popular, eh, not with the Tranby Croft affair so recent. Illegal game.'

Walter's stomach lurched. The chits added up to a lot of money. Petersfield was not a rich man. But, married to Stockbery's daughter, no one would dare to touch him . . . His answers to Rose's questions grew more perfunctory and, as soon as was possible, he left Rose alone. He decided he needed air, the confines of the house were becoming stifling.

Rose paced around the room. It was all too neat. Motives, means and evidence, all before him. But which tied up with which? Who had donned the livery and crept behind the baize door? Who had seen that plate of sandwiches and added a twentieth grain of aconitia to each one? And which of them had knocked a fifteen-year-old boy over the head and left him to die?

Walter donned ulster and hat and went into the gardens. There he found Lady Jane on the croquet lawn viciously attacking the course with more determination than skill. It was a cold day and, between the fur collar and the large-brimmed hat, little of Jane's face could be seen. What he could see of it did not bode well for an amicable conversation. Yet for once she did not seem disposed to vent her wrath on Walter.

'A game's always better with two,' he remarked cordially. 'I'll join you.'

'It's a stupid game,' she said. 'And I'm tired of it. It makes me feel like something out of *Alice in Wonderland*.'

Ungainsaid, Walter fell in beside her as she strode off towards the wilderness that divided the park from the farmland.

'Let's go up to Seven Acre Field,' she said.

'We can't,' said Walter. 'That's where the next shoot is. The keepers won't be pleased if we go striding through the coverts. Let's go up the hill.'

'Nothing but shooting, shooting at this time,' she said moodily. 'All those dead birds strung out, the men talking of nothing else. Disgusting.'

'There I agree with you,' said Walter mildly.

'I can't wait for the hunting to begin again,' she said. Father won't allow it while the pleasant shooting's on.'

'Bloodthirsty woman,' he said.

She looked at him, startled. 'Bloodthirsty? Oh, the fox – but that's different.'

'Why?' enquired Walter. 'I don't expect the fox thinks so.'

'Because –' She frowned and kicked a stone with the toe of her elegant black boot. 'Well, it is,' she said crossly. 'Don't you hunt?'

'No,' said Walter. 'Nor shoot. I find them both unrewarding.'

'Why do Mother and Father keep inviting you down here then?' said Jane belligerently.

'I've often wondered that,' said Walter thoughtfully. 'I've long since given up flattering myself I'm on your mother's list of prospective suitors for your hand.'

Startled she looked up. 'You,' she said witheringly. 'I should think not indeed. Anyway, I –'

He cut across her. 'You're hardly flattering to my self-esteem. You don't have to dismiss the idea quite so out of hand. I'm what is known as an up-and-coming man. If you listen very hard, you can hear my name spoken of in the ripples round the circle that circles the circle round the inner circle.'

'You're talking nonsense,' remarked the Lady Jane. 'Anyway, I don't know anything about politics, and moreover I'm going to marry Lord Arthur Petersfield.'

'So you are,' said Walter Marshall politely. 'I'd forgotten.'

She glared at him, then suddenly she said in quite ordinary tones, 'Walter, who do you think is doing all these awful things?'

He glanced at her, surprised by the use of his Christian name. 'I don't know. I thought I did – but now I don't.'

'Surely,' she said, 'it *must* be one of the servants. It couldn't be one of us, could it? That steward man was killed in the servants' quarters, so that means it couldn't have been one of us. And Mrs Hartham must have known who it was, and that boy –' Her voice trailed off unhappily.

Walter was silent. He could not, even for the sake of reassuring her, speak what he knew could not be the truth.

'Walter,' she went on in a low voice, 'I'm so worried. Inspector Rose has had Father and Mother talking to him for hours. Arthur hasn't even had a chance to ask them about us, yet.' She stole a look at him. 'You don't think – I mean – what motive could either of them have had? He *can't* think they did it, do you think? What reason could they possibly have for killing Greeves and then poor Mrs Hartham? Why, she was Mother's best friend. And Father's –'

'No, I don't think and none at all,' said Walter firmly, putting an arm round her waist, unrebuked.

Walter was still in the garden as Auguste came up to him half an hour later, Jane having departed to change for luncheon.

'How is the boy?' enquired Walter.

179

Auguste sighed. 'Bad. Still unconscious. The doctor says if he regains consciousness he will be all right, but otherwise – A boy,' he said fiercely, 'a mere insignificant boy.'

'An important boy to someone,' Walter observed. 'Unless of course his assailant thought he was another footman. John is the same height. Perhaps it was not Edward who was with Mrs Hartham at the ball.'

'No,' said Auguste. 'I have asked the other Freds. It was not them. What reason would they have for lying? So tell me, monsieur, what happened there – at the ball?'

'Mrs Hartham had sent him off with a message to someone, I think the Prince, which I – and I think,' he hesitated, 'the Duke took to be a message of assignation.'

'Why, monsieur?'

Walter thought. 'She was very pleased with herself,' he said slowly. 'Very full of how beautiful she was, in the way that such middle-aged women have. Preening. She was being arch, twitting Petersfield about something and tapping him with her fan which was annoying him. Then she said she would tell his secret to the Duke, she'd tell all our secrets to the Duke. Then I saw the Duke was still standing there – and the footman who had come back.'

'Makes our work a lot easier having gentlemen like you to help us.' Rose had come up silently behind them.

It was Auguste who replied, taking his words at face value. 'If we can help, monsieur, then we are delighted to do so.' It was always difficult for him to adjust to the English sense of humour.

They had come to the end of the long walk and face to face with a naked Venus. Rose inspected her gloomily. 'We like our statues in London with more clothes on,' he pronounced at last. 'You can have too much nature.'

'You don't enjoy working here, Inspector?' asked

Walter surprised. Used though he was to the smoky pall of London, he could not understand someone preferring it to the country.

'I work best in the fog,' said Rose, thinking longingly of one of those peasoupers, the smell of the gas lamps, the muted sounds. A man's mind could work in that, better understand the murkier machinations of men's minds. Here in the country, by the harsh light of day, he couldn't seem to get to grips with evil somehow. Though evil existed just as much here, perhaps more. 'Different sorts of crime, of course.'

'In murder too?'

'Yes,' said Rose, considering. The stabbings, the garrotters, the railway murders, Jack the Ripper. It was what he was used to. 'Your villains leave clues, bloodstains, you track them down, step by step, until you find their mistake. Bloodhound. Out here it's different. I don't say it's not interesting, but it's not like you find in the brothels, up the Haymarket. You feel you're doing some good there. Sorting out things, like. Making life more decent. Cleaning up a mess, like in Cleveland Street.'

'Cleveland Street?' asked Auguste, at a loss.

'A male brothel run by two gentlemen, Veck and Newlove. Their premises were raided and closed down yet they received notably light sentences when their case came up. There had been red faces in high places, as they say. Then a local paper took it up, started naming names, and an earl sued for criminal libel. He won, but it didn't stop the rumours. The Prince of Wales' friend fled the country, and plenty of others are keeping very quiet. Very quiet indeed.'

'You were involved?' asked Walter.

'When it was raided, yes. Us lesser folk at the Yard were kept out after that. It was a mistake it was discovered at all, we suspected. They knew about it at the top, but let it be. All

181

the patrons were men with plenty of money and position; all went there anonymously. No names, no pack drill. We only got on to it through some missing money from the GPO. Telegraph boys were very popular there, you see.'

He stopped abruptly. Auguste too.

'Telegraph boys!' they breathed in unison.

'*That's* where I seen him before,' said Rose triumphantly.

'Edward Jackson!' exclaimed Auguste, simultaneously.

Chapter Eight

'The Duchess! It's the Duchess!'

'*Tiens*, Gladys, clarify, clarify! How often have I told you you must clarify the butter. Of course you will not get the perfect results if you do not pay attention to detail.' A ruined panful of *pommes de terre duchesse* headed for the waste bin and Gladys, cast down, laboriously puréed yet more potatoes.

Muttering exasperatedly under his breath Auguste continued preparing the sauce for his soufflé. For his part, he did not like duchess potatoes; give him the *gratin dauphinois*, or the *pommes de terre Cendrillon,* Cinderella potatoes, or *à la lyonnaise*, or – ah, but so many choices for that humble vegetable the potato. Yet was any taste more superb than the first scrubbed new potatoes from the Home Farm, simply boiled? Always there were so many different ways of preparing a particular food, yet in the end one dish was chosen. He remembered one of his lessons from the maître, Escoffier; he read out a long menu, offering many rich dishes. All sounded fascinating; all tempting to the palate. Yet when one had studied this menu carefully and analysed its contents, it resolved itself into one or two choices. Those that fitted the mood, the day, the individual. But *which* are the choices? had asked the maître. That is the secret that will single out the maître chef or the maître eater from the rest.

183

So with this murder, Auguste reflected, so many suspects, yet when one thought, when one analysed, there were only two or three people who could have committed it . . .

Dinner at Stockbery Towers that Monday evening was a gloomy affair, despite Auguste's *soufflé au saumon et aux écrivisses*. His Grace was more than upset. He was uncomfortable, especially with Mr Hartham acting as a depressing reminder of tragedy. How the deuce were they to get through to Thursday, the day of the inquest, and then the funeral on Friday? Would Hartham expect him to trail up to Hertfordshire? Now Honoria was dead, the Duke felt strangely remote from her. He stole a look at Laetitia, so able to cope even with this situation, charming that bore Hartham, filling the role of hostess so ably. Yes, he was lucky to have such a loyal and devoted wife. Damned if there'd be any more Honoria Harthams.

His loyal and devoted wife, concentrating her charm on Hartham, was in fact resting her gracious foot on that of the Prince, once more obediently attentive, now that Honoria was no more. None of the guests was at ease. It was possible that one of their number was a murderer. What if the Duke himself . . .? Stranger things had happened. It was not so long ago a viscount had been tried by his peers and found guilty of murder. And His Grace undoubtedly had a vile temper. It had been much in evidence at a recent shoot when a rash newcomer had shot at a bird over His Grace. He had wasted no time in finesse. He had turned purple with rage and only a belated realisation of his position as host had saved the young man from physical injury. He would not be invited to shoot again at Stockbery Towers.

Even Auguste's best *tournedos bearnaise*, following the soufflé, and *blanc de volaille de la Vallée*, specially created in honour of the Marquise, failed to cheer the party and, after dinner was concluded, guests hung about morosely. It did not seem cricket to play billiards too often in a house where two had met unnatural deaths in the last two weeks and a third either had or would die, and conversation was stilted to say the least.

Finally His Grace could stand it no longer. He cleared his throat. 'Thought of a shoot in the morning. What do you say, Petersfield?' He avoided looking at Hartham.

Petersfield brightened. 'I'll take a gun.'

'I also,' chimed in the Prince.

'You, monsieur?' The Duke felt honour bound to ask the Frenchie. François looked unhappy and dutifully murmured he was *enchanté*.

Walter looked amused. 'Not I, Your Grace. Glovers wouldn't thank me for joining the party.' The gamekeeper had made it clear his opinion of Walter as a shot. Of François also, but François lacked Walter's determination.

Laetitia glanced at Mr Hartham. What she saw in his face made her realise that all her powers of tact would be called upon. 'George,' she said firmly, 'that seems to be an excellent idea. I'm sure Mr Hartham would agree that it is in everyone's best interests that the police be left to carry out their enquiries without falling over us all day. After all, we must find out what happened to dear Honoria. She would want us to.'

A hint of a wisp of lacy handkerchief to her eye to still the merest hint of a tear was all it needed to persuade a censorious Hartham that this indeed was the best idea. Particularly if a Duchess suggested it, it might be added.

'Splendid,' said the Duke, relieved. 'Then we needn't call off the Saturday shoot either. Get some air in our lungs, what? Picnic lunch. Glovers has been getting the birds ready for the last week up at Seven Acres.' Thank God the big shoot wouldn't be affected, the climax of the shooting season. Everything would be over by Saturday, the inquest, the funeral, and perhaps they could get back to normal. He was disagreeably aware, however, that things would not get back to normal until the triple murderer was safely behind bars.

'Any more news of that footman?' asked Petersfield casually.

'Poor boy, they don't expect him to live,' said the Duchess. 'He's unconscious, and his aunt is with him.'

'Aunt?' cried Petersfield in amusement. 'One doesn't expect footmen to have aunts. I thought they just sprang up fully liveried from the earth.'

Marshall's lips tightened. They were all under strain and showed it in different ways. He found Petersfield's way peculiarly unpleasant. He thought of the man's arms round Jane and the packet of gambling chits, and a spasm of emotion shook him, and he had to turn away from the spectacle of this odious man nonchalantly topping up with the Duke's brandy.

Rose had other things to do than worry about the proprieties of a shoot; he was telegraphing to Scotland Yard. Thus it was that a very senior official indeed was speeding to Berkshire, to interview an irritable Lord Brasserby.

'Thought we'd got all this over once. No news, have you?'

'Nothing definite, Your Lordship.'

Brasserby sighed. How could he have been such a fool? Fell right into the trap. And, moreover, he had been forced to face the unpleasant thought that one of his own guests was responsible. Any of the five hundred of them! Of course that had narrowed down to a mere twenty or so in practical terms of possible culprits and it had been the PM's decision not to make a hullabaloo about the theft. It would have done more harm than good; he'd been right. No public scandal had ensued.

'Is it possible that anyone from outside could have broken in?'

Brasserby shook his head gloomily. 'Not a chance. Been over it time and time again. Had to be inside. Couldn't have known where it was. Only my secretary and a few of the guests could know where I keep my working papers.'

'And now some of those guests are at Stockbery Towers – and so is a rough copy of one of the papers.'

'Stockbery? Where Mrs Hartham's just died? Sudden attack of food poisoning, so *The Times* said.'

'Yes,' replied the senior official unblushingly.

'Who's there?'

'Lord Arthur Petersfield, Prince Franz of Herzenberg, Walter Marshall, and a Frenchman, François Pradel, and the Marquise de Lavallée, and, of course, the Duke and Duchess.'

'Well, any of them *could* have done it,' said Brasserby doubtfully. 'But I know the horse I'd back.' He glared at his interrogator. 'And the Prime Minister needs to know who as well. And Gladstone. Hurry up, my dear fellow. Get him.'

Next morning, the gentlemen, duly deer-stalkered and Norfolked, set off for Seven Acre Field. It promised to be a good day.

Inspector Rose appeared mid-morning, somewhat unexpectedly, in search of the Marquise. She had accompanied the shooting party.

'I ll show you, if you like, Inspector, where they are,' said Jane nobly. True, she could see Arthur – but all those dead

187

birds again – ugh! 'Do you think you can find out who did it quickly, Inspector?' Jane asked hopefully, on the walk up to the field. 'It must have been one of the servants, mustn't it?'

Rose looked at her morosely. 'Too early to say yet, miss,' he intoned.

'But that boy, we none of *us* knew him. It's ridiculous, keeping us all cooped up like pigeons.'

'Why should one of the servants want to kill Mrs Hartham?' Rose countered. 'Tell me that, miss – er – Your Ladyship.' Seemed a silly word to apply to this slip of a girl, but there it was.

'I think,' said Lady Jane stoutly, 'it just got in the sandwiches by accident – they must have been meant for one of the other servants, and Mrs Hartham got the wrong plate. Something like that.' She paused. She was a fair-minded girl, and she had no quarrel with the cook. Indeed, she rather liked him. Auguste used to cook her special dishes when she was still officially in the schoolroom and, despite Nanny's disapproval, had had lots of talks with her about France. He made her laugh. He had attractive twinkling eyes, too, for a servant.

'You must find out soon,' she went on firmly. 'It's dreadful for Mother and Father not knowing.'

Rose glanced at her and wondered whether she had any idea of what her father and mother were really like. Perhaps she, too, would be like her mother one day if she married that Petersfield man. Shifty-looking. Didn't like the man's eyes; they were cold. Reminded him of Art the Mobsman, up Pimlico way. Sooner have that tailor dummy Prince himself.

The guns were in sight now, the air punctuated with the crack of shots as each new flush of birds volleyed into the air, loaders bent to their task. The spoils were already being strung out on a line erected between two beech trees; partridge, pheasant and the odd hare. Rose turned his eyes away. You didn't see sights like this in London, not in his area anyway. Good honest beef was good enough for him.

Lone amongst the women the Marquise had accompanied the men, to the Duke's disgust. Women were all very well in the picnic tent, but they got in the way on a shoot and distracted the guns. Even Honoria, who even insisted on taking a shot herself from time to time, had been a mixed blessing by his side. He'd been captivated at first but, looking back, it was a – well – not done. Fast, that was what Laetitia had said about her. Fast. He took aim at an overlow pheasant and reddened when it fell to earth, hoping nobody had noticed, this transgressing against the code. Damned women, even the thought of them put him off.

The Marquise was sitting on a canvas chair, a gracious figure in a dark grey walking suit, gloved hand on cane, large feather hat obscuring her face. She greeted Rose with a nod. She at least did not treat him as an annoying tradesman suddenly thrust in their midst.

'Monsieur *l'Inspecteur*, you have come to shoot?' Her eyes twinkled at him.

'No, ma'am.' Against his will he found himself twinkling back. Perhaps it was true what they said about Frenchwomen. She must have been a stunner in her time. 'No, I've come for a word with you.'

'With me? But I am honoured. Flattered that I am one of your suspects. At my age I am expected to sit quietly and amuse myself with gossip, not commit murders. Now come. There is a shooting stick. You sit here and we will talk of your murders, *hein*?'

It wasn't what he would call comfortable, but it was a seat.

189

'Funny occupation for a lady like you, ma'am, if I may say so, coming all this way to watch men shooting birds.'

'Ah.' Her eyes wandered to where a young man was inexpertly firing at a pheasant. 'Ah, Inspector, there are many unusual occupations for an old woman.'

He followed her eyes. 'Yes, ma'am, that's who I've come to talk about.'

She turned to him, for once shaken. 'Monsieur?'

'Your secretary,' he said. 'How long has he been with you?'

'For four years,' she said, frowning.

'And no trouble with him?'

'You do not suspect my secretary, Inspector, of killing that man, or that foolish lady? Or of hitting a child over the head with a bronze lamp?' Her voice was ice-cold.

'I'm not concerned with that just at present. I want to know about a house party at Chivers in June.'

'For Ascot. Yes, I was there and François was with me.'

'Did your host discuss his work at all?'

'Lord Brasserby – he is in the Admiralty, yes? And François's father is an admiral. There is some connection . . .?'

'Perhaps, ma'am.' He looked at her with respect.

'Tell me.' It was a command.

Rose hesitated. Somewhat unwillingly, he told her of the Rivers papers.

'When were they stolen?' Her voice was quiet.

'So far as we can tell, during the Sunday night.'

She relaxed. 'Then I can tell you you may look elsewhere for your thief, Inspector,' she said with a slight smile. 'François was with me that night.'

'Working, ma'am? Till what time?'

'No, Inspector. Not working. Just with me. And all night.' She watched him as the import of her words sank in

190

and he blushed. 'I shock you, Inspector?' she said amusedly. 'So be it. You will know by now that Greeves was a blackmailer; he attempted to blackmail me. I am sure he blackmailed others. Mrs Hartham was one of them. She told me. Asked me what to do. I advised her to do nothing. Ignore him. But she was a stupid creature.' She sighed. 'And now she is dead.'

'Monsieur Auguste.'

'Just Auguste,' said Auguste tenderly. It was ridiculous to be sitting in a barn in a stolen hour of leisure with your arm round a girl as pretty as Ethel and for her to be murmuring 'Monsieur Auguste' for all the world as though they were in Pug's Parlour.

'Do you think they'll ever find who did it?' she said in a low voice, trying to ignore the arm which was stroking hers in a rather insistent way.

Auguste sighed. It was an unpleasant subject and there were matters much more pleasant to think about at this moment. However, Ethel was clearly not in a mood to have her mind taken off murder so he did his best to answer her. He withdrew the arm to avoid temptation.

'*Oui*, doubtless, *ma chérie*, this inspector will find who did it.'

'But he thinks it's me. I'm sure he does.' Her voice rose in fright.

'Now why would he think a little maid like you would kill a man, then a woman, then hit a strong boy over the head?'

'Because he knows I did those sandwiches. Besides he found out about me and Greeves wanting to give me the sack.' Her voice was a trifle reproachful.

Auguste was shocked. 'I told them nothing, and I am sure that Edward would not.'

'He asked me about it, if it was true, and when I said no,

it wasn't, he told me Greeves had told someone about it. I think it was Chambers. He never did like me. I know it's wicked to say so, but . . .' The tears rolled down her face.

The arm was quickly back in position, this time quickly followed by the other arm encircling her warm body.

'There, my precious,' he whispered. 'You must not worry, I told you. I, your Auguste, will find out, very soon, and put an end to this. You will see.'

Her eyes turned on him adoringly, so adoringly that it seemed only natural to move from this uncomfortable position to one of more comfort reclining on the straw. After that, it seemed quite natural to kiss away the tears from her eyes, and then to move his lips to hers, then for his fingers gently to unbutton her coat and the first few buttons of her blue and mauve print dress. As his fingers found her breast, she stopped crying and became quite still. Then: 'Oh, Monsieur Auguste,' she breathed and her arms crept round his neck. Gently he eased himself on top of her, her body soft beneath his and relaxed. She gave a little gasp as his hand encircled her breast and began to caress it.

'Monsieur Auguste, I know you'll take care of me always.' Her trusting face looked up into his.

Had Auguste not been half French, these words would undoubtedly have ensured the end of Ethel's maidenhood. As it was, his native caution reasserted itself, difficult though it was. His body told him one thing, his head that this was Ethel, not just any village girl, and that 'always' for Ethel meant just that. Slowly, and with many endearing kisses, he commenced the rebuttoning of Ethel's dress.

That evening Auguste Didier himself once again took the tray to the nursery where Inspector Rose was waiting, pleasantly anticipating by now his evening meal.

'Ah,' he said cautiously on seeing Auguste again bringing

it personally. He was an astute man. Auguste was not here for the sake of Inspector Rose's stomach, though it was to be hoped that he had paid due attention to its needs.

'Monsieur *l'Inspecteur*,' announced Auguste, as he laid before the inspector *poussins à piémontaise*, navarin of lamb, with a *bavarois* to follow. (Mrs Rose would have died of apoplexy had she observed the amount of cream going into an authentic Didier *bavarois* and a *charlotte aux poires*, together with some of the Duke's best grapes, and a half a bottle of Château Margaux to wash it down.) 'I am not a barbarian. I do not normally interrupt gentlemen at their suppers. But when I return, monsieur, is it permitted that I talk with you?'

Rose grunted. He liked the evenings to himself, to let the information of the day swill around in his mind, even as his stomach was digesting its supper, but he could hardly refuse. Anyway, he believed in letting people talk. A lot of villains would be alive today if they'd kept their mouths shut.

One hour later Auguste Didier reappeared. Rose was in benign mood. He was not used to wine, but he had a strong head and, though it might dim, it never obscured his judgement. Not when it was necessary.

'Mr Didier,' he said cordially. 'That was a right fine meal you gave me there. I wish Mrs Rose –' But this rare confidence was bitten back in a sudden rush of loyalty to the tough liver and the boiled cabbage, and their creator.

'Monsieur *l'Inspecteur*, the staff they are worried. They wish to find this murderer. May I tell them perhaps it is unlikely to be one of them now? We are all openly at odds now in Pug's Parlour. Miss Fawcett does not speak to Mr Chambers; no one speaks to Miss Gubbins save myself; they only speak to me because I am the cook and they need me. Mr Chambers is nasty to everybody; Mr –'

'Can't do that, Mr Didier, not yet awhile.'

'Then will you tell me, Inspector, so that I may think more about this crime, in what order the gentlemen returned to the bootroom? This way it is possible to guess – is it not? – who might have put the livery on. Mr Marshall only remembers when he came back and who came back after. He returned with Lady Jane and entered the bootroom as Lord Arthur Petersfield came out. After him came François Pradel and the Prince. But who was first – Petersfield or His Grace?'

Rose studied him carefully. 'Don't see as it would matter telling you. His Grace was apparently first.'

'So,' said Auguste. 'Monsieur François or the Prince are the most likely, they arrived later. Either could have hidden till everyone else was back –'

'You can count Monsieur Pradel out,' said Rose laconically. 'Leastways for the moment.'

'Because he was not being blackmailed?' asked Auguste inquisitively.

'Oh, I think he was all right,' rejoined Rose blandly. 'You just take my word for it, Mr Didier. Now, as to Mr Edward Jackson –'

'How is he, Inspector?'

'You'll see right now.' Rose got to his feet and led the way down to the housekeeper's room. 'He's had a nasty blow on his head, and cuts, but as I said, the wig saved him. But he's a clever lad, that one; he'll go along with us. He knows there's someone out to kill him, and that's why he's locked up here. We're going to smuggle the lad out of here, back to his aunt in Maidstone for a while. Only myself, Sergeant Bladon, Constable Perkins and the two nurses know he's come to, and I put the fear of God into them two about the consequences if anyone else knew. Now you know, too, Mr Didier. I'm taking a chance on you. Edward here thinks you're okay.'

A pale, bandaged, but still sharp-eyed Edward Jackson

peered up at them. 'You'll maybe get more out of him than we can,' remarked Rose. 'Don't think much of the police, do you, lad?'

Edward gave a weak grin.

'So you can't tell us, lad, who hit you?'

The boy looked anxious. 'Didn't see nothing, Mr Didier. Just remember coming out to look for food. Then nothing else.'

'You saw no one?'

'No one, Mr Didier.'

Rose sighed. 'Not helpful. Now lad, we know you was with Mrs Hartham at the ball. You took a message to someone. Now think hard, lad. What you heard the lady say, and what exactly the message was.'

'Flower. I took a flower, and some sort of message about being cross.'

'What? Try again, lad, come on, one last try.'

The boy obediently tried again. 'Wilde. She told him to think about Mr Wilde's story.'

'Don't seem much like an invitation to the last dance to me,' muttered Rose to himself. 'Well, go on. What happened when you went back to her?'

'She was standing there, laughing, waving her fan about,' said Edward in adolescent disgust for the ways of womankind. 'There was a group of men standing round her –' He stopped short, and a look of fear came over his face.

'Go on, go on, Edward,' said Auguste firmly.

'She was saying something about secrets, giving away people's secrets.'

'Secrets, eh?' said Rose thoughtfully. 'Talking of secrets,' he went on conversationally, 'I remembered where I seen you before, lad. Cleveland Street, wasn't it? A year or two back. You were the one they called Jimmy. Very sought after, you were, very.'

'Don't know what you're talking about,' said Edward, after a quick glance to size up his enemy.

'That's all past history, son,' said Rose comfortingly. 'Don't have no worries on that score. But what I want to know is, maybe there's someone you recognise here that was known to you from those days.'

'No,' said the boy. 'No, there ain't.' Wide-eyed he stared at Rose and Didier until his glance fell.

'Useful chap, Cricket. Keeps track of me suits and boots.'

Rose remembered His Grace's verdict on his valet, as he looked at the weak-looking individual in front of him.

'Like your job, do you?' began Rose, pleasantly enough.

Cricket simply nodded, eyeing him warily.

'Wouldn't want His Grace to know, would you?'

'Know what?' ventured Cricket carefully.

Rose smiled almost cosily. 'Don't need to play games, do we, Mr Cricket? He used you to sound out the other valets and ladies'-maids, didn't he?'

Cricket was white, but said nothing this time.

' 'Course I don't know how you did it but I've little doubt you persuaded the valets to cooperate. Acted as go-between. Collected the material. Paid them off.'

Cricket found his voice, albeit a squeak. 'I didn't.'

'Didn't you? What, may I ask, was your role then?'

Cricket eyed him, clearly counting up the risks. Then he decided that of murder outweighed that of blackmail. 'I used to sound them out,' he said sulkily. 'But they handed the stuff straight to Greeves. Didn't trust me, Greeves didn't.'

'Can't think why not,' murmured Rose.

Chapter Nine

Solemnly they filed into the ballroom, decreed by the Duke as the most suitable room for an inquest: Archibald Tong, baker; Edward Tibbins, druggist; Leonard Gander, grazier, four, five, six, seven, eight, nine, ten, took their seats for the second time in ten days for an inquest into sudden and violent death. They were acutely aware that the body they had just viewed had but days ago been watching the proceedings from the spectators' benches wearing a large purple-feathered hat. Jacob Pegrim took his seat: it had taken him some time to become accustomed to being a policeman and judge rolled into one; before the demise of Archibald Greeves nothing more exciting than a collection of old pots dug up on Jim Gubbins' West Field had presented itself. Even then it had never in his wildest dreams at the Swan hostelry occurred to him that His Grace and Her Grace would be sitting in front of him in their own castle, respectful, deferential, while he presided over a second death in the house. And soon there'd be a third, so they told him. He was The Law, he told himself. Yet he was essentially a modest man, and he evaded His Grace's eye as he surveyed his temporary kingdom. Nevertheless he had to impress this Scotland Yard fellow with the way things were done in Kent.

The innocent occupier of his thoughts sat gloomily next to Sergeant Bladon. It had not been an easy couple of days.

Mr Hartham had been at him every two minutes demanding justice, that somebody be arrested, *anybody*, a servant naturally. It had been difficult for Rose to dissuade the Chief Constable from ordering the instant arrest of half the kitchen staff, beginning with Auguste Didier. He had to make long and slow explanations to which the Chief Constable listened with scant interest and rising impatience. It was pointed out that should there be another death when Didier was safely in custody, His Grace's ire would undoubtedly fall directly on the Chief Constable; a present duke being a greater threat than a soon-to-be-absent Mr Hartham, Auguste Didier remained at liberty.

Pegrim was easy on Ethel. After all, he knew her father and had known Ethel since the day the old Rector christened her in the little grey stone church at the top of Hollingham village.

'Now, Eth – er, Miss Gubbins, you made the sandwiches sent up to the deceased.'

Ethel was paralysed with fright.

Eventually she managed to confess she had.

'Duck. And where did you get that duck from?'

'From –' Ethel's voice became inaudible.

'Speak up, my dear.'

'From the kitchen.'

'From the kitchen. You mean the duck was just lying about on the table?'

'No –' she said, quavering. 'The leftovers had all been put in the larder by then.'

'And you went to the larder to get it?'

'Oh *no*,' said Ethel, shocked. 'I'm a housemaid. I wouldn't presume.' Her voice wavered again, and her glance slipped to Auguste. He nodded encouragingly. 'It was – Mr Didier – he gave it to me. But,' her voice gathered strength, 'he just went straight in and brought it out

198

and carved it off and gave it to me on a plate. Ever so quick. He didn't have time to –'

'To what, my dear?' said Pegrim blandly.

'To put poison in,' declared Ethel stoutly.

Auguste closed his eyes at this double-edged help from Ethel.

Two of the jury wrote on their pieces of paper – 'cook'.

'Do you know what aconitia looks like?' asked the coroner.

'No,' said Ethel doubtfully.

'Did you know it is extracted from a common garden weed and is completely colourless, once extracted?'

'No,' said Ethel again. 'But he didn't anyway,' she added defiantly, if inconsequentially.

In love with him, concluded all the ladies in the court.

French Casanova, thought all the men of the court, with a variety of emotions ranging from fatherly protectiveness to lechery.

Rose gave evidence of a technical nature, including confirmation of the presence of aconitia in the sandwiches, and the amount of time they had lain undisturbed outside Mrs Hartham's room.

'How did they get there?' asked the coroner puzzled. 'Who put them there?'

Rose stared stoutly ahead. 'The lady herself, Mr Coroner. I understand they were a signal.'

'Signal?' repeated Pegrim, puzzled.

'That – ah – the lady was ready to receive visitors.'

'But, as I understand it, it was one-thirty in the morning. Visitors?' said the coroner, completely flummoxed now.

'Of – er – a clandestine nature,' said Rose, his face the colour of his name.

From the Duke's best leather chair, Mr Hartham's face suddenly bleached. The Duke's guests kept their eyes resolutely away. One and all were appalled. This was a matter that should not be touched on, far worse than murder. This broke the bounds of public decency.

'A lover,' breathed the coroner, eyes gleaming, before he recollected his duty and the company. He hastily bent his head over his notes and reassumed his judicial air. 'She was a married lady, Mr Rose. You realise what you are saying?'

'Yes, Mr Coroner,' said Rose stolidly.

The Duke, suddenly alert, diverted his thoughts from Hoo Wood and the newly created clump to its right where he had been mentally counting the possible Saturday bag. Dammit, suppose – that letter – suppose that idiot Scotland Yard fellow had got the wrong end of the stick . . .

The Prince sat immobile, staring ahead, apparently impassive. He cast his mind wildly over the chances of the Kaiser or Kaiserin reading of the dark doings at the Towers. No chance now of it remaining a sad case of food poisoning so far as the press were concerned, after this evidence. He would be recalled. His career in ruins. Better to bluff it out. Deny it. The police could have no proof he visited Mrs Hartham's room. There was none. He had seen to that.

'*Nein*,' he replied to the coroner's first question. Already hesitant over how to address a prince, this staccato answer, combined with Prussian aloofness, nonplussed Pegrim. He cleared his throat and sought to regain authority. 'So you deny you were anywhere near the deceased's room that night.'

'I do.'

'This message which the deceased sent you by way of the footman. What was it?'

'That she wished the last dance of the evening with me.' Eight centuries of diplomatic lying stared Jacob Pegrim in the face.

After a welter of evidence, the jury fastened on to the one

concrete fact before them. When they brought in their verdict of murder by persons unknown, once again they added a rider condemning the carelessness of the cook. Jacob Pegrim blenched, having forgotten to instruct the jury more carefully than last time on the finer points of their duty, but something that might have been a smile twitched at the corners of Egbert Rose's mouth. It was speedily removed when faced with a righteously indignant Mrs Hankey.

'Now that that's settled, Mr Rose, I'll trouble you for my bottle of aconite back.'

Hartham, face pale but resolute for his duty, completed arrangements for the removal of his wife's body for burial in rural Hertfordshire, where, he hoped, probably in vain, that few would be privy to the details of a Kentish inquest. With his departure on the Friday, an air of relaxation permeated the house; it returned to normality or as far normal as the presence of the police, and one boy nigh unto death, could make it. Albeit it was the climax of the best weeks' shooting of the season, there were signs of impatience from the imprisoned party. It was time an arrest was made. Any arrest, though both His Grace and Her Grace had their own reasons for wishing a certain amount of care taken as to who should be selected.

Meanwhile, the Duke busied himself with the enjoyable task of choosing the guns for the morrow's grand shoot; the best drive of the season it would be. Closeted with his keepers, he viewed with pleasure estimates of a bag of thirty brace of partridge and one thousand pheasant. Never mind if the stocks did get depleted; a good bag tomorrow would rid minds of murder, restore his popularity with the village, too, with the extra beaters to be employed. It would not make him popular with mothers, but that was of little import. The Duchess busied herself with the task of supervising the huge picnic lunch. Arrangements were made with Hobbs for the erection of a marquee large enough for the accommodation of the resident party and family together with the extra guns invited to join them from the Kentish hierarchy. With an anxious eye on the weather, the Duchess pointed out to her Maker that He owed them a fine day at the very least in exchange for all the inconvenient thunderbolts He had tossed their way recently; she made clear to all the ladies that they were expected to attend. With her usual sweet smile, perhaps with a touch of determined frost in it, she negotiated a menu with Auguste.

Were it not for the fact that the Duchess could see no earthly reason why Auguste should have wished to rid the world of Honoria Hartham, Her Grace would already have taken steps to ensure his employment ceased at Stockbery Towers. However, as he was an excellent cook and reflected on the glory of the Towers, she was determined that Christian charity should grant him every chance. His Grace, not so farseeing as his wife, had expostulated with the Chief Constable at the non-arrest of Auguste Didier, and when with some stumbling it had been made clear that Inspector Rose of the Yard (His Grace's request) had been instrumental in at least delaying Didier's arrest, he turned his ire on him: 'Dammit, man, biggest shoot of the season coming up. Don't want half the county poisoned off with wolfsbane by a lunatic cook.'

'I doubt that will happen, sir,' replied Rose firmly.

The Duke glared. He was not satisfied, that was clear.

Rose sighed. 'I'll have one of the Maidstone men watching every step he makes, Your Grace,' he offered.

The Duke grunted. After all, Didier had prepared the best pâtés and pies he had ever tasted. And where was he to get another cook for the grand luncheon at this short notice?

Rose was, privately, a deeply worried man. Friday evening found him again in the schoolroom, staring into the fire. He preferred this room to the study he'd been allotted with its Chippendale chairs and elegant escritoires. He felt at ease in its homely atmosphere; liked the view on to the herb garden and the apple tree outside its window. The room disciplined his mind into concentrated thought, as though the ghosts from its previous use still hovered over it. It had not been easy this time to fight off Naseby and the Chief Constable. They had been out for blood. Only a firm statement that he needed two days more, and that he would name those responsible if events went against him, had stayed their hand. Faced with this ultimatum and with the knowledge that they could only produce a case of opportunity and not motive against Didier, they had capitulated for the moment. But the weekend had to produce a solution. Rose had sounded a great deal more confident than he was.

He sifted through his huge pile of notes once more, but without hope. Notes could only take you so far. You needed notes, and nose, and something extra. He knew what it was his nose told him; it tied up with the notes all right, but there was still a missing factor. It tied up with none of the motives so far revealed, and he had enough of them, goodness knows. What was it his old chief used to say? 'Murder's either the work of a maniac, son, or it's logical.' There was no maniac at work here, he'd swear to that. So, right, let's take it steady now. A good hour before Didier would bring his supper in. Some thinking would sharpen his appetite. Then he could let the results swill round his insides till they were digested, and turned into good solid conclusions.

But for once his mind refused to obey him. Instead the thoughts swirled round in chaotic order. Then he brought to mind what Mrs Rose so often said to him: 'Egbert, take a hold of yourself.' He dutifully obeyed his absent spouse. Slowly the kaleidoscope began to settle. But the pattern it formed he did not like at all. Three motives: two men.

He was still savouring this unpalatable thought as Auguste Didier came through the door with a trolley of food collected from the dumb waiter. The aroma drifted over to him. So did the cold atmosphere emanating from Auguste. He had repulsed three attempts by Auguste to see him after the inquest.

'Ah, Mr Didier, not upset, are you, by the inquest verdict?' he asked blandly, ignoring the waves of ill-suppressed rage. 'I'm glad you've come. I was just thinking a little chat with you and Mr Marshall might be most rewarding, now I've cleared you two gentleman from *my* enquiries,' he added provokingly, 'but –' as Auguste eagerly stepped forward – 'I'm sure you must be the first to agree I've just got to give my full attention to this – now what is it?' he enquired, eyes riveted on the trolley.

'*Confit de canard*,' muttered Auguste, torn between the undoubted truth of this statement, and his personal agony. Art and the *confit* won.

'Come along in about an hour say,' said Rose kindly, knife and fork already poised.

Auguste compressed his lips and turned to go. However, one small revenge was his. '*Attention*, Inspector, it is *very* rich.'

When he returned with Walter an hour later, the warning did not seem to have deterred Egbert Rose from doing full justice to what was before him. Brushing aside his compliments – they were after all only to be expected – Auguste plunged straight into his grievance: 'But you knew, Inspector, that the Prince was not telling the truth at the inquest, and yet you do not intervene. No, once again it is the French cook to blame, no one speaks to me, I am a foreigner. I am a Frenchman. All Frenchmen are evil men. But am I to blame because Bonaparte wanted to invade this country? Am I to blame that William the Conqueror did? No, but I am convenient; I cannot defend myself, I am among strangers –'

'Now Mr Didier, don't take it to heart,' said Rose soothingly. 'We didn't want the gentleman insisting on his diplomatic rights, did we? We've got to give the pheasant time to hang, eh?'

Auguste fumed. These English. Yes, they believed in letting their pheasant hang. Hang, and hang again. Till it was overripe and unfit for eating.

'Do I take it, Inspector, that you have decided Prince Franz is your man?' asked Walter slowly.

'Trouble with this case,' said Rose, 'begging your pardon, Mr Didier, too many cooks, too much broth. But when you boil it down there have been two murders, and so far as the guests know, three – I told His Grace that Jackson died this afternoon. In fact he's tucked up in bed in his aunt's home in Maidstone. At the moment we three, and the valiant Auntie Elsie, are the only ones that know Jackson's alive.'

'But for how long can you pretend this?' asked Walter.

'Won't be long now,' said Rose soberly. 'I think things are warming up nicely. Assuming Mr Didier's right about this livery theory, to my way of thinking we can discount the ladies, and His Grace, and you too, Marshall.'

'Thank you,' murmured Walter.

'Leaving us with Lord Arthur Petersfield, Monsieur Pradel and Prince Franz. All three of whom were probably being blackmailed by Greeves. We've got an awful lot of gambling debts from Petersfield. Don't seem much of a motive to me, but you assure me, Mr Marshall, that in his circles it would be quite enough. The law doesn't look too kindly on baccarat at present, nor does the Prince of Wales. He can't afford to turn the old Nelson eye. Petersfield stood to lose quite a lot: reputation; position in the Prince of Wales set. He would have to resign from his regiment, leave the country and –'

'And Jane,' whispered Walter to himself.

'Quite, sir.' Rose had sharp ears. 'As regards the Rivers plan, Prince Franz is our man, for we know Greeves was blackmailing him, and the copy of the plan was in the safe, probably handed over to Greeves by the Prince's valet at Stockbery House – no doubt in return for a large bribe – when they were there in August for the ball. If the theft is laid at the Prince's door officially he could say goodbye to his job here, for the Kaiser could not ignore one of his diplomats being openly discovered spying. That's worth a murder or two to an ambitious man.'

'But, Inspector,' said Auguste, frowning, 'I understand the murder of Mr Greeves for these motives, but why the attacks on Mrs Hartham and Edward Jackson?'

'You're forgetting, Mr Didier,' said Rose smugly, 'that, according to young Edward, Mrs Hartham was talking at the ball about revealing secrets. With at least three in her audience. Maybe our villain thought it might be his.'

'True, Inspector,' replied Auguste with dignity. 'I *had* overlooked that point.' Rose should see that he could accord honour when it was due. 'But Edward?'

'That puzzled me,' admitted Rose. 'Maybe there's something young Edward hasn't told us. Or maybe our man heard Mrs Hartham was chattering about his secret in front of Jackson thinking a footman wasn't a person and didn't count. Then when I arrived he panicked. Or it could be the attack on young Jackson was because someone recognised him from Cleveland Street, but then we're looking for two

206

murderers because that villain would have no reason to rid himself of Greeves and Mrs Hartham. Edward says he doesn't recognise anyone here. Maybe he does, maybe he doesn't, but he wouldn't keep quiet if that someone was the person who tried to kill him.'

'Suppose that person was completely separate – someone who was staying in the house that Saturday night and recognised Jackson, but who was not here before and who took advantage of the cover afforded by the other two murders?' Walter said.

'Unlikely,' said Rose, considering, 'but possible.'

'After all,' said Auguste, 'our three contenders do not seem to have interests towards little boys – the Prince is most attractive to ladies, I gather. Monsieur François also, and – er – Lord Arthur Petersfield.'

'I have heard rumours,' began Walter unwillingly, but let his voice drop.

'Versatile some of those customers at Cleveland Street,' recalled Rose. 'Some of them straight nancy-boys, others respectable as you like.'

'But it is too much of a coincidence,' objected Auguste. 'Greeves began this. And his murder was planned.'

'You're thinking like a mutton cutlet, Mr Didier. Not straight,' pointed out Rose, with some glee. 'If someone was being blackmailed because of young Edward, how did Greeves know about it in the first place?'

'Perhaps Greeves knew of Cleveland Street,' suggested Walter hastily, seeing the look of chagrin on Auguste's face. 'Though not of Edward himself.'

'Rum coincidence,' said Rose.

'Or perhaps,' said Auguste loftily, 'the murderer had seen Edward before, on a previous visit. *No*,' he caught himself immediately, '*pas possible*! He would not then have been taken by surprise at the ball.'

'Suppose young Edward saw our villain earlier and told Greeves,' put in Rose mildly.

'When we came down at New Year, perhaps,' said Walter.

'But yes, at the Servants' Ball.' Auguste was excited. *'Mon cher Inspecteur*, I congratulate you.'

'Too kind, Monsieur Didier,' murmured Rose, as Auguste swept on.

'Suppose Edward saw this person, and his expression of surprise was noticed by Greeves, who twisted the information out of the boy after the guests had departed? Surrounded by a hundred or so servants' faces at the ball, the murderer would not necessarily have seen Edward, even if Edward had spotted him. Then Greeves could have started blackmailing the murderer the next time he saw him. At Chivers in June, or in London at the Stockbery House ball in August.'

'So Greeves goes up to our villain and says, "I know you're a pansy and here's Edward Jackson to prove it", does he? Then,' said Rose, darting in as swift as a dipper's hand, 'why does he kill Greeves first and not Jackson?'

A second's pause, then: 'Because, *mon cher Inspecteur*,' Auguste replied with dignity, 'Greeves did not *tell* the murderer what his evidence consisted of. Merely that he knew about Cleveland Street. The charge alone would be sufficient. Our man plans murder, he obtains the poison – and yet,' mused Auguste, 'though it is easy to hit someone over the head, it is not so easy to obtain pure aconitia.'

'Unless you're a cook,' pointed out Rose meditatively, 'with access to a garden.'

'Inspector! This ceases to be –'

'Only my little joke. No, it's easy enough to get hold of the stuff. Dr Lamson just went into the chemist, said he'd

left his prescription book at home, and gave the name of a
real doctor in the medical directory; when the chemist
checked the book it tallied, and Bob's your uncle . . .
'Course they've tightened things up since then, but it could
still be worked. Now,' he ruminated, 'let's suppose the
motive isn't Cleveland Street. Suppose it's the Rivers
papers and our prince. Aconitia's very popular on the other
side of the Channel, I'm told, as a medicine; he could work
out some stunt pretending to be a German doctor. He had
time to plan it all out. The papers were stolen in June.
Greeves probably obtained a copy of the drawing at the
time of the Stockbery House ball in August. Easy enough
for our villain to pay up till October, then bring down the
aconitia with him. That could apply to the Prince, Pradel
or Petersfield. They worked the livery trick, popped the
poison into the sandwiches outside Mrs Hartham's door –'
     'How did they know which one she would take?'
observed Auguste.
     'Only a midnight visitor could know that,' said Walter
slowly. 'And it was hardly likely to have been
Petersfield – he was after bigger fish that evening. Nor
François.'
     'Herzenburg,' said Rose, 'Prince Franz of Herzenberg.
No doubt then.'
     'There is always doubt,' said Auguste, frowning. A
maître should never be sure till the final taste. His brain may
tell him that he has put the right ingredients, the right
quantities into a receipt, but a maître can have an uneasy
feeling that the receipt will not work . . . It has nothing to
do with reason.

Saturday dawned golden and clear. Looking out of her
window, after May had drawn back the curtains to reveal
the world, the Duchess congratulated herself on the success

209

of her word with God. It was without doubt going to be a good day, a day when she might flirt a little with the Prince, making him hope she might return to him. She would not of course. He bored her now. Already she was planning future house parties, future conquests. She had heard of a certain actor she might invite . . . now that the profession had become respectable. She would introduce him to Society.

Leisurely she sipped her coffee. After she had breakfasted, she rang the bell for May.

'My bath, Fawcett,' she commanded sweetly.

'Yes, Your Grace.'

May Fawcett disappeared into Her Grace's bathroom. Bathrooms were still a rarity; had it not been for the insistence of the eleventh Duke's wife, none would have been built at all at Stockbery Towers and the family, as the guests, would have had to make do with hip baths in front of the fire. As for the servants' quarters, it was considered not a seemly subject even to discuss the question of servants' cleanliness. Her Grace vanished into the warm scented depths of the huge porcelain bath and contemplated her day ahead, while May Fawcett laid the paraphernalia of Her Grace's toilette in the dressing-room.

Down below in the servants' wing, the day had begun somewhat earlier. Normally beginning at six, today even the upper servants were on the scene without insisting on their prerogative of the extra half-hour.

Hobbs was supervising, somewhat nervously, for it was his first 'simple picnic', the exit of chairs and tables, the wine emerging from the cellars in Messrs Farrow and Jackson's wine bins, the arrival of the marquee, the chivvying of footmen. Ethel was up betimes, intent on getting all the daily household work done in time that she might accompany Mr Didier, as he had promised Hobbs he

210

would condescend to attend in person. With the help of the still-room maid she was preparing breakfast for the servants. Auguste Didier, a frown on his face, was once more surveying his kingdom.

One oak scrubbed table was allotted to the preparation of breakfast for the family. Ethel was supervising the dispatch of trays to the ladies, and the preparation of the huge silver salver chafing dishes that would be laid along the sideboards waiting for the gentlemen to descend.

Auguste Didier had even more important concerns. He had dismissed from his mind all thought of murder, and concentrated on the luncheon. Hampers were laid out symmetrically as on a chessboard. One of the Freds was dispatched to the ice chamber at the far end of the long walk in the south gardens; Gladys was detailed to get everything out of the refrigerators; Annie to coordinate sauces with the entrées; he, Didier, was the all-seeing eye, as each item was carefully lifted into its hamper. There had not been a minute to lose when the Duke confirmed that the big shoot would still take place on the Saturday. Straightaway the aspic had to be put on the stove for preparation, the stocks prepared, the pies raised. His Grace never appreciated the problems of the kitchen. Mr Tong, the butcher, had had to be disturbed at nine o'clock in the evening for more calves' feet, the Home Farm's supply having been used at the ball. He had not minded. Few would, considering the business he got from Stockbery Towers.

Eight-thirty. The pace was quickening now.

'The spit, Mr Tucker –' William rushed in to adjust the guinea fowl.

'Oh, Mr Didier, I been and dropped a junket –'

'Mr Didier, this mayonnaise 'as gone funny.'

Auguste rushed hither and thither: rescuing the plovers'

eggs from where they had been hidden behind a large boar's head in aspic; checked the syllabub; reactivated the mayonnaise; added the touch of sloe gin to the *coq au vin*; tenderly removed the coverings from the terrine of partridge and truffles; inspected with critical eye the chicken pie with port; and checked Mrs Hankey's cranberry jelly for the spit-roasted turkeys. He approved the desserts produced with a flourish: his speciality, the Nesselrode pudding made from chestnuts all picked on the estate; the *croquante* of walnuts; the *crème aux amandes pralinées*. And the cheeses. Auguste drew a breath, as he admired the cheeses disappearing beneath their vast china canopy. He came from a country of over three hundred cheeses, and yet the sight of the English cheeseboard never failed to move him. They seemed to him a stately progress of the sturdy English lords of old: My Lord Stilton, My Lord Leicester, My Lord of Cheshire, and his own favourite, My Lord Wensleydale. French cheeses were wonderful, but they were dainty by the side of these oaks: Monsieur Camembert; Madame Brie; *les petits chèvres*.

On the other side of the green baize door preparations were also being made, but not with the same speed or desperation as in the servants' hall. Lady Jane was pondering whether to wear her dark blue merino costume with the matching blue velvet hat and blue silk blouse that had been so much admired by Walter Marshall, or the dark brown severely cut Paris tailored walking dress that Arthur said matched her eyes so wonderfully.

'Which shall I wear, Mary?' she cried imperiously to one of Ethel's underlings.

Mary had no hesitation. 'Oh, the dark brown, Your Ladyship. Without a doubt. It's so *distungwee*.' She had been conversing with the Marquise's maid.

Lady Jane was annoyed. 'You don't know what you're

talking about, Mary? I shall wear the blue.'

With a sigh Mary hung Lord Arthur's choice back in the vast wardrobe. Lady Jane began to look forward to the day with a sudden pang of excitement . . .

In the bachelors' wing, unaware that his judgement was being favoured by his lady, Walter Marshall hesitated between the Norfolk jacket and knickerbockers, or a country suit. With some reluctance he donned his sporting gear. Not that he intended to shoot. It was all a ridiculous charade, but even he could hardly ignore the Duke's – 'Counting on you to be there, Marshall. Lend a hand, even if you won't take a gun, what?'

Walter shrugged and accepted it. He had an inkling that there would be more hunting than that of flying birds today. Rose had a look in his eye that smacked of the bloodhound taking the scent. He'd taken breakfast with him, Rose making his first appearance in the ducal dining territory, and Walter had taken this as confirmation that the hunt was nearing its end. The sooner it was over the better, but all the same he had his doubts as to the day ahead. There might be trouble, and if so he didn't want Jane around . . .

Lord Arthur Petersfield hummed complacently as he donned his shooting coat. He always had been a good shot, ready to take chances, where others hesitated. The Guards' training. He too sensed the day ahead would be unusual. And tonight he would ask the Duke for Jane's hand. A decent enough interval had elapsed since Honoria's death. Just get the day over first. He was always one to face up to a challenge . . .

Franz von Herzenberg stared at his reflection in the mirror. Strange, three years in England, and still when he donned English clothes, made in Savile Row, he did not look English. Who would want to after all? He was

213

German. He had the honour of the Fatherland to maintain in the field. The English were hypocrites, pretending they did not care who had the biggest bag, when all the time they cared very much indeed. At the end of today *he* would have the biggest bag. At the end of the day . . . It required some effort to complete the intricacies of his toilette.

The Marquise de Lavalleé wrapped herself warmly in her cloak. All very well for these younger women who could dash to and fro doing this and that, but for her it was to be hours of sitting still in the fresh October air. There was a knock at the door. Her maid went to open it.

'*Entrez*, François. I am ready you see, prepared for the feast.'

'Madame, it is too cold. Do not go, I beg you.' His eyes met hers squarely. 'I feel you should not go today.'

She sighed. '*Non, François. Vous avez raison.* But still I shall go. We shall see the end of the play together, yes?'

He bowed and then, as the maid went into the dressing-room to fetch her hat, stepped forward and fastened the button at the neck of the cloak, murmuring possessively, 'Together, madame.'

His Grace had no doubts over weather, or over the advisability of so many passions being brought together on a shooting field. His Grace was looking forward to the day, simply because His Grace liked shooting, and the prospect of a golden October day with the best drives of the season ahead of them was pleasing. All other thoughts were far from his mind. Even that of Rose. The sight of Rose, in what he fondly thought was a country suit, hastily acquired in Maidstone for the occasion, only aroused a slight impatience that the fellow didn't know how things were done. That such an improperly dressed fellow might nevertheless have it in his power to ruin the best shooting day of the year never entered his head.

Rose himself, little dreaming what emotions he was arousing in the ducal party, or perhaps fully aware of it, was closeted in the schoolroom with Auguste and Edward Jackson, smuggled in from Maidstone now greatly recovered, though the Towers was officially mourning his death.

'Got it, Mr Rose, sir,' he chirped. He was sitting on his bed, only a small bandage now round his head, and this almost hidden by a large cap.

'And above all, you are to stay with Mr Didier. Not leave his sight, you understand, lad?'

'Rightio.'

Auguste remained worried. 'But it is a risk, Inspector, is it not? A risk with a boy's life. Even though we watch him all the time.'

Egbert Rose looked sober. 'I'm aware of that, Mr Didier,' he said stiffly. 'But unless we flush our trickster out, this lad is going to be in fear of his life all the rest of his born days. You still want to do it, Edward? Remember I explained this is for your country. Someone who means to harm England. You want to catch him?'

The boy nodded enthusiastically.

'It's not like your hero Sherlock Holmes,' said Auguste quietly. 'This is real, you understand, Edward? You must be by me all the time, *all* the time, you understand?'

Edward nodded. 'I want to get home to see me auntie again,' he said unexpectedly. 'Anyway, this cove's promised me a trip to London if I do it.'

Auguste fixed Rose with a steely look.

Rose blushed. 'I'll be watching, Mr Didier, and you'll be watching. Nothing can go wrong. You've my word on that.'

Constable Perkins put his head round the door. 'Beg pardon, sir, Mr Marshall wants to see you urgent in the library.'

Rose frowned. 'Right, I'll be along.' It was not an interruption he welcomed.

He found Walter pacing the floor of the library agitatedly, a stranger with him. He turned quickly as Rose entered. 'Inspector,' he said, 'thank goodness. I was afraid you'd left for the shoot. Lord Brasserby, this is Inspector Rose.'

A reluctant handshake portrayed that Brasserby would much rather be preparing for the shoot than talking to Scotland Yard, but that he was prepared to do his duty for England.

'Marshall here tells me you're thinking Franz von Herzenberg had something to do with this spot of bother. That he took the Rivers papers and was being blackmailed by this butler fellow.'

Rose looked none too pleased.

'I told your other chappie only one chap could have done it,' said Brasserby impatiently. 'Assumed we were both thinking the same way. Couldn't be Prince Franz.'

'Why not?' Rose rapped out.

Brasserby blinked. He was not used to being rapped at.

'As Marshall tells me, your idea goes something like this. Herzenberg is a von Holstein man, Holstein ordered him to obtain plans of Britain's future navy so that he can build up Germany's navy for an eventual war. Right?'

'Something like that,' said Rose cautiously. He was not pleased. The initiative seemed to have left his hands.

Brasserby shook his head. 'Got it all wrong. Firstly, the Prince is a Kaiser man, and the Kaiser's the one with the bee in his bonnet about the British navy. Jealous, you know. And the Kaiser and von Holstein are at daggers drawn.'

'So the Prince stole the plan for the Kaiser, not for von Holstein. What does it matter whom for?'

'No,' said Brasserby. 'Franz wouldn't dare. You don't know von Holstein. He has black files on all his underlings, ready for use, just in case. He doesn't allow the Kaiser's men to work for him – and prosper. He allows one in from time to time, but keeps a careful eye on them. Franz would not dare spy for the Kaiser without von Holstein's approval.'

'So,' said Rose impatiently, 'even if this von Holstein and the Kaiser don't like each other, why couldn't von Holstein be equally keen to get the plans?'

'Because,' said Brasserby, 'just at the moment von Holstein is doing everything in his power to keep England sweet; whatever his long-term plans are he doesn't want to move a step to antagonise England at present. He's holding the Kaiser back.'

'So what you're saying,' said Walter, his feelings mixed, 'is that it couldn't possibly have been Franz who stole your plans.'

'Of course not,' said Brasserby with scorn. 'Only one fellow could have done it. Petersfield. Blast him. Lord Arthur Petersfield. It's my view von Elburg is behind it all, Franz's superior. Now he is a Kaiser man, but von Holstein can't touch him. Even so he couldn't risk getting the plans himself. He set up Petersfield to do it. Got some hold over him –'

'Gambling,' said Rose gloomily.

'That it? Arranges for rumours of a break-in at the Foreign Office and hey presto. One good thing though –' Brasserby paused and smiled – 'A word in your ear . . .'

At ten-thirty on the front steps of Stockbery Towers a large party of persons convened, the house party plus another thirty guns from the county. The younger and more robust men and the loaders strode off towards the first coverts;

217

ladies and the more elderly gentlemen piled into carts. Round by the servants' quarters, their own party was mustering, carts piled high with staff and hampers.

Last of all to leave were Rose and Auguste, the latter now aware of the new development. After all but they had gone they were joined by a pale but excited Edward.

'Nice day for a shoot, eh, Mr Didier?' said Rose cheerily.

Auguste cast a look at him. 'The hunt is on, I think?'

'Oh yes, indeed,' said Rose. 'The beaters are out, the birds will fly, eh, Mr Didier?'

Chapter Ten

It was a text-book battlefield. Both sides ranged neatly, opposing each other, ready for the signal that would set the war in motion. Not that it was any kind of equal contest, thought Walter wryly. The beaters, representing the yet unseen pheasants, were lined up in Shorne Wood, their cream-twill smocks gleaming intermittently between the trees. Opposing them the guns, in some places double-banked on this day of the big shoot, loaders behind them at the ready, their masters' honour their own.

The keepers had been up since dawn, coaxing and driving the birds into the clumps. Shorne Wood, famous throughout England for its pheasants, would take two drives this morning; it was a large wood, carefully cultivated into coverts, and its conditions were ideal. For two days now there had been no noise on the estate; all farm machinery had been silent, the tracks passing the wood closed to traffic; even Hollingham Mill had been paid to be silent, lest the noise disturb the birds. The miller made no objection; he earned twice as much from the Duke this way as from his daily grind, not to mention the additional money he picked up from beating. Farm workers, even footmen, became beaters for the day, enjoying the break from routine, and either ignorant of or ignoring the fact they themselves were in the running to be winged or even worse, with the unknown quantity of some of the guest guns. 'What was a peasant or

219

two in the interests of the day's sport?' was the attitude of some of the more die-hard landowners of Europe. The Duke, however, was not of that ilk. When a beater had been wounded a year back by one of his guests, he had not only been fully compensated but had received the honour of a ducal visit, a situation he made the most of, thus doubling his official compensation.

There was a tension hovering, for all the world like a medieval field of battle waiting the order to change. Women had no place in this world, though some stalwarts stood behind their menfolk. The Duchess set an example; her solidarity was especially noteworthy nowadays, as though she were gaining good points in store against her next lover. Behind Lord Arthur's loader stood Lady Jane, bravely, palely doing her prospective wifely duty. She hated the noise of guns, and had it not been that she knew Walter's eyes were probably on her, nothing on earth would have kept her standing there. The rest of the women were some way back, squatting uncomfortably on shooting sticks. The Marquise was today comfortably installed, to the indignation of the staff, by the luncheon tent; this was some way away since it had to be estimated where the drive would have reached by lunchtime; however she could hear distant shooting and yet be comfortable. She had no great wish to see François shooting. He was not a good shot, and only took a gun because the Duke had insisted, in the blind belief that the fellow enjoyed it and was only reticent in taking a gun because of his lowly position.

The hunting horn was raised to the Duke's lips, the clarion call given and the drive began. The keepers first, driving the birds out carefully, not too quickly, in ones and twos, concentrating them, directing their path of flight, the beaters and stops, as the far escort, wheeling round in a flanking movement ready to circle in.

A moment's silence, then: crack, staccato shots and the terse 'Right', 'Left' as the loaders, working as a team with the gentlemen, directed the line of fire on to the next target from their rear position. The race was won by the surefooted; nimble footwork was necessary if the best angle of shot was to be obtained. To Walter, watching from his vantage point on top of a wall, it was then the different personalities emerged; he watched the Frenchman, excitable and erratic, and passed a prayer for the beaters. If left to himself François would probably be a reasonable shot, but egged on by the scorn of his loader and his unfortunate position between the Duke and Lord Arthur Petersfield he did not stand a chance. By a lucky shot aimed at a partridge he brought down a pheasant, but it was one above the Duke, a feat that earned him a scathing look and further unnerved him. Moreover the bird was a hen and the Duke had decreed a cocks only day. François' hands trembled and he ceded his place to the man behind.

The Prince was a dead shot; the Germans usually weren't, not being used to the British methods of shooting, but he had been in Britain several years and his calm Prussian efficiency and determination was rapidly bringing his score to rival the Duke's. The Duke was not amused. An Englishman maybe, but not this Prussian fellow.

Lord Arthur had a reputation to keep up. However, used to shooting with the Prince of Wales, he was also a diplomat. He knew when to fire and when to miss, when to shout a quick 'yours, sir'. His diplomacy was well to the fore today.

Walter, contemplating the spectacle of a Lady Jane with her eyes fixed in a determined expression of admiration and adoration on her intended, scowled.

The world was all noise. Dogs barked, rifles cracked, the women, to the men's disapproval, laughed and chattered. It was a good drive: two hundred and two pheasant, six brace of partridge, and only one unfortunate incident, when a pheasant falling to earth inconsiderately failed to avoid a portly industrialist from Thanet who fell to the ground as though poleaxed and had to be revived by an anxious Duchess and two spare loaders.

Back at the luncheon tent Auguste Didier supervised the final garnish of the cold buffet. Edward Jackson was blithely uncorking wine under Ernest Hobbs' supervision, polishing glasses and arranging napkins. Egbert Rose stood fidgeting by the marquee entrance listening to the shots now coming from the near quarter clump of Shorne Wood.

'Rules for murder,' he said at last. 'Funny thing, Mr Didier. Here am I trying to catch a murderer, and there's a whole line of menfolk up there banging away bringing death with every shot.'

'Not unlawfully, monsieur.'

'Depends on whether you're a bird or not,' said Rose, then reddened as though ashamed of being caught out in this flight of fancy.

'You are not a countryman by birth, I think, monsieur,' said Auguste. 'In the country we cannot think about such things; for the cook if the bird is raised for eating we do not think whether it is right or wrong to kill it; it is part of our day.'

'But –'

'You and I are not meant to change the world, monsieur, merely to do our job within it. You catch criminals to make the world a safer place; my part is to make it a little happier by my art. Look what happens when your Mr Gladstone decides to save women of the street. He is accused of having other motives towards them, because the world thinks of him as a statesman, not as a saviour of fallen ladies. No, he should have left that job to you.'

'To me?' said Rose, momentarily diverted in thinking of

Mrs Rose's reaction had be returned home with a Haymarket belle on each arm and announced he was saving their souls.

'Like your Cleveland Street.'

They cast a surreptitious glance at Edward busily polishing a glass at the far end of the marquee. Edward caught Auguste's eye and winked. How could such an innocent-looking face have survived such a life, thought Auguste.

As if following his thoughts, Rose said soberly, 'It's the lads that suffer. We never laid hands on the real villains, the customers. Only the owners, and the boys. That's how we got on to it. There was a question of some stolen money from the post office; we tracked it down to one boy and the trail led us to Cleveland Street. All the records showed on the clients was Mr Smith, Mr Jones; you could hardly expect them to put in the Earl of this or that. And Veck and Newlove didn't give them away. They were too busy looking forward to comfortable retirement for their pains when they'd done their time. It hasn't stopped at Cleveland Street either. All these fashionable greenery-yellery young men taking over London. Oscar Wilde – I had a look at his book at the Yard – *Picture of Dorian Gray*. If that's literature, give me Mr Dickens. Yet it's caught on. Some say it stems from the top – that Prince Eddy was implicated in Cleveland Street and that's why there's all this talk of his being married off quickly. It often happens, of course, to cover up –'

The same thought struck them both: Petersfield and Lady Jane.

'Too much of a coincidence,' said Rose slowly.

'It would explain why he attacked Edward, however.'

'No, it ain't logical,' reasoned Rose. 'The fellow poisons a blackmailer over the Rivers plans and then by chance sees this Cleveland Street boy and bumps him over the head. Villains don't work that way.'

223

'He would have no opportunity to *poison* Edward, though,' Auguste pointed out. 'But, now I think, why did Edward say nothing? He recognised him. Why should Edward lie?'

Rose said soberly, 'Ever been to one of these brothels, Mr Didier? It ain't just the money. Some of the customers get attached to the boys and vice versa. Now perhaps young Edward thinks of Petersfield as a friend, as a –' he paused awkwardly – 'a lover.'

Lover? Auguste thought about Edward, a strange mixture of stubborn loyalty combined with native cunning and distrust. Perhaps – yes. 'And, Inspector, did we not tell Edward that the man who tried to kill him had endangered England's safety? He would not connect that with Petersfield.'

'Hell and Tommy, you're right, Didier. But –' They looked at Edward. 'What'll happen when he sees –' As they spoke, the advance party of luncheon guests came into view. Auguste quickly hurried to see whether the hot dishes had yet arrived from the house. He kept a not obvious eye on Edward. Rose would be watching Petersfield. Hobbs was standing by the champagne table and the wine – the shooting would show a marked deterioration after all those bottles of claret had taken their toll.

The women arrived first. The Marquise, with the wives of the day guests, lastly the Duchess and Lady Jane. The men came in either self-consciously proud, or studiously avoiding the gaze of their fellow guns. The Duke was happiest. He had shot the biggest bag of the morning. Over twenty per cent of the total kill. Loaders and beaters went off to a well-earned beer and a sandwich lunch a couple of fields away. The main party sat down at the three long tables, as the donkey carts from the Towers arrived with the hot food, the mulligatawny soup, the *coq au vin*, the *filets de sole*.

The talk was, as usual, disappointing to the ladies: it was concerned with one topic – the shoot, the bag, the estimated bag for the afternoon, the missed shots, the lucky shots, bags of the past, bags of the future. The women might not have been present. So much for their gallant effort in accompanying their menfolk and talking an intelligent interest in their sport!

At the entrance to the tent stood a footman with a tray of sherry. He was not in dress livery. He was not one of the Freds. He was Edward Jackson. Watchful beside him stood Rose, and from the other side of the tent from where he could observe the expressions on those entering, Auguste Didier.

Last into the tent was the Duke's party: the Duke himself, Lord Arthur, the Prince, Walter and a nervous François. He had not shot well.

The Duke was slightly ahead of the others. He did not look at the footman. He was simply a Fred. He helped himself to a sherry. Then he observed the bandage and frowned in some perplexity: 'Egad, aren't you the lad – ?'

At that moment pressing behind him an arm – Auguste could not tell whose – shot up and the tray of drinks went flying. In the split second that the eyes followed the glasses, both Auguste and Rose missed the reactions of those entering. It was immaterial. The tension was in the air. Someone, somewhere, had reacted.

Edward went scarlet, as Hobbs rushed forward grim-faced. It would have boded ill for Edward had not Rose stepped forward and said blandly: 'Not his fault, Mr Hobbs. Trust you won't reprimand him. Straight out of sickbed, you know. Now, lad, behind the tables,' and, with curious eyes upon him, the ripple having spread round all the tables, Edward slipped thankfully from the doorway to behind the trestle tables. Heads bobbed to and fro as guests strained to see this first-hand evidence of Murder at the Towers, the word having quickly gone round of the miraculous recovery.

The Duchess's lips were set tight, but she was ever percipient of guests' moods, and glancing round, she gave a light laugh. 'Dear Edward,' she cooed. 'Such a favourite with us all.'

The slight uneasiness that the presence of a policeman, with its unpleasant reminders of Honoria Hartham's death, not to mention that of a murderer's victim, albeit still alive, was quelled once tastebuds had a whiff of Auguste's cooking. The guests had heard of this chef, rumoured to be a killer, yet he seemed to have a hand with the capon pie that was almost English, damned if he didn't. And, after all, he'd hardly poison off *them*, would he? By the time they reached the spit-roasted turkey, the galantines and the aspics, they were captivated. Their hungry stomachs after the morning's shooting made murder a good subject for mirthful discussion, once it was seen that the Duke had no objection. He looked a little grim at first, but cheered up once it became apparent that no one was blaming him personally. The Duchess resolved to make capital out of the disaster, and enlivened her guests with a low-voiced witty appraisal of the investigation so far, and the capabilities of the Yard.

'Poor Honoria,' she sighed. 'How she would have despaired. Her standards ruined. To be investigated by a detective in a green-checked suit.'

A trill of laughter greeted this sally as ten pairs of eyes glanced at the inspector and his Maidstone purchase.

'He doesn't quite look like a Sherlock Holmes,' breathed one purple-hatted lady, her fox fur coming perilously near to sampling the mulligatawny as she twisted in her chair to look.

'He's Lestrade, not Sherlock Holmes. Lestrade of the

Yard. My dear, do you have to entertain him at meals? Imagine having to be hostess when at any moment he might suddenly get up and say I arrest you, Laetitia!'

Her Grace felt this was going too far. A cold eye was turned on the offender. 'Are you implying, dear, that any of us – ? This is a servants' murder,' she said, and a short silence fell. A servants' murder was not nearly so interesting as speculation that His Grace had rid himself of his lady love by foul means. But one could hardly mention that to dear Laetitia.

The buzz of conversation from the ladies rose and fell. They were mostly forced to chatter across their menfolk, who were talking in short incomprehensible monosyllables of jargon, nodding in satisfaction, and unaware of feminine distraction. Egbert Rose surveyed the groups from the doorway. Petersfield couldn't try anything now, not with them all seated there and Didier with his eye on the boy. The cold buffet was removed and the desserts took their place. Then coffee. In deference to the need for accuracy in the shooting to come, no brandy or liqueurs were served, but the Duke gave the signal for the men to congregate, to rise from the table and to retire to one corner of the tent to smoke.

Rose gave an exclamation of annoyance. He had not expected this. Still, Didier was in that corner. He would watch Petersfield.

'Which wood this afternoon, Stockbery?' enquired a guest.

'Cranesback,' replied the Duke. 'Fifteen minutes, gentlemen. It's a half-mile walk.'

Auguste, keeping his eye on the Duke's group, listened with gloom to all talk of bags. He was so tired of inventing new recipes for the partridge and the pheasant. The pâtés, the pies, the roasts, a glut of game and then it would be over. But meanwhile his game larder was a forest of hanging birds,

227

and Gladys and Annie would be spending half their days plucking, not cooking. He had noticed the kitchen-maids often decided to get married in the middle of the shooting seasons, giving in their notice. He hoped devoutly that Gladys wouldn't. She was beginning to turn a nice hollandaise, and her pastry was almost better than Benson's.

He began to compose a receipt for pheasant stuffed with quail stuffed with *foie gras*, whilst watching the group of men. No, that could not be right. Too heavy. The *foie gras* would detract from the meats. He was looking at the problem the wrong way up. He must look at the whole, not the parts. The whole was too rich. From *foie gras* to plans, Cleveland Street. The truth exploded on him. They were looking at the problem the *wrong way up*. They should start with the whole and work back. And in a blinding flash he knew and turned for Rose. But he was there already, gripping his arm painfully.

'Quick, man, where is he?'

Startled, Auguste looked round. *Mon Dieu*, Edward had disappeared. A moment ago, he had been carrying coffee cups back from the tables, now where was he? He must be outside taking the crockery to the carts. Auguste peered in panic through the flap of the tent, but there was no sign of Edward Jackson.

'You fool. I told you to keep an eye on him. Petersfield's gone too.'

'But, Inspector –'

This did not make sense. Could he be wrong after all?

The inspector was blowing violently on his police whistle. All noise in the tent stopped instantly as ladies jumped and men turned angrily to see what the disturbance might be. The birds were uppermost in their minds.

'What the devil do you think you're doing, man? Upset the birds.' The Duke's face was purple.

'Calling reinforcements, sir. Petersfield's gone, and he's got the boy.'

The Duke gaped. 'Petersfield?'

'Your murderer, sir. He's got Jackson; he's given himself away, like we thought, but he's got the boy and he'll do away with him, like enough. And we won't have a thing on him.'

There was a shriek from one of the ladies. The Duchess had fainted. Oblivious to his spouse's distress, the Duke battled with the thought for a moment; then years of army discipline came to his aid and he glared at Rose: 'By God, if you're wrong . . .'

'I'm not wrong.'

'Where are the police?'

'Other side of the lake, sir.'

'Right. Gentlemen!' Centuries of expectation of instant obedience brooked no denial. 'Form a line. Can't have got far. In Hoo Wood most likely. Nearest to here, furthest from beaters.'

Loaders appearing for their two-fifteen call were surprised to have guns snatched from their hands by their lords and masters, surging out of the luncheon tent with an enthusiasm unequalled even in the annals of the Stockbery game records.

'What the devil's going on?'

Thirty men turned round to find Lord Arthur Petersfield facing them, a surprised look on his usually imperturbable face. Sheepishly, they drifted back into the luncheon tent.

'Where's the boy, Petersfield?' said Rose. 'What have you done with the boy?'

Behind him, Auguste gasped in sudden alarm.

'Boy?' said Petersfield blankly.

'Jackson.'

'Jackson?'

'Jackson.'

'Forgive me, Inspector,' said Petersfield, 'if I'm wrong, but isn't Jackson the name of the boy who died the other night? Who was here just now handing me a glass of His Grace's most excellent sherry?'

'You know right enough he is.'

'And how am I involved with this young gentleman?'

'Because he was here and now he ain't. And you've got him. What have you done with him? Strangled him?'

Petersfield blinked. 'Strangled, Inspector? This ceases to be amusing. Do I take it you are accusing me of having murdered this young lad, either now or a week ago?'

'Yes, sir, I am,' said Rose solidly.

Petersfield's face grew red, suffused with anger. 'By God, I'll have your blood for this, Rose,' he said viciously. He looked round the faces of his accusers, now not quite so certain.

'Very likely, sir. But before that just inform me where you have been. Are you saying you were alone in the woods just now?'

Petersfield hesitated and a slow smile crossed his face. 'No, Inspector, I'm not saying any such thing.'

'And, if it wasn't Jackson, someone'll bear witness to that?'

'Certainly, Inspector,' said a cold voice. Lady Jane's face was flushed.

'You, miss? *You* were with His Lordship here? What were you doing in the woods, may I ask, with him?'

Lady Jane's face grew pink and she looked haughtily at the inspector.

'I was kissing her, Inspector,' said Petersfield. 'Do you require to know how often – or where?'

There was a cry of rage. The politically pacifist, objectively minded, quietly spoken Walter Marshall leapt forward and with one blow from his right fist made

230

contact with Petersfield's jaw, propelling him backwards into the cold buffet. The trestle tables, not built to withstand the rage of a jealous man, collapsed in the middle, the far ends swinging up like Tower Bridge in reverse. A lemon syllabub hit Her Grace, newly recovered from her faint, full in the face; the Marquise received a *croquante* of walnuts in her lap and the sauce Melba now adorned her hat; and Lord Arthur staggered to his feet his face covered with aspic of turkey, one pea of the garnish balancing on his nose.

Auguste covered his face amid the screams of the ladies and the righteous indignation of the men, and then tried to protect the ruins of his best *banquet de picnique*. In vain the Lady Jane picked up from the floor the one *plat* that had survived the carnage intact – a *bavarois* – and balanced it thoughtfully in her hand, looking balefully from Marshall to Lord Arthur. Walter waited for the blow. Her glance passed from one to the other, resting on Walter who stood submissively in front of her. The Lady Jane giggled, turned round and with one swift movement plunged the *bavarois* into the lugubrious face of Egbert Rose.

It was a just revenge.

The other females, starting with the most praiseworthy motives of coming to the aid of their own sex apparently under attack, completed the wreck, as they slipped, slithered and finally deposited satin-bustled backsides in the ruined remains of Auguste's art. Menfolk coming to the aid of their distressed women soon found themselves as liberally adorned as the gentler sex, as frantic besauced and bejellied hands grabbed at their lapels for assistance.

'Lor' love a duck, what's bin going on?' A shrill cockney voice squealed in amazement. In the midst of the carnage, Edward Jackson had strolled back into the tent.

The Duchess was the first to speak. 'Is this the boy?' she

231

said, in awful tones, pointing at Edward, and fixing Rose with a stern eye.

Jackson, the cynosure of all eyes, turned to his one ally and announced plaintively: 'I only went for a piss, Mister Didier.'

Once again the Duke showed the powers of leadership that his family had had bred into them for centuries. The ladies were dispatched to the house and ordered to bedeck themselves in their choicest teagowns, the visitors being assured of the comforts of hot baths and alternative raiment where necessary. Only the Marquise and Jane elected to stay, the Marquise because the mere advent of a *croquante* of walnuts and a sauce Melba did not disturb her in the slightest, and Jane because she had somehow remained immune from the ravages of the occasion.

The men were quickly gathered for a shoot, in the hope that their minds – even with luck Petersfield's – might be distracted from the unfortunate happenings of the luncheon period. Just as they set off, the police arrived: Sergeant Bladon, Naseby and several lesser fry. They were amazed to find the staff of Stockbery Towers clambering around the floor of the marquee picking up broken china, and wiping custard from the walls.

'An orgy,' remarked Bladon with satisfaction. His best fears were confirmed about the goings-on in the luncheon tents at the big shoots. 'Drunken revelries.' His eyes surveyed the empty champagne and claret bottles. He looked round for Rose but he was in discussion with that Froggie again.

'Inspector, we have been wrong – this was a red herring what you heard from Lord Brasserby. The smell, the taste – all wrong.'

'Are you saying it really isn't Petersfield?'

232

'No, Forget the plans. Mrs Hartham's message, Cleveland Street, Oscar Wilde. The Prince, the *Prince*!'

Rose stared at Auguste, his face suddenly pale. 'Cripes' was all he said at first, simply. Then, in sudden fear, 'Where's the boy?'

Jackson had gone again.

With one accord they rushed outside. Hobbs was still sadly loading broken china and effects into the carts.

'Jackson?' he said. 'Why, he went to the shoot. They wanted extra beaters, they said. Went off early afore the rest of the party.'

'Which wood?'

'Why, up at Cranesback,' said Hobbs, puzzled.

Auguste tore off his cook's hat and apron, dropping them on the ground as he turned to run, closely followed by Rose and more slowly Bladon, panting heavily.

Even as they came up to Crook Field and the lines came in view, they heard the Duke's horn. It was the sign for the beaters to move, slowly, slowly, towards the birds, the gun fodder. And Edward Jackson, conspicuous because of his lack of smock, would be in the direct line of fire. An accidental shot, no one would know which gun, and –

'He'd never dare,' said Auguste, but without conviction.

'Without that boy, I've no case,' grunted Rose.

One minute, two minutes, Rose was scrambling over the last stile, closely followed by Auguste.

The firing line was on the alert, guns ready.

The first birds were already put up by the time Rose burst through the line, shouting, 'Stop the drive!'

The Duke was apoplectic. Two guns went off, their aim thrown wide by the suddenness of Rose's appearance, one killing a cow peacefully grazing in the adjoining field.

'By God, I'll have your skin for this, Rose,' the Duke promised grimly. 'Hold your fire, gentlemen.' Two hoots on

233

the horn followed for the beaters to stay put. The pheasants, however, did not recognise the signal for what it was and craftily took advantage of the situation to sneak out of the clump to safer territory, a few daringly taking to the air followed by wistful eyes and itching fingers on the firing line.

The front line gathered indignantly round Rose, dogs yelping, the Duke muttering.

'Well, Inspector, what have I done this time?' asked Petersfield sarcastically.

'Not you, My Lord,' said Auguste, quietly. 'The boy. He's one of the beaters.'

'What of it? demanded the Duke, bristling. 'And, my God, what's my cook doing wandering about in the middle of a shoot? World's gone crazy. See here, Didier, none of your French ways here –'

'Sir,' said Auguste, turning to explain. He did not get so far. '*Ma foie*, Inspector, where is he? The Prince – where is he?' He seized the Duke's arm. 'Sir, the Prince –'

The Duke was more aware that this damned Frog he'd imported was clutching the ducal arm than of the purport of his words. 'He was here a minute ago. Damned cheek,' he snarled.

'But it is he, Your Grace. Your murderer.'

The Duke blinked. 'Now see here, Didier. Bad enough having Scotland Yard gone crazy, now me own cook –'

Rose interposed: 'There's no time to lose, Your Grace. He's in the wood now. He's only got to separate Jackson from the other beaters . . .'

The Duke regarded them stonily for a moment. Then: 'By God, I never liked that man,' he roared and, as on the field of battle, gave his orders. 'Gentlemen, wheel round, semicircle, flank the wood. We'll beat the bastard out.'

One could have sworn the Duke was enjoying it.

Once again his guests, some still under the impression this

was a new-style house-party game, obediently formed a
flanking line and wheeled up to Cranesback Wood. Thirty
men encircled it. Rose's police reinforcements, panting to
the site, were ordered to the rear. There were guns enough;
no need to risk unarmed police.

When all were in position, the Duke put his horn to his
lips, a latter-day Childe Roland. Three blasts for the beaters'
recall. Slowly the cream smocks broke cover, emerging from
the woods, their owners in wary hesitation as they saw the
shooting line close to them, guns cocked. A new kind of
drive perhaps? Themselves the prey? The Duke was a rum
'un . . .

The Duke nodded when all were out.

'Let the boy go, and come out.'

There was no reply to Rose's shout. 'I'm going in,' said
Auguste suddenly.

Rose put out a hand to stop him. 'He's armed, Didier.'

Auguste removed the restraining arm. 'I let that boy go
into danger once before. If I can stop it this time I will.'

Rose pursed his lips and simply said, 'I'm coming with
you.'

They plunged into the wood, their path punctuated by the
odd bird that flew up under their feet in alarm.

They stopped and listened. Not a sound. Then a sudden
bird flew up not twenty feet from them.

'There, my friend,' breathed Auguste.

They ducked behind some bushes.

'Let the boy go,' called Rose again.

This time there was a reply and a laugh. 'Let Edward go?
Nein, nein. He comes with me. He is my friend, my very
good friend.'

There was a whimper by his side.

'Inspector, I am leaving now. I will go out of the end of the
wood towards the house. You will call your men off, yes, or

235

this boy dies.' There was a pause, and another whimper.

'Now, stand up, Inspector, so I can see you. And your companion.'

Slowly they stood up. The Prince, clasping Jackson in his arms, gun cocked and ready, was a mere ten feet away. He was dishevelled, his face tense and set. Slowly he walked towards them, feeling his way carefully along the path, dragging the boy with him, gun in front.

Jackson's face was white and strained. He was babbling as they passed. 'But he's my friend. He won't hurt me. It was a mistake last time. He told me. He's sorry. He loves me, he does. He hasn't done nothing. It wasn't him.'

Slowly the Prince passed them and they could do nothing but watch. 'Call your men off, Rose, no shots in the back, if you please.'

With a shout from Rose the men lowered their guns, reluctantly scattering, and the Prince began to back across the open fields, Jackson half finding his way for him, half looking back to safety. The path was clear to the house. Clear of all save one.

The Marquise had come to watch the rare afternoon sport with the only weapon at her disposal. Climbing delicately over a stile, holding up her trained walking dress with one hand, she unerringly aimed one of Auguste's capon pies (with truffles) at the back of the Prince's head.

'Sedan,' she hissed.

Feeling the jerk, Edward swung to one side, and upset the Prince's balance. Knocked sideways, they fell together down the steep slopes above the Duke's lake. The Prince's grasp slipped from Jackson. It was a deep lake; it was meant for fishing. And Edward Jackson could not swim. The Prince might yet have swum to the other shore and safety. He did not. He seized the panicking boy and thrust him out on to the bank. But he chose the wrong place. The gun had

236

slipped down the bank after its owner. The boy, landing on top of it, dislodged it and discharged its pellets into the Prince's belly, staining the water of Stockbery Lake red.

The Prince was not quite dead when Rose and Auguste reached him. With the only smile that Auguste had ever seen on his lips he murmured, 'I shall claim diplomatic immunity, *Herr Inspektor*,' and died.

The only mourner was Edward Jackson.

'So we were right,' said Rose to Auguste as the police went about their business and the Duke, reluctantly abandoning thoughts of re-starting the shoot, shepherded his guests back to the house. 'Right in the first place. And Edward thought the fellow loved him. Misplaced loyalty.'

'So he did,' said Auguste soberly. 'He saved him at the end.'

'Yet he tried to kill him a few days ago,' Rose pointed out matter-of-factly. 'Not too much love there, not with his career to think of.'

'You are right, Inspector.'

'No, you were,' said Rose, generously. 'You saw the truth before me. I was swallowing the Petersfield hare easy as a basinful of your fish soup, Mr Didier. It all fitted. Petersfield fitted for the Cleveland Street connection, too. In with Lord Arthur Somerset who left the country after the case; he was not married and clearly anxious to get spliced for the look of the thing. And there's the Prince, women falling over themselves for him. Last chap you'd think of who needed to amuse himself with little boys. Still, I did say some of the clients were very respectable. What made you realise it was him after all?'

'A receipt, Inspector. Just a dish I was composing. We thought Edward was a – a – garnish, if you like, but he was the centrepiece all the time. Edward had brought that message to the Prince: "Think about Mr Wilde's story". Mrs Hartham would have been thinking about his fairy tale, or of a private joke between the two of them, yet from the lips of Edward Jackson it meant only one thing to the Prince – *Dorian Gray* – the story of a degenerate.'

'Poor Edward,' swept on Auguste inexorably. 'As soon as the Prince saw him at the dance, he recognised him, even in his footman's livery, and realised that he had killed Greeves in vain. Greeves had not just been relying on gossip or hearsay when blackmailing him, he had evidence right here in Stockbery Towers: Edward Jackson himself.'

'Ah, yes,' Rose at last managed to contribute. 'And, when he followed Jackson back to Mrs Hartham, there was the good lady talking about revealing everybody's secrets. And he knew Jackson had been talking to her, so some of the aconitia left from Greeves' murder promptly silenced her. Jackson, he thought, could wait – he'd frighten him into silence. Then he saw me! He did not recognise me, but he heard that I'd been in on the Cleveland Street affair and knew that I'd recognise the boy.

'Greeves obtained the ship's plans from *Petersfield's* valet, not the Prince's,' continued Rose. 'But what he must have gleaned from the Prince's valet was the power that von Holstein had over all the diplomatic staff – and that the Prince, being a Kaiser man, would be an especial target for his pile of incriminating dossiers. So Greeves threatened to tell von Holstein of the Prince's homosexuality. That would mean the end of his career, as the Kaiser would be the last person to take a tolerant view where that is concerned.'

'So, the livery,' said Auguste. 'He returned to the house as soon as Petersfield had left the others, and entered the livery-room. If he'd passed anyone unexpectedly before he went in he could always delay his attempt till another day.

He was lucky, except that the Duke saw his back view disappearing into the the servants' quarters. On his return he checked through the window on to the garden that no one was coming; climbed through it and made a second entrance in the garden door to the bootroom. And when,' Auguste was carried away by his own rhetoric, 'he visited Mrs Hartham's room, he poisoned the sandwich, made sure which it was he handed her, waited till it had taken effect – he must have given a very large dose – pulled the bell rope and left.'

'But –'

'And all for the love of Edward Jackson,' went on Auguste unheedingly.

'A shooting accident. That's what it will be put down as at the inquest. Looks better in the press,' said Rose gloomily, sidetracked. He sighed. Promotion would continue to elude him.

The following morning the ducal party attended church to give thanks in their various ways for the enjoyable shooting party of the last three weeks. That evening the guests would return to London, and Stockbery Towers to normal.

'One moment, Inspector,' Petersfield said, 'before you go. A word in your ear.' He smiled, not at all pleasantly. 'I have not forgotten. Before long you will find yourself *Sergeant* Rose of the uniformed police again. A charge of murder is not a pleasant threat to make before witnesses. Such witnesses.'

Egbert Rose faced Lord Arthur uncowed. 'You're right, sir. I apologise. I got the wrong man.'

'You did indeed, Inspector. And you will not forget it, that I promise you.'

'But I think you will, sir,' said Rose slowly.

Petersfield laughed. 'You think in vain, Inspector.'

'You were being blackmailed by Greeves, weren't you, sir?'

Petersfield stiffened. His eyes were watchful. 'Take care, Inspector.'

'I shall, sir, thank you. I don't think the Duke would like it if he knew one of his guests was handing the plans of the British navy over to Germany, for all he's an army man himself. I don't doubt you were forced to do it, sir. Wouldn't have wanted those stories about your baccarat debts to get to the Prince of Wales, eh? I don't expect you'd be prosecuted over the plans, of course . . . You see, you could say you did England a good turn in the long run. What you didn't know, Your Lordship, is that when Rivers started reworking the plans after the theft he realised he had made one fatal error in the first lot. If the Kaiser builds to that pattern, his ships will most probably sink.'

Rose let out one hearty guffaw. Then his face grew grim again. 'But word will get to the Prince of Wales all right. I shouldn't drop your calling card in at Sandringham for a while, if I were you, sir.'

Sunday luncheon was over. It was a warm day for the end of October, and several people were strolling in the grounds. The Kentish trees were at the height of their autumn glory. Lady Jane had – quite by chance – come across Walter Marshall in the gardens, and had suggested, offhandedly, he might be amused to investigate the maze.

With some misgivings Mr Marshall agreed. It would indeed be an interesting experience. He had no doubt that Lady Jane knew its secrets intimately and had little more doubt that it would appeal to her sense of humour to abandon him there. However, reasoning that it was no more than he deserved, he meekly consented to be led to the middle of the maze. Not directly, Lady Jane was too cunning for that;

240

but with many twists and turns on the way. There was a small fountain at the middle with a late rambling rose around it, and two stone lovers in an embrace which were it not art could well have been thought just a little risqué. Perhaps it was this that brought back to Walter's mind his own plight for, instead of availing himself of the inviting place by Lady Jane's side on the stone seat surrounding the centre, he placed himself on the wooden bench at the edge of the circle.

Lady Jane frowned and carelessly twiddled a rose between her fingers. Walter watched intently. He would not be first to speak. Revenge should be hers.

'Walter,' she said suddenly. Her voice did not sound angry at all. 'Arthur intends to speak to my father this evening. He could not last night because of – well, obviously not.'

Walter said nothing, but a muscle twitched in his cheek. He folded his arms and endeavoured to look disinterested.

'What shall I do?' she said so artlessly that he had but one desire. He suppressed it.

Lady Jane sighed to herself. Really, he was making this very difficult. 'I do not think,' she said, her eyes on the rose, 'that I could marry anyone who looked so silly as he did with aspic of turkey all over his face.'

Walter's heart leapt up, and it was all he could do to keep from leaping after it.

'You could,' he said slowly, his eyes fixed on her, 'you could always marry me instead.'

In a trice, there were two figures on the wooden bench reclining in a position uncommonly reminiscent of their stone counterparts facing them.

'You won't be horribly schoolmarmy with me, will you, Walter?' she whispered after a while.

Walter, his heart at her feet, could only assure her he did not feel in the least schoolmarmy towards her.

*   *   *

The maze was obviously a popular place for rendezvous that afternoon. Ethel too had a problem and, since on Sunday afternoons the upper servants were allowed the use of the gardens, she had earmarked the maze for the discussion of this problem with Auguste.

'You see, Monsieur Auguste,' she said confidingly, her hand in his, 'it's Constable Perkins.'

'What is Constable Perkins, my dove?' murmured Auguste, wondering whether they were deep enough into the maze to risk kissing her without fear of exposure to Mrs Hankey.

'He wants me to go the village dance with him.'

'Then go, my sweet.'

This was not the answer Ethel sought. 'But, Auguste,' she said, raising her eyes to his, 'I told him I was promised to you.'

The little hand once so confiding now seemed to exert a monstrous grip. Auguste loosed it gently and gazed at her. No, she was still his sweet Ethel. He sighed. Here was a problem he must deal with delicately. He put his arm round her as they walked, Auguste noting the way they were going in case he needed to exit quickly.

'My love,' he said, tenderly kissing her. 'I am not intended for such happiness.'

He held his breath, wondering whether this was going too far. Apparently not, for Ethel's face betrayed adoration besides bewilderment.

'Since I came to the Towers, my little star, you have been the light of my life, the one bright spot in my dull work, the only thing that kept me from total despair. But I am beholden to the memory of another. Such happiness is not for me.'

There was a little intake of breath. 'You're betrothed to another, Auguste?'

'Not betrothed. *Beholden*. My Tatiana. In Paris.'

Ethel held her breath. This was romance indeed, like what she read in her *Girls' Companion*. 'Who is she, Monsieur Auguste?'

'Tatiana,' he paused momentarily. 'Tatiana is a Russian princess. You understand that is not as grand as one of Her Majesty's daughters in this country, for Russia has many princesses, but she is a princess nevertheless. She lived in a large house in Paris, where I was apprenticed. She is beautiful, my Tatiana. We fell in love when she was still a little girl and I took her her meals in the schoolroom –'

Behind the yew hedge one of the two eavesdroppers held her breath. Something seemed rather familiar about the recital, to Lady Jane.

'Then she grew up and came to the schoolroom no more. She was destined to marry a noble prince. But one day she was out riding in the countryside and her horse bolted. But I, Auguste, was there to save her. I seized the reins of the galloping horse and helped her to the safety of my arms. We sat beneath an apple tree that she might recover her spirits and we talked, she and I. Oh, how we talked. We talked until the twilight came and, as the last bird sang his song of farewell to the day, we realised we were in love. Ah, it was love, the truest love. But we could not marry. No, she is a princess and I a mere cook. But we took a vow never to marry another while the other remained single. She is single still, my Tatiana.'

Ethel drew a deep breath; tears were welling in her eyes. 'That is beautiful, Monsieur Auguste, beautiful. I couldn't come between you and Tatiana, could I?'

'My love, it is a great sacrifice to me, you understand. But I think Constable Perkins must claim his partner for the dance.'

'He is very good-looking,' said Ethel doubtfully. 'And I

243

do like him. But, oh, Monsieur Auguste –' She gazed up at him again sorrowfully.

'Away, child. Leave me to sorrow alone,' said Auguste, giving her a gentle push of self-sacrificing renunciation – not all assumed.

With a backward glance, she went. As soon as he was out of sight, he leant back against the hedge, weak with exhaustion.

Walter Marshall's head appeared over the top, followed by a giggly Lady Jane.

Auguste regarded them reproachfully. 'You were listening?'

'You did it to me,' Jane pointed out, giggling.

'That was by mischance, My Lady,' he said with dignity. 'I would not have done so intentionally. I –'

Walter had no such inhibitions. 'Tell me, Auguste,' he said with interest, 'is there really a Tatiana?'

Auguste looked him straight in the eye. 'Sir, when a lady's honour is at stake, we *Frenchmen* do not talk of such things.'

And to the strains of Walter's laughter he began to beat a retreat to the maze's exit.

'This is a really nice cup of tea, Mr Hobbs. Say what you like, Mr Greeves' tea was not of the best.' Mrs Hankey had given the seal of approval to Pug's Parlour under its new management.

'Sugar, Miss Fawcett?'

'Thank you, Miss Gubbins.' May smiled at Ethel.

'Mr Chambers?'

'Not for me, Miss Gubbins. That's a pretty dress you're wearing this afternoon. And yours, Miss Fawcett,' added Chambers hastily, remembering his duty. A smile of acknowledgement was his reward.

'May I be of assistance with that cake, Mr Hobbs?' In the

absence of Edward Jackson, who was spending a few days with his aunt, Cricket was anxious to oblige. His offer was accepted. But Mrs Hankey intervened.

'No need, Mr Cricket,' she beamed, 'I was just going to cut it.' She smiled fondly at Mr Hobbs. 'I know Ernest here has a sweet tooth.' There could be worse fates for her old age than looking after Ernest Hobbs.

Pug's Parlour was back to normal.

Rose stood at the entrance to the kitchens. Regret for *sole au chablis* and a hundred dishes of Auguste's creation not yet tasted assailed him. Tomorrow it would be Mrs Rose's mutton pie, as heavy as the *Mrs Beeton* she used to prop up the kitchen cupboard. Ah well, a man would get tired of this all the time, he told himself firmly as he surveyed the kitchen team preparing now for just a small family luncheon: roasted sweetbreads, partridge pie *chasseur*, almond *gauffres*, *capon à la Perigueux*, *Salade à la Pompadour*, salmagundy . . . He turned his head in momentary anguish.

Auguste, cap on head, the devoted eye of the maître chef upon his sauces, was hard to distract, but when he saw Rose he came over.

Rose regarded him. 'Tell you what, Mr Didier, you teach me to be a cook, I'll teach you to be a detective.'

Auguste bristled with indignation. Was it not he who – ?

'I *am* a detective already, Inspector. Was it not I who solved how Greeves' murder – ?' Then he saw Rose smile. Ah, these English with their straight faces . . . 'Ah Inspector, you may mock me. But I tell you there is much the same in our two jobs. There is much patient reasoning, composing of menus – just as you build in your background; we assemble our ingredients as you your suspects and evidence. And then comes the art: the basic skills; the careful attention to detail; then the cooking; the seasoning; the knowing when and where to act; and finally –' He paused.

'Yes, Mr Didier?' asked Rose.

'There is the touch of a maître,' said Auguste reverently. 'Only a maître can achieve the supreme result.'

'I've heard of a maître d',' said Rose. 'Now I'll know it means maître detective. First time I've ever thought crime could be solved in the kitchen. I must tell Mrs Rose.' With this warming thought he was disposed to be generous and added, 'That was a fine bit of work you did at the end, Didier.' Then he remembered something. 'How do you explain the pulling of the bell rope? That's why we thought the murderer and the visitor to Mrs Hartham's bedroom weren't the same person.'

Auguste said quietly, 'Because I am a Frenchman, monsieur. And he was a German. And Frenchmen have feelings about Germans, born of a war fought twenty-one years ago. Madame la Marquise cried, "Sedan". Memories of the massacre at Sedan go deep in France, monsieur. We remember.'

'But the bell rope?'

'He was a Prussian,' said Auguste simply. 'And Prussians are correct in their behaviour. Through centuries of obedience to orders, they do what is required automatically in a given situation. Mrs Hartham needed assistance. He pulled the bell rope. It seems ridiculous, perhaps, monsieur, but the Germans are not so. You see just a man whom the cartoonists love. We French see a German. Never underestimate the Germans, monsieur. This Kaiser, he is no joke, Inspector Rose. You will see, we will all see.'

'Oh, not in England, Mr Didier, not in England.'

MARGERY ALLINGHAM

"The best of mystery writers!"
The New Yorker

THE RETURN OF MR. CAMPION 71448-5/$3.95 US

MR. CAMPION AND OTHERS
70579-6/$3.95 US/$4.95 Can

THE BLACK DUDLEY MURDER
70575-3/$3.50 US/$4.50 Can

CARGO OF EAGLES 70576-1/$3.99 US/$4.99 Can

THE CASE OF THE LATE PIG
70577-X/$3.50 US/$4.25 Can

THE CHINA GOVERNESS
70578-8/$3.99 US/$4.99 Can

THE ESTATE OF THE BECKONING LADY
70574-5/$3.99 US/$4.99 Can

THE FEAR SIGN   70571-0/$3.95 US/$4.95 Can

THE GYRTH CHALICE MYSTERY
70572-9/$3.50 US/$4.50 Can

THE MIND READERS
70570-2/$3.95 US/$4.95 Can

MORE WORK FOR THE UNDERTAKER
70573-7/$3.95 US/$4.95 Can